Identity Found

Also by Ray Green
Buyout – A Roy Groves Thriller (Book1)

For five ordinary guys and one rather extraordinary woman, the only escape from the corporate rat-race is to buy the company they're working for: take it all to a new level, save hundreds of jobs and make some serious money.

But it quickly becomes clear that nothing is as easy as it seems. The bid is quickly undercut as twisted corporate politics and personal vendettas take over.

When the buyout becomes *all or nothing* for the management buyout team, it all spins out of control: marriages fall apart, lurid secrets are discovered; life savings are spent on the stock market; illegal insider dealing becomes a matter of fact; and blackmail, theft, betrayal and manipulation are the new rules of the game.

A once-in-a-life-time opportunity turns into a lurid nightmare.

BUYOUT is a gripping and compulsive page-turner about the power of money to unveil the deepest in human nature. It's also a story about chasing one extraordinary dream. At an extraordinary price.

Also by Ray Green
Payback – A Roy Groves Thriller (Book 2)

Roy Groves is Operations Director of a successful company manufacturing dashboard instruments for luxury cars.

A fatal motorway fire is traced back to a fault in the product supplied by Roy's company. Was it a tragic accident or something more sinister? As Roy and his colleagues battle to establish the cause of the fire, and save the company from bankruptcy, they discover that they have been the victims of sabotage.

Eventually, it emerges that an old enemy of Roy and the rest of the team has reappeared and is intent on destroying the company and every member of its management team. Once just a business adversary, their nemesis is now so consumed with hatred that he is on the edge of insanity; he resorts to blackmail and even murder in the pursuit of his goal.

PAYBACK is a chilling tale of how hatred can twist and corrupt the human soul.

Also by Ray Green
Chinese Whispers – A Roy Groves Thriller (Book 3)

Chuck Kabel is on a business trip to China, visiting the factory to which his UK-based company subcontracts the manufacture of its products. He unexpectedly collapses and dies at the airport before he is able to report on his visit. When the Chinese authorities are evasive about the exact cause of death, the suspicions of his boss, Roy Groves, are raised.

Roy decides to investigate further; it soon becomes clear that there are serious financial irregularities within the Chinese company, and that dark forces are in play, intent on ensuring that these do not come to light. When Roy edges closer to uncovering the truth, he is warned off but refuses to back down, unaware that he is about to confront the Chinese Mafia, who will stop at nothing to achieve their objectives.

When his own family are targeted by his opponents, Roy embarks on a desperate battle to protect them, now well aware that if he should turn to the police, their lives will be in even greater danger.

CHINESE WHISPERS is a frightening tale of organised crime and the way in which it uses and abuses legitimate business for its own illegal purposes, relentlessly destroying the lives of anyone who stands in the way.

Also by Ray Green

Horizontal Living: A Tale of Expats Abroad - A Roy Groves Thriller (Book 4)

Roy Groves has led a colourful career in business, during which he battled with corporate politics, deception, and even vicious criminals. But now Roy has retired, and he is looking forward to a quieter life. He and his wife, Donna, have bought an apartment in an exclusive development on Spain's Costa del Sol.

He soon learns, however, that there are financial problems: the community is, in effect, bankrupt. Roy is persuaded to take on the role of President of the community, confident that, with his extensive business experience, he should easily be able to sort things out. It soon becomes clear, however, that nothing is as simple as it seems. As he tries to come up with a rescue plan, Roy discovers that a poorly constructed retaining wall has begun to collapse, threatening the development with a landslide. And this is just the start ...

As the problems mount up, Roy becomes entangled with an astonishingly diverse cast of characters: the devious building developer; the vengeful former President; the Russian prostitute, and her mafia minders; the deranged Middle-Eastern doctor; the devastatingly glamorous French girl next door; and many more ...

HORIZONTAL LIVING is an illuminating insight into the shenanigans which pervade an ex-pat community abroad: sometimes hilarious, sometimes hard to believe, but sometimes darkly disturbing.

Also by Ray Green
Lost Identity - The Identity Thrillers (Book 1)

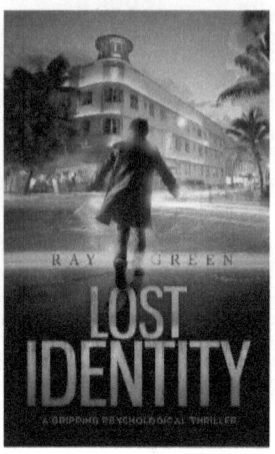

When research scientist, Stephen Lewis, wakes from a coma in a Miami hospital bed, he remembers nothing about his head injury, how he came to be in Florida, or even who he really is.

As fragments of his memory return, Stephen is shocked to find that even those closest to him seem not to know him. And when another man turns up, claiming to be the real Stephen Lewis, he begins to doubt his own sanity.

Desperate to learn the truth, Stephen is unwittingly drawn into a murky web of drug trafficking and murder. At its heart lies a terrifying conspiracy and a secret so appalling that, even if he survives, he knows his life can never be the same again.

Also by Ray Green
New Identity - The Identity Thrillers (Book 3)

Jason Hardwick and Gabriela Suarez have been on the run for almost three years – pursued by a network of professional assassins. Now they are living under false identities in the Market town of Chichester, in England.

Mark Bowman was the detective who helped the couple escape from a terrifying confrontation with their pursuers in New York City some fifteen months ago. Now he has been murdered. His killer is Jade Lacroix: a beautiful, highly intelligent, bisexual assassin. Jason and Gabriela are her next targets.

When Jason and Gabriela learn of Mark's death, they realise that these people will never give up. What can they do to fight back?

Alexis Miller – also an NYC detective – was Mark's girlfriend. She has vowed to bring his killer, and those she works for, to justice.

Will Alexis track down the assassin before she gets to Jason and Gabriela? Will she become a target herself? Who is the shadowy figure behind this murderous network?

'New Identity' is the thrilling, shocking conclusion to the 'Identity Thrillers' trilogy.

Identity Found

Identity Found

The Identity Thrillers – Book 2

By Ray Green

Identity Found

Published in Great Britain by Mainsail Books in 2019

First Edition

ISBN 978-1-9999406-2-1

Published by Mainsail Books
www.mainsailbooks.co.uk

Cover design by Ana Grigoriu-Voicu
ana@books-design.com

Chapter 1

New York City – A Friday Afternoon in April

Julia Turner was feeling upbeat as she shut down her laptop and prepared to leave the office. Just twenty-four years old, she had recently landed her dream job as an investigative journalist at the New York Times. That was six months ago, and so far, she was enjoying every moment of her new job. So far, she had only been given fairly mundane assignments, but that was only to be expected while she was still a rookie, learning her craft. The bigger, more exciting projects would come in time.

But perhaps she wouldn't have to wait too long. While working on her current assignment, she had stumbled across something big – something that might turn out to be very big indeed. She had wondered whether she should involve one of her senior colleagues, but Julia was ambitious, and she wanted to make quite sure that when this story was cracked open, *she* would be the one to get the credit. This could catapult her fledgling career right into the fast lane, and there was no way she was going to pass up that opportunity. No, until it was time to inform the police of her findings, she was going to run this one on her own.

As she gathered her things together and put them in her purse, she glanced around the open-plan office, with its tightly packed rows of desks, noting that quite a few people had already gone home. She checked her watch: 7.05 p.m. It was rather later than she would normally work on a Friday; she must have been so engrossed in the case that she had lost track of time. Now there just wasn't enough

1

time to go home and change before meeting her boyfriend, Mark, for dinner at eight. She reopened her purse, withdrawing a hairbrush and makeup compact. She dabbed a little powder on her face before pulling the brush through her long, wavy, black tresses, checking the results of her efforts in the small mirror attached to the inside of the lid of her compact. A deft application of lipstick and a couple of squirts of perfume around her neck completed the running maintenance. That would have to do.

She replaced everything in her purse before glancing out of the window, to see the golden orb of the late-afternoon sun reflecting off the windows of the building opposite. It had been a glorious spring day, which had completely passed her by while she was ensconced in the office. The restaurant was only just over a mile away, right in the heart of Central Park. She had plenty of time, so she decided to forgo a cab and, instead, take a gentle walk. Slipping into her jacket and slinging her purse over her shoulder, she stepped out of the office and into the corridor, making for the elevator which would take her down to ground level.

As she stepped out of the climate-controlled environment of the building – an unchanging seventy-one degrees Fahrenheit, sixty per cent relative humidity, summer or winter, rain or shine – she took a deep breath of the cooler, fresher air outside. She gazed up at the towering buildings around her; the last rays of sunlight still glinted off the upper-floor windows of some of them, but down at street level, everything was enveloped in the shadows cast by these massive edifices.

She walked the short distance into Times Square; it buzzed and hummed with life. Although there was still a little daylight left, all the brightly-coloured lights on the towering billboards were illuminated now, dancing and pulsing as they competed for the attention of the throng milling below. Julia never tired of this spectacle, which seemed to her to encapsulate the very essence of New York City – a restless, vibrant cauldron of energy. It was a far cry from the sleepy little town in Maine where she had grown up. She made her way across the square, savouring the sights, sounds, and smells of this life-affirming scene, finally passing by Carnegie Hall as she neared the entrance to Central Park.

She smiled as her thoughts turned to her dinner date with Mark. She had first met him around eighteen months earlier when her car had suffered a puncture on a busy highway, and a passing police car had stopped to help. As soon as Mark stepped up to the window of her car she was immediately drawn to his sparkling blue eyes and infectious smile. As he set about changing her wheel for her, his easy humour and soft, but rich voice captivated her. It seemed the feeling was mutual for, by the time she was ready to continue her journey, they had exchanged telephone numbers and Julia had vowed to buy him dinner as a thank you. Well, the 'thank you' extended well beyond dinner and they saw each other twice more within a week. It wasn't long before the relationship developed into a deep love affair.

It was a little unusual for Mark to suggest eating out on a Friday evening. Often Mark's shift times would not accommodate this, and even when they did, Julia was usually exhausted come Friday evening, so they would, more commonly, settle for a takeout, curled up in front of a movie at his place. So what was special about tonight? She had a bit of an idea, but could she dare to hope that she was right?

***

Mark Bowman sat at a table by the window of the Loeb Boathouse restaurant, in the heart of Central Park, gazing out over the lake, its surface bathed in the dying rays of the Spring sunshine. A raft of ducks began making their way lazily across the lake towards whatever spot they had chosen to spend the night, their slowly spreading wake disturbing the mirror-smooth surface. He glanced at his watch: 7.40 p.m. He was ridiculously early, having arranged to meet Julia at eight, but tonight of all nights, he didn't want to risk the possibility of her arriving first and having to sit on her own waiting for him.

He took from his pocket a small, deep red, fabric-covered box, flipping it open to reveal a sparkling diamond solitaire ring, nestling in the black velvet lining. He hoped he had the size right; he had borrowed one of her other rings and taken it to the jewellers to have it measured, but she wore that one on her right hand. There was no telling whether the ring finger on her left hand would be the same size. The jeweller had, however, assured him that the size could be adjusted up or down if necessary. He took a nervous sip of his beer before closing the box and returning it to his pocket.

3

He glanced around the restaurant, which looked to be about three-quarters full, with more guests still arriving; it was a good thing he had booked in good time. This had been the venue for their first dinner date – the one Julia had treated him to as a thank you for his help with her puncture. He smiled as he thought back to that evening, which had suffered none of the awkwardness or tension which so often characterises a first date; it was as if they had known each other for years. And when they had gone back to his place for a 'nightcap' the lovemaking had been so easy, so natural, so passionate, that he just knew, right from that day, Julia was 'the one'. It seemed only fitting that this should also be the setting where he would ask her to be his wife. But what if she wasn't ready to make that commitment? All the signs were there, and it wasn't as if he had rushed things, yet …

He took another sip of his beer and checked his watch again: 7.55 p.m. She would be arriving any moment; now he was nervous as hell.

***

As Julia stepped into Central Park, and away from the shadows of the Manhattan skyscrapers, she was finally able to feel the very last kiss of the Spring sunshine on her skin. Another few minutes, though, and the sun would be gone. Even so, the temperature was still pleasant enough. The park wasn't as busy as she would have expected on such a fine evening: just a few couples out walking, some teenagers scooting around on skateboards, and one or two joggers. She checked her watch: 7.35 p.m. She still had plenty of time, and she didn't want to arrive too early, so she decided to take a longer route, using the smaller, less-direct paths.

She set off, in the rapidly fading light, down a narrow path she knew well. Now there were hardly any other people around, and before long, none at all. The silence was punctuated only by occasional birdsong as the creatures settled down for the night. The temperature was dropping rapidly now, sending an involuntary shiver down her spine. As the last vestiges of sunlight disappeared, she realised that this little-used path had very meagre lighting, the lampposts spaced far more widely apart than on the main thoroughfares. In a few fleeting moments her contented mood evaporated as the silence and isolation began to unsettle her. She pulled her jacket a little closer around her neck and quickened her step. She was no longer concerned about arriving at the restaurant too early and now just wanted to get there as quickly as possible.

She heard something: it sounded like the rhythmic thudding of distant feet pounding on the pavement somewhere behind her. The sound became gradually louder; for some reason this sound unsettled her even more than the silence which had preceded it. She turned to look: coming toward her, at a very brisk clip, was a young, Lycra-clad woman, wearing headphones and holding one of those water bottles shaped to provide a handgrip. As she sped past Julia, she flashed a breathless smile and muttered some sort of greeting which Julia could not discern. Julia silently chided herself for her foolishness and continued on her way. She was only about ten minutes from the restaurant now. She hurried on, anxious to leave this gloomy path behind her and reach the comforting light and warmth of the restaurant.

After a few more minutes, she heard another sound behind her: a sort of rustling noise which she could not identify. Instead of turning to check what it was, she pressed on a little faster still. The rustling noise faded away, and she began to relax a little. But then she heard something else: footsteps – yes, definitely footsteps this time. They seemed to be speeding up to match her pace. Now her heart began to race. Why on earth had she chosen this quiet path, especially as it was now almost completely dark?

As she rounded a sharp bend, she came across a payphone booth. She stepped off the path and crouched down behind the booth, struggling to control her ragged breathing. She waited … and waited. Nothing happened: no footsteps, no-one approaching … nothing. She stayed like that, huddled behind the phone booth for what felt like several minutes; still nothing happened. *Get a grip*, she admonished herself, standing up and smoothing down her clothes with her hand. *You're only five minutes away now.* She stepped out on to the path and made to continue on her way.

Then it happened. A large, shadowy figure stepped out from the trees and onto the path, around ten yards in front of her. He looked like a bald, white guy, of muscular build, as far as she could tell in the meagre light. He didn't say anything or make any attempt to approach her; he just stood there, facing her, blocking her way.

'What do you want?' she demanded, in a voice which carried far less conviction than she had tried to muster.

He didn't reply.

'What do you want?' she repeated.

Still no reply. The man just stood there: motionless, silent, and menacing.

Now the cold tendrils of fear snaked down her spine. What should she do?

She slipped her hand into her purse and withdrew the self-defence spray which she always carried, thrusting her trembling hand forward. 'You'd better back off,' she cried. 'I have a pepper spray here, and I'm not afraid to use it.'

The man chuckled: a low, sinister sound which chilled her to the bone. 'From that distance?' he taunted. The accent sounded British.

She didn't know whether to step forward and use the spray or turn and run. Paralysed with fear, she did neither.

'What do you want?' she repeated, once again, dismayed to hear the involuntary tremor in her own voice.

'You shouldn't be poking your nose into business which don't concern you.'

'Wh-what do you mean?' she stammered. 'What business? Leave me alone.'

'Sorry, love,' he said, now raising his right hand towards her.

As Julia strained to discern what he was holding, a creeping horror permeated her entire body. It was a gun, its muzzle elongated by the fitment of a silencer.

'P-please,' she pleaded, 'I don't know what you want, but there must be some terrible mistake here. I'm just—'

Her words were cut short as she saw the muzzle flash and felt the pulverising impact to her chest, punching her backwards and onto the ground. She lay on her back, unable to move, gasping for breaths which would barely come. The only thing she could see was the deep blue-black evening sky through a gap in the overhanging trees.

And then the sky disappeared as his face loomed over her; finally, at this very close range, she could see him clearly, in spite of the poor light. Cold, dark eyes; broad, flat nose; sallow cheeks; lips set in a thin, straight line; thick, bull-neck; shaven head. The evil intent evident in that face cut through even the searing pain in her chest.

'Wh-why?' she gasped.

'Nothing personal,' replied the flat, featureless voice. 'Just business.'

She felt something hard, hot, and metallic being pressed into her ear. A bilious terror rose in her throat as she realised it was the muzzle of the gun.

The last thing Julia Turner ever saw on this earth was the evil smile on the man's face just before he pulled the trigger.

Chapter 2

Toronto, Canada – Sunday Morning

James Connolly had hardly slept at all the previous night. It was the disturbing news report he had seen on the TV the previous evening which was preying on his mind. Murders in New York City were not exactly rare events, but there was something about the reported killing of the young New York Times journalist which had grabbed his attention and was now tormenting his every thought.

The first light of dawn was beginning to filter through the thin drapes at the window, suffusing the room with a soft glow. He turned over and laid his head on the pillow, his face just inches from Juanita's. She was still fast asleep, her olive complexion smooth and her expression untroubled. They had been together for just over a year, and still, James was utterly captivated by her striking features: strong, angular cheekbones; aquiline nose; and dark, penetrating eyes – now closed as she slumbered peacefully. He kissed her lightly on the forehead, eliciting from her a little snuffling noise as she shifted her position slightly. She did not wake, though.

James had been wrestling all night with the issue which was on his mind. Now he knew he had to make an important decision … or rather *they* did. They needed to talk.

He decided to get up and make some coffee. Then he would wake her and share what was troubling him. He slid out of bed, slipped into his bath robe, and made his way through to the kitchen, flipping on the under-cupboard strip lights, which cast a far more agreeable light across the room than the harsh overhead lights. He spooned some ground coffee into the filter machine, poured in some water, and pressed the power switch. As he waited for the coffee to brew, he reflected on the events which had led to their fleeing from mortal danger in Miami to make a new life together in Toronto, Canada.

***

It was just over a year earlier that he had awoken from a coma in a Miami hospital bed, remembering nothing about his head injury, how he came to be in Florida or even who he really was. The only thing he knew, with near-certainty, was that he was British, his own accent contrasting sharply with those of the medical staff in the hospital. As fragments of his memory gradually began to return, though, he embarked on a quest to discover his true identity and find out what had happened to him. His enquiries eventually led him to Juanita who, it transpired, he had previously tried to rescue from some vicious thugs who had attacked and tried to rape her in a darkened alley in Miami Beach. For his trouble, he had received the blow to the head which had put him in hospital, robbing him of his memory and his identity.

Juanita, feeling a debt of gratitude to the stranger who had come to her aid, decided to help him in his quest to discover his true identity. As the two of them began to piece things together, James discovered some very dark and unpalatable things about himself and his past life: things which, at first, he just could not believe. Eventually though, as the evidence mounted up, he was forced to accept the truth: he had previously been a paid assassin. The reason he had been in Miami was that he was part of a plan to assassinate an eminent research scientist and several of his team in order to suppress the discovery of a revolutionary new treatment for cocaine addiction; his paymaster was a powerful drug cartel who had a vested interest in preventing the new treatment from seeing the light of day.

Horrified by what he had discovered, and wracked with guilt, James vowed to disrupt the assassination attempt, going to war with the others involved in its execution. Juanita was at his side every step of the way, saving his life on more than one occasion. Two innocent people died in the desperate struggle which ensued – one of them Juanita's best friend, Sylvia. In the end, however, James and Juanita succeeded in foiling the assassination attempt, ensuring that the new addiction cure would indeed become a reality. In the process, though, they had made deadly enemies of those they had thwarted, several of whom had also died in the battle to disrupt the assassination.

And it was not only those behind the assassination attempt who now sought to hunt James and Juanita down: the police were after them too. From the police's point of view there were far too many unanswered questions about both the assassination attempt itself and the various deaths which had also occurred. If the police caught up with them, it was by no means certain that they could avoid being falsely accused of murders which they had not committed. And if they should be charged and tried, it was equally doubtful that they would be able to convince a jury of their innocence, particularly once it emerged that James had originally been part of the assassination plot. Who would believe that one of the assassination team could turn himself around so utterly and completely as to become the architect of the plan's downfall?

In the end, they decided that their only course of action was to disappear: to just slip under the radar and try to make new lives for themselves in another country. They faked new identities as Canadian citizens and fled to Toronto; James and Juanita were not their real names.

A year had passed, and no-one had tracked them down; it seemed that their strategy had been successful. Surely, by now, both the police, and the assassins they had battled, would have lost interest in pursuing them. They had a good life together now and had fallen deeply in love with one another. It would be lunacy to do anything to jeopardise all that. And yet he just could not shake his nagging suspicion about why the young journalist had been murdered. If he was right, more innocent lives might well be in danger.

He had to know.

***

The glurping sounds emitted from the coffee machine, announcing the impending end of the filtering cycle, interrupted James's introspective musing. He poured the coffees and set them down on a tray, before grabbing a few cookies from the jar on the counter top and laying those on a plate alongside the coffees.

When James returned to the bedroom, Juanita was still fast asleep. He kissed her on the cheek; she stirred, turning her head to one side but still, she did not wake. He gently shook her shoulder, calling her name; she gradually began emerging from sleep's embrace, her eyelids flickering as she spread her arms and stretched her whole body, arching her back and giving a contented sigh. She smiled, putting a hand behind James's neck and pulling him towards her for a kiss.

'Coffee?' said James, moving over to the window and pulling back the drapes a little.

'Mmm,' she purred, her nostrils wrinkling as she picked up the delicious aroma. She propped herself up on one elbow, turning towards the tray that James had set down on the bedside cabinet. 'Cookies too?' she said, raising an eyebrow and brushing aside an unruly mass of long, dark hair from her face. 'What's this ... some sort of special occasion that I've forgotten?'

He chuckled. 'No, nothing like that. It's just that I couldn't sleep.'

Her finely tuned antennae had obviously picked up on his troubled mood, for suddenly, the veil of sleep had slipped from her completely. She shuffled herself into a sitting position and locked eyes with him. 'What is it?'

'I need to talk to you about something.'

'So talk away,' she said, her wrinkled brow telegraphing a mix of puzzlement and concern.

He passed her coffee to her and took a sip of his own. 'You remember last night's news report?'

'Well, yes ... I guess so ... but what exactly—?'

'You remember the main stories?'

'I ... uh ... yes, I think so. There was the earthquake in Mexico, more horrific bombing in the Middle East ... the government shutdown ... What are you getting at, James?'

'You remember the report about the young journalist murdered in Central Park?'

'Oh ... yes. She worked for the New York Times ... only twenty-four years old, I think they said. Horrible.'

He nodded, slowly. 'Why would anyone want to kill a young girl like that?'

She shook her head in puzzlement. 'I don't know ... it's New York City. All kinds of crazy stuff goes on down there. I don't get it – why are you asking me about this?'

He fixed her with a steady stare. 'I think I might know who killed her.'

Chapter 3

They sat opposite one another at the breakfast bar while James shared what was on his mind.

'You remember what they said about the way she died?' he began.

Juanita visibly shuddered. 'Well, if what they reported was true, she was shot once in the chest and once through her ear … absolutely barbaric.' The colour drained from her face at the retelling of the horrific details of the murder. 'But didn't the police refuse to confirm that?'

'They did, but these news channels often have a knack of getting hold of information long before the authorities are prepared to confirm it.'

She nodded. 'I guess so. But you still haven't told me how you think you know who the killer was.'

James's face was grimly set. He hated delving into this murky chapter from his past, but now that he had raised the subject, there was no going back. 'You know what I was before … well, before we met … before it all happened.'

'Yes, of course' she said, 'but what does that have to do with any of this?'

'Look … I don't remember too much about that time, but …' He cast his eyes downward, trying to compose himself for what he was about to say.

'But what?' she urged.

'These professional assassins … they will often bring down their victim with a body shot – easiest and biggest target, you see – and then …' – he hesitated as he felt the fragile barrier of self-control within him begin to falter, but forced himself to continue – '… then finish the job with a shot to the head.'

That was it: the dam burst, and the emotion overwhelmed him; tears sprang from the corners of his eyes and he began to weep, his shoulders heaving with each anguished sob.

Juanita jumped to her feet, rushed around the breakfast bar, and pulled his head towards her, hugging him to her breast. 'James … oh, my love … what is it? Tell me.'

He clung to her, for a minute or so, immersing himself in her warmth and comfort while he struggled to regain control. Eventually he eased himself away from her arms, wiping away the tears with the back of his hand.

'It's just that … well, I can still hardly bring myself to believe that *I* was one of those people … that I could have—'

'Stop it!' she cried, cupping his face in her hands and locking eyes with him. 'I don't care what you *were*; *this* is the man I fell in love with – the man you are *now*. Come on – you need to tell me the whole story now.'

'Can I have another coffee?' he said. 'I just need a minute or two to … well … compose myself, I guess. I'm all over the place right now.'

She smiled, kissing him on the cheek. 'Sure … take as long as you need.'

She moved over to the coffee machine to pour him another cup. When she returned to the breakfast bar, setting down the coffee cup, he was ready.

'As I said, I still don't remember all that much about my former life, but I do remember one man in particular: a professional assassin who worked within the same network as I did. They had operatives all over the world, but this man, like me, was English. I think the reason I remember this guy, specifically, is because of the way he operated … the way he *was*.'

Juanita tilted her head, enquiringly. 'What exactly do you mean?'

'This guy didn't do what he did just for the money; he *enjoyed* it. Even if he had the opportunity to take down his victims cleanly, he wouldn't always do so. He liked to bring them down first, without killing them, and then close in and see the terror in their eyes as he put the muzzle of the gun into their ear before delivering the killing shot.'

Juanita's hand flew to her mouth, her eyes wide with shock as she drew in a sharp breath. She took a second or two before she could speak.

'I can't … I mean, how could anyone be such a sadistic monster?'

James shrugged, shaking his head. 'That, I can't begin to explain. It's just the way he was.'

'Incredible,' gasped Juanita.

James continued, 'This guy was always so arrogant – so sure he'd never be caught – that he never made any attempt to disguise who had done the killing by varying his *modus operandi*. It was almost as if he *wanted* the authorities to know … to taunt them.'

'And you think this is the man who murdered the journalist in New York?'

'Well I can't be sure, of course, but the chest shot – which, by accident or design, missed her heart – and the killing shot though the ear … it has all the hallmarks of his work.'

'Anyway,' continued James, 'here's the thing: although, as I said, the money wasn't important to him – he was already well on his way to becoming a billionaire – his reputation was such that he could easily command a fee running into millions, or even tens of millions, for a single hit.'

'My God!' gasped Juanita. 'Can these hit men really earn that sort of money?'

James shook his head. 'Only a very, very few … and a client will normally only pay this kind of money to take out someone *very* important, like a head of state, or a major crime boss, or head of a drugs cartel for example.'

The dawning recognition of where he was going with this began to register on Juanita's face. 'You mean, not …'

'Not a junior journalist,' he confirmed.

'So why …?'

'I can only think of two possibilities: either it wasn't the guy I'm thinking about at all, or this girl was onto something very big … something which certain people would be prepared to pay almost anything to keep under wraps.'

She nodded, slowly, pursing her lips as she digested his words, an expectant silence between them.

After some seconds, she said, 'So it could be nothing to do with this man at all … it could be a random mugging by some low-life criminal, couldn't it?'

'It could,' agreed James, pausing before adding, 'but if it *is* him, then …'

'Oh, James … please tell me you're not going to get involved in this. We have a good life here now, I couldn't bear to see you get mixed up with those hideous people again.'

He met her gaze; the pleading in her eyes pierced him to the core, but he knew he couldn't just ignore what he felt in his gut. 'I'm sorry, Juanita, but I'm worried that someone, somewhere, is planning some horrendous crime. If I stand back and let more people die, I just wouldn't be able to live with myself.'

'Then why don't you give the police an anonymous tip-off … let them deal with it.'

He shook his head. 'I don't even know this man's name, and I have no idea where he lives or where he would be. The cops would most likely just dismiss it as a crank call.'

She sighed, her shoulders slumping in defeat. 'So what do you want to do?'

'There is a way I might be able to find out for sure whether it was this man who killed her, but I'd have to go to New York City for a few days to dig into it.'

'And if it's not him?'

'Then I promise you I'll step away and leave it to the cops.'

'But if it is?' she pressed.

'I … I don't exactly know, but—'

'OK, stop,' she cut in. 'If you insist on doing this, then I'm coming with you.'

'No … there's no need for that. I can just—'

'I'm coming,' she insisted, her mouth firmly set, her eyes fiery with determination. 'I'm not going to sit here, worried sick that you're doing something stupid. In any case,' she continued, 'you might just need some help.'

James had seen that look before: it was one of the things about her which had captured his heart during their terrifying ordeal in Miami. Although he felt deeply apprehensive about the prospect of Juanita getting involved, he knew her well enough by now to know that she would not be dissuaded. And, he had to admit, in a tight spot, there was no-one in the world that he'd rather have by his side.

Despite his unease, he couldn't stop himself from cracking a small smile.

'We'd better get packed then.'

***

James and Juanita had come away from Miami with a very substantial sum of money. They had found the cash, and numerous fake passports, concealed beneath the false bottom of a briefcase which James had been carrying before sustaining the head injury which had robbed him of his memory. James didn't know where the money had come from or why he had been carrying it, but he wasn't about to try and find out – and, in the process, risk one or both of them being discovered by their pursuers.

They decided not to rely on this windfall for their everyday living expenses, though; instead, James had taken a job as a security guard working on armoured vehicles transporting cash around the city, while Juanita – a talented artist – was making a modest income from selling her paintings. As James had pointed out, 'You never know when we might just need some of that money: if either the bad guys or the police ever look like catching up with us, we might have to run again.' Well, it hadn't happened yet and, as a full year had now passed, it didn't look as though it was going to. Nevertheless, they had stuck to their resolution not to use too much of the cash and, so far, they had spent very little of it. They were also conscious that if they suddenly became big spenders, they might draw unwanted attention to themselves.

The situation in which they now found themselves, however, meant that they had no alternative but to dip into their cash reserves. James had already used up most of his two weeks annual vacation allowance, and when he approached his employer to request an additional one week's unpaid leave, the response had been distinctly unhelpful. They told him that if he wanted more time off, he'd have to quit his job and re-apply for it when he returned. They couldn't guarantee that they'd still have a job for him, though. Although Juanita had, initially, been very uneasy about this mission which James was intent on, she backed him to the hilt when he said he wanted to quit his job and take his chances on picking it up again upon their return to Canada.

And so, just two days after hearing of Julia Turner's murder, they found themselves sitting together on a plane bound for JFK Airport. While Juanita dozed alongside him, James was wide awake as his brain grappled with the difficult question of how he might discover the crucial piece of evidence which would confirm whether the perpetrator of the murder was the man he suspected.

And if it is him, he thought, *what exactly am I going to do next?*

Chapter 4

Kyle Richards had never been able to come to terms with the vicious and brutal murder of his girlfriend, just over a year ago. Sylvia had been the love of his life, whom he had intended to marry, but she had been cruelly snatched away from him. The Miami-Dade Police had been unable to find the killer or even come up with any plausible reason why Sylvia had been targeted. It was, they said, an apparently random and motiveless murder – perhaps a mugging which had gone too far.

Kyle didn't buy it. Sylvia had been killed just inside the entrance hall of her own apartment block, with a single shot to the centre of her forehead, and none of the little cash she had in her purse had been taken. He had long felt that the police just hadn't put enough effort into investigating the murder; they were probably too preoccupied with the high-profile bombing at the Palm Grove hotel which had almost succeeded in killing the brilliant research scientist and his entire team responsible for the revolutionary new cocaine addiction cure, which was now being hailed as a breakthrough in the war against the illegal drugs trade. Ironic, he reflected, that in spite of the vast resources they had deployed on that case, compared to the cursory dismissal of Sylvia's murder, it too, remained unsolved.

There was one other thing about Sylvia's death which gnawed incessantly at his brain: the cryptic note from her best friend Carla which he had received soon after Sylvia's death, together with $20,000 in cash. How could Carla, on a restaurant server's modest salary, have laid hands on that sort of money? And what on earth did her puzzling note actually mean? He took the creased and yellowing piece of paper from his pocket, unfolded it, and read it for the hundredth time.

Kyle,

I can't tell you how devastated I am by what happened to Sylvia. I can't imagine what you must be going through right now. The fact that Sylvia's funeral has had to be delayed while the authorities carry out an autopsy must have made things even worse – if that is possible.

For reasons which are too complicated to explain, I have to leave Miami for good. Before I go, though, I need to tell you something – I know what happened to her.

You know full well that she – and I – got involved with some pretty bad people, but she never did anything to cross them and that's not why she died. Sadly, she was just in the wrong place at the wrong time and became an innocent victim of something else entirely.

I wish I could explain more, but really, I can't. To do so might put other lives in danger, so all I can say is that she did nothing to deserve such a fate.

I know money can't begin to compensate for the loss of such a wonderful person, but I'd like you to be able to at least give her a fitting send-off, so use as much of the $20,000 as you need for this. Whatever is left over is for you to use as you wish.

You're probably wondering how I have come by that sort of money. I'm afraid that's another part of a very complicated story which I just can't tell you, except to say it wasn't through my doing anything criminal.

Sadly, I won't be able to attend the funeral of my very best friend. In fact, I can't ever come back to Miami, and you will never see me again. You know, though, that my thoughts and prayers will always be with you – and Sylvia.

All my love, Carla x

Sylvia, a Brooklyn girl, and Carla, a Mexican immigrant, had been the very best of friends. Although he had only actually met Carla once himself, he knew, from everything Sylvia had said about her, that the two of them were like sisters. Why on earth would her friend have taken off like that? Where did she get the money from? Where was she now? And the biggest question of all: what did she know about Sylvia's murder?

Somehow, he had to track her down.

***

James and Juanita had checked into The Manhattan at Times Square hotel in New York City. It had probably been built in the sixties, with evidence of some retro art-deco details here and there. It had obviously been refurbished though, and inside it was modern and comfortable. It was only a short distance from the New York Times office and from the scene of the murder – a good location to work from.

Once they were settled in, James wasted no time in getting down to business. 'I need to get a copy of the autopsy report. If I can see all the details, I should be able to figure out whether this killing was the work of the man I told you about.'

Juanita shook her head. 'Surely, they'll only release that to a family member.'

'So, I'll have to pose as a family member.'

'But they'll want to see I.D. – proof of who you are.'

'I know,' he said, 'but look, we managed to fake completely new identities when we fled to Canada, didn't we?'

Juanita's forehead creased in a frown. 'Well yes but—'

James stepped over to the suitcase which lay open on the bed – they hadn't even finished unpacking yet. He withdrew a thick, brown envelope.

'We still have these,' he said, emptying the contents of the envelope onto the bed.

The dozen or so passports – a legacy of his former occupation – spanned a variety of nationalities. James picked up a U.S. passport, opening it to reveal that the title page was blank, the plastic sheet which covered it not yet sealed down.

'You're planning to fake an identity as a relative in order to get a copy of the autopsy report?'

He nodded.

'What relative?'

'I don't know … maybe her father.'

'Risky … he may well have been to identify the body already.'

'Maybe a brother then.'

'Hmm … not wishing to be disparaging, but aren't you a bit old to be the brother of a twenty-four-year-old?'

'Hey you,' he laughed, 'I look young for my age.'

'Maybe, but there's something else you need to consider.'

He inclined his head, enquiringly. 'And that is?'

'Have you seen a photo of the dead girl?'

'Well, no,' he admitted. 'I don't think the news report included a photo.'

'The original one didn't,' she agreed, 'but they've released one now. Get your laptop.'

A few minutes later they were huddled around the laptop looking at the latest report on Julia Turner's death. They gazed at her photograph.

'It never occurred to me,' muttered James, 'with a name like Turner, who'd have guessed that she was a Latina?'

'Well, probably not first-generation but, from her skin tone and features, she clearly had some Hispanic blood in her.'

Suddenly, he knew where Juanita was going with this. He raised his hand towards her, palm-outward.

'No,' he said, firmly, 'absolutely not. I won't have you risking—'

'Shhh,' she said, taking his raised hand and gently easing it downward. 'Look at it logically. Which of us stands the better chance of pulling this off?'

'Well, that's not the point,' he spluttered.

'Isn't it? I look like she did, I'm nearer her age, and my accent is going to be way more convincing than yours. I could easily be her older sister.'

'Well, I suppose that's true,' he admitted, but—'

'No "buts",' she insisted, her face displaying that look of fierce determination he knew so well. 'If you want that report, I'm the one who stands by far the best chance of getting it for you.'

He knew there was no arguing with her when she became set on any given course of action, besides which, he had to admit she was probably right.

'W-ell, I suppose …' he began, but Juanita was already rummaging through the pile of blank passports. She held up a U.S. one.

'I assume – since you were planning to fake a passport for yourself – that you've brought the portable printer with you?'

He nodded.

'Come on,' she urged, 'you get busy on the laptop, while I go out and find a photo booth. I'll leave you to decide on her sister's first name.'

With that, she grabbed her coat and purse, and swept from the room.

Chapter 5

Kyle Richards stood just across the street from Eduardo's Restaurant. It was hardly worthy of the title: from the outside it looked more like a basic diner. The most noteworthy feature on the rather drab frontage was a logo of a leaping swordfish alongside the title. But he hadn't come for the culinary experience. This was where Carla had worked before she fled Miami and went to ground; it was the only starting point he could think of to find some clue as to where she had gone.

Not wishing to dice with the heavy traffic moving in both directions, he walked about fifty yards to the nearest crosswalk and then doubled back to the diner.

When he stepped inside, he found that the interior looked barely more salubrious than the exterior had suggested. The tables were topped with plastic laminate, of a garish red tone, accompanied by basic steel-framed stacking chairs, which had definitely seen better days. The floor was covered in beige-coloured ceramic tiles, some of which were cracked, and the cream paintwork on the walls was in need of some attention. Nevertheless, the whole place was clean and tidy, and despite its unprepossessing appearance, it was almost full; they must have been doing something right. Most of the customers, and staff, appeared to be of Latino descent.

There weren't many vacant seats, but he spotted a small booth at the back wall which was empty; that would do. He went over and claimed his seat.

He picked up the rather dog-eared menu card propped up between a ketchup bottle and the salt and pepper mills. As he scanned the list, he was struck by how very reasonable the prices seemed; maybe that was why the place was so popular. Before he had a chance to make his lunch selection, a heavily accented voice interrupted him.

'Hi, my name's Ana. I'll be your server today.'

He looked up to see a young, rather attractive girl of Latina appearance, smiling down at him.

'Are you ready to order, sir?'

'Hi … uh, I'm still choosing just now.'

'Oh, sure … I'll give you a few minutes. Can I get you something to drink?'

'Yeah … thanks. I'll take a coffee, please … black, no sugar.'

'Coming right up.'

When she returned with his coffee, she took from her pocket a small notebook and pen. 'Ready to order now?'

'I am,' he said, smiling.

'What'll it be then?'

'I'll take the Spanish omelette please … with a side of fries and a small salad.'

'You got it,' she replied scribbling the order in her notebook.

'Say, Ana,' interjected Kyle, just as the girl was about to turn away.

'Uh-huh?'

'How long have you worked here?'

'Oh … about a year or so, I guess. Why?'

'It's just that I'm trying to catch up with a friend that I've lost touch with. She used to work here, and I wondered if maybe you knew her.'

'I might … what's her name?'

'Carla … she's from Mexico.'

The girl pinched her chin between thumb and forefinger, drawing her eyes together and pursing her lips It took her just a few seconds to recall. 'Oh, yeah … sure. She left just a couple of weeks after I started here.'

'Any idea where she might be now?'

She shook her head. 'Sorry, no idea. I hardly knew her.'

'Oh,' said Kyle, 'well, I guess it was a bit of a long shot.'

'But María might know,' she said.

'María?'

'Sure. She and Carla were real good friends; she still goes on about what a shame it was that Carla left so suddenly and moved away.'

Kyle's heart jumped; this sounded much more promising. 'Great! Does María work here?'

'Sure, but—'

'Any chance I could have a word with her?' cut in Kyle, eagerly.

'Not today … that's what I was about to say. She's not working today … but if you come in around the same time tomorrow, she'll be here.'

Kyle smiled. 'I will … thanks so much, Ana.'

'Sure … now let me get you that omelette.'

***

The Edward Mason Pathology Laboratory was an impressive, marble and smoked-glass creation, its frontage presenting an almost-perfect, reflected image of the building opposite. Juanita's heart was pounding as she approached the front door: what, the previous day, had sounded like a feasible plan, now felt like the height of folly – fraught with danger. James was waiting in their rental car, just around the corner, ready to whisk her away quickly if things went wrong, but there were just so *many* things that could go wrong. She swallowed hard – her throat already dry as sand – and pushed the door open.

Inside, everything was white: the walls, the ceiling, the floor, even the two couches in the reception area – not to mention the crisply tailored shirt worn by the woman behind the desk. She was probably in her early-to-mid thirties, sporting an abundant shock of tumbling blonde tresses and immaculate, if a little over-heavy, makeup. As Juanita approached her, she looked up, her face displaying a smile which somehow managed to be both sympathetic and tragic at the same time. When she spoke, her tone matched her facial expression: soft, concerned, and understanding.

'Hello,' said the receptionist, 'how can I help you today?'

I wonder how long she has spent in front of a mirror perfecting a tone and demeanour appropriate for this place of death and sorrow? thought Juanita – perhaps, she had to admit, a little uncharitably, considering she didn't even know the woman.

She did her best to compose herself before replying, trying to ignore her racing heartbeat and sweaty palms. Even so, her voice, when she uttered her first words, sounded unnaturally tremulous to her own ears.

'My name is Susan Turner. My late sister was recently admitted here for an autopsy.'

'Oh, I'm so sorry,' said the other woman, but the compassionate smile had turned into a puzzled frown.

'Did you say your name was Turner?'

'Yes … I'm Julia Turner's sister.'

The woman's frown momentarily deepened, before the sympathetic smile reasserted itself. 'Of course. Please accept our condolences on the shocking death of your sister.'

Juanita cast her eyes downward, as she effected her very best impression of a suppressed sob. She pulled a tissue from her purse and dabbed at her eyes.

'I realise how upsetting this must be for you. Please, take a seat and let me get you a coffee.'

Juanita shook her head, dabbing away another imaginary tear. 'Just a glass of water, please.'

She sat down on the white couch, before accepting the glass of water which the woman drew from the water cooler in the corner of the room.

'Thank you,' said Juanita, taking a grateful sip of the cooling liquid.

'Now … how can I help you today?'

This was the critical moment. Julia took a deep breath before replying. 'I've come to get a copy of my sister's autopsy report.'

The other woman's smile slipped, as her eyes narrowed slightly. 'Its normal procedure to phone ahead and make an appointment for anything like that.'

'Oh, I'm sorry … I didn't realise. You see I've just flown in from Los Angeles, and I thought it would save time to come straight here.'

'I see … well, please wait there for a moment while I get Julia's file.'

She moved back to her desk and withdrew a key from the top drawer, before turning towards a door in the back wall of the room. She unlocked the door and went into the room, leaving the door open; Juanita could see that it contained several tall filing cabinets. She watched closely as the woman opened the second drawer from the top of one of the cabinets, leafing through the hanging files until she found the one she wanted. She laid it on top of the open drawer and began perusing the papers it contained. Seconds passed, and then minutes. *Why is she taking so long?* thought Juanita. She took another swallow of water to lubricate her throat which, by now, felt like blotting paper.

At length, the woman picked up the file and closed the drawer, coming back into the main reception area and closing the door behind her. She sat on the other couch, set at right angles to the one on which Juanita was sitting.

'Now, according to my notes,' she said, maintaining the soothing, concerned tone of voice, 'your parents have already identified the body and have had a copy of the autopsy report. And it seems that—'

This seemed like the right time to try to evoke more sympathy. 'Oh my God,' wailed Juanita, 'how can my lovely sister be just "the body"?' She grabbed another couple of tissues, wiping her eyes and smearing her makeup.

'I'm sorry … I didn't mean to … do you need a few moments to—?'

'No … no, I'm alright, thank you,' she sniffed, doing her best to sound anything but.

'OK, well I'm sorry to have to ask you but … well, there's no mention of any sister in the file.'

'There isn't?' said Juanita, widening her eyes in fake surprise. 'Then I guess Mom and Pop must have forgotten to mention it. You see, I haven't seen them for around fifteen years … they didn't exactly approve when I got pregnant at sixteen, and they more-or-less disowned me. I've been living in Los Angeles ever since.' As Juanita looked into the other woman's eyes she could not discern, from her expression, whether she believed any of this story. She pressed on anyway. 'But when something like this happens,' – she managed a slight hitch in her voice – 'well, it kinda puts everything into perspective. I'm going to go and see them right after this to try and build some bridges.'

Juanita stopped, looking up at the other woman again to try and ascertain whether this tale was cutting any ice. From the pursed lips and furrowed brow, it didn't look too good. Nevertheless, the woman continued to maintain the caring and considerate tone of voice, even though her body language and facial expression gave the lie to its sincerity.

'I'm sorry to have to ask you this, but do you have any I.D. with you?'

'Oh, sure … I have my passport here.' She fished in her purse for the fake passport and handed it over, hoping that the confirmation of her fictitious name and Los Angeles address would help validate her story.

The woman's expression softened a little. 'Thank you. That all seems to be in order.' She paused for a few moments before adding, 'Would you mind just confirming your parents' names?'

Thank goodness I did my homework thoroughly, thought Juanita. She replied without hesitation. 'Sure … Richard's my father, and Isabella's my mom.'

Juanita's confident reply seemed to mollify the other woman's apparent concern: her expression relaxed as she glanced at the file, open in front of her, giving an almost-imperceptible nod. However, Juanita wasn't out of the woods yet.

The woman closed the file and placed it on her lap as she made eye contact. 'I'm afraid I'm going to have to clear this with my boss before I can release a copy of the report,' she declared, standing up.

Shit! thought Juanita, now starting to panic. 'Oh sure … of course,' she said, trying to sound as calm and composed as she possibly could.

The woman went back into the other room and returned the file to its original location. When she came back into the main reception area, she locked the door behind her and returned the key to her desk drawer. 'I'll just be a few minutes,' she said, striding towards a corridor at the side of the room.

Alarmingly, she was still holding the passport. Juanita was wracked with indecision: should she ask the woman to return the passport before leaving the room … or would that look too suspicious? But, within a couple of seconds, the woman was gone: too late now, anyway.

Juanita leapt to her feet, heart pounding furiously, and rushed over to the desk, pulling open the drawer. To her horror, the key was nowhere to be seen. She began frantically rummaging through the contents of the drawer: no sign of the damned key. *Shit, shit, shit!* Suddenly, it occurred to her that, from where she had been sitting, the perspective may have distorted her view of which drawer the key had been placed in. She slammed the centre drawer shut and wrenched open the top left-hand-side drawer. There was the key, lying on top of some papers.

Taking a deep breath to try to calm her nerves, Juanita stepped over to the door. Her hands were trembling so much that she took three attempts to insert the key in the lock, but once in place it turned easily. She rushed over to the relevant filing cabinet; this time she made no mistake about which drawer to open, and quickly located Julia Turner's file.

She opened the file at the first page and laid it on top of the open drawer, rummaging in her purse for her cell phone to photograph it.

Shit! Her cell was out of charge. *How fucking stupid of me not to check it before coming here.*

She had, however, already noticed that the filing room contained a photocopier; she'd have to use that and smuggle out the hard copy. However, the autopsy report was spiral bound down one edge, so she wouldn't be able to feed the sheets automatically; she would have to laboriously copy each page individually, folding them back each time to place on the glass bed. But how much time did she have before the other woman returned? There was no time to waste; she set about her task, working as fast as her trembling hands, and the painfully slow scanning speed of the machine, would allow.

She had only copied around half of the pages when she heard something outside the room. She stopped what she was doing for a moment to listen; the distant click-clack of heels on tiles was overlaid with the sound of two voices: a woman's and a man's. Her heart jumped in her chest as she realised the sounds were getting louder. *Fuck!*

Chapter 6

When Kyle Richards returned to Eduardo's Restaurant, the girl, Ana, who had previously served him, was not there. In her place was a shorter, slightly more heavily built woman – also of Latina appearance. She smiled at him as she came to take his order.

'Hi, my name's María. I'll be your server today. What can I get you sir?'

Same script as the other girl, thought Kyle. *Must be standard here.* It was an absurdly trivial observation, he realised. *I need to concentrate on the task in hand.*

He smiled back at her. 'Can I just get a cold beer to start while I choose?'

'Oh, sure,' she replied. 'I'll get that for you right now. Any preferences?'

'Bud Light'll be fine, thanks.'

She was only gone for a minute or two before returning with his beer.

'Thanks, María. Uh, can I ask you something?'

She laughed. 'Well that's what I'm here for, so ask away. The cheeseburgers are real good.'

Kyle chuckled. 'No, not about the food.'

She inclined her head, little crinkles appearing at the corners of her eyes as she gave a curious smile. 'Well … what then?'

'I was in here yesterday and had a chat with the other girl who works here, Ana.'

'Yeah, well so do most of the guys who come in here,' she laughed. 'I gotta admit she is kinda cute.'

'Well, yes she is,' laughed Kyle, 'but that's not what I meant.'

'Go on then.'

'I'm trying to get in touch with someone, and Ana said you might be able to help.'

Her expression became even more curious. 'So, who is it that you're looking for?'

'Her name's Carla – she used to work here, and I gather you were good friends with her.'

Her eyes narrowed and her tone immediately changed. 'Yeah, she and I were friends. Why do you want to get in touch with her?'

It was an obvious question to ask, and Kyle was prepared for it: he had decided that it would be best to be completely honest. He swallowed hard before replying.

'About a year ago, my girlfriend was murdered.'

She gasped, her eyes widening and her mouth forming a perfect 'O' shape. There was an almighty crash as the metal tray she was carrying fell to the floor; every face in the diner turned towards them at the sound. Fortunately, she had already set down the beer on the table. She seemed rooted to the spot as the colour drained from her face.

'Let me get that,' said Kyle, leaning over and picking up the tray.

The other diners quickly lost interest and returned to their meals and their conversations.

'Sorry to have shocked you like that,' said Kyle, 'but I wanted you to realise how important this is.'

María finally found her voice. 'I … well, when you just come right out with something like that it's kinda …well …'

'I know. I'm sorry.'

'Look,' she continued, 'I'm real sorry to hear about your girlfriend but what does that have to do with Carla?'

'Carla was her best friend. I think she might know something about the murder.'

María shook her head. 'No … Carla would never—'

Kyle raised his hand, palm-outward. 'No … I'm not for a moment suggesting Carla was involved but, before she disappeared, she left me a note. The police never solved the case but, from Carla's note, I'm sure she knows something about what happened.'

María backed away slightly. 'I … I'm sorry, but I can't help you. I haven't seen Carla for over year. I have no idea where she is now.'

'Do you at least have a phone number or email … any way I could contact her?'

She shook her head. 'Sorry, no … nothing.'

But Kyle had picked up the way she broke eye contact as she made this assertion.

'Are you sure there's no way? I'm desperate, and you're my only hope.'

He thought he detected a hint of sympathy in her eyes, but she remained resolute. 'I'm sorry, but I don't know where she is or how to contact her.'

'OK,' he replied, shoulders slumping in defeat, 'well, I guess it always was a long shot. I'm really sorry to have upset you like that just now.'

Suddenly, the mood changed; she seemed to shake free of the nervous veil which had descended upon her. 'It's OK … like I said, I'm real sorry about what happened.' She hesitated before taking a notebook from her pocket and adding, 'You still want something to eat?'

'Sure,' said Kyle, smiling as he sought to continue lightening the mood, 'I'll go with your recommendation and take the cheeseburger.'

She nodded, jotting down his order and turning away towards the kitchen. He had the sense that she was relieved to have terminated their discussion.

Kyle was convinced that this woman knew more than she was admitting to. He was, however, ready for this eventuality. Now he would put into action his pre-prepared plan.

Chapter 7

Juanita was out of time. There was no way she could return the file to its proper location, get out of the room, lock the door behind her, return the key to the desk drawer, and get back to the couch in the few seconds – at most – that she had left. The only thing to do now was run.

She gathered up the pages she had copied, grabbed her purse from where it lay on top of the filing cabinet, and rushed back into reception, leaving the original report on the photocopier and the key in the lock of the open door to the filing room. The clacking of heels on the hard floor sounded alarmingly close now.

She rushed towards the main entrance, wrenching open the door just as a woman's voice sounded behind her.

'Excuse me Miss Turner, but—'

Juanita didn't look back; the moment she was outside, she broke into a run. She didn't break stride or glance back once as she sprinted away. It took her but a minute or so to reach James in the waiting car. He must have seen her coming, for he already had the engine running and the passenger door open as she approached. She leapt into the passenger seat and slammed the door; with a brief chirrup from the tyres, the car pulled out into the dense stream of traffic. Only once they were underway did Juanita risk a glance over her shoulder, her heart pounding and her breath coming in desperate gasps; there was no-one following. *Thank God!*

'What happened?' said James, stealing an anxious glance in the rear-view mirror.

'They ...' – she had to pause to gain control of her ragged breathing – 'they almost caught me. The woman in there seemed suspicious: she asked me a bunch of questions ... which ... well, I think I answered them OK, but I could tell she wasn't entirely convinced. In the end she asked me to wait in reception while she went to check with her boss.'

James glanced anxiously across at her. 'So,' he said, checking in the mirror before twirling the wheel to make a left turn, 'what did you do?'

'Well, while she was talking to me, she had the report right there in her hand, but when she went off to see her boss, she didn't take it with her; she put it back in the filing cabinet where she had got it from. It was in a locked room, but while she was gone, I managed to get hold of the key and find the report.'

'Is that it?' he said, casting a glance towards the slightly crumpled pile of papers on Juanita's lap.

'No. I thought it would be too risky to take the original report, so I decided to copy it. I thought I'd have time to make the copy, put the original back in its proper place, and lock the room before she came back. That way they'd never even know that a copy had been made.'

'So what happened?'

'Unfortunately, she wasn't gone for as long as I'd hoped. I was in the middle of copying the report when I heard her coming back. She was talking with some guy – probably her boss. There was no time to do anything but run.'

'Oh Christ!' he breathed. 'Thank God you managed to get away. If they'd stopped you and called the cops, we'd be in deep shit now.'

'I guess so,' she agreed.

'Anyway, how much did you manage to copy?'

She sighed. 'Only about the first half, I'm afraid.'

'Well, I guess we'll just have to hope that's enough. At least you got away safely; that's the main thing. I should never have let you take such a risk.'

'There's something else,' she said.

James had obviously picked up the anxiety in her tone. 'What? What's the matter?'

She exhaled loudly enough for him to swivel his head towards her. 'They have my fake passport.'

'What? But how—?'

'The woman took it away to show her boss, and when they were coming back before I'd finished copying the report, I had no choice but to run for it and leave the passport behind.'

'So that means …'

'… they have my photograph,' she confirmed.

'And it won't take the police long to discover that the passport's a fake,' he added.

Juanita summed it up. 'So, they know what I look like, they know I was using a fake I.D. and they know I was digging into the autopsy details of a murder victim. That probably makes me …'

'… their prime suspect,' muttered James. 'Shit!' he hissed, slamming his hand down on the top of the steering wheel.

Chapter 8

Kyle Richards was a telecoms engineer by profession, and this was one occasion when his technical knowledge would serve him well. While waiting for the server to return with his cheeseburger, he took from his pocket a device which looked rather like a normal smartphone, except that it was a little bulkier and had four conventional keys below the touchscreen. He put it down on the chair alongside him, next to the baseball cap he had laid there when he first sat down. He pressed the on/off key, and within a second or so the home screen appeared. A couple more taps and swipes took him to the screen he wanted. Now he would be ready to activate his plan with just a single key press at the appropriate time. He covered the device with his baseball cap to ensure that no-one would be able to see it. Now he waited, taking occasional sips of his beer. In spite of the over-zealous aircon, Kyle was sweating profusely.

Where the hell was María? She seemed to be taking far too long just to fetch him a cheeseburger. Did she suspect something? Had she spoken to her boss … or even called the cops? His pulse was racing now; maybe he should just abandon his plan and get out of there. He checked his watch: it was only five minutes since he had placed his order; somehow, it felt more like twenty. *Calm down*, he told himself. *Just wait – she'll be back.*

At that precise moment she reappeared, making her way towards him with his burger. He tried to conceal the huge sigh of relief which he exhaled.

She still looked a little wary as she set down his meal on the table: her smile was present and correct, but her eyes told a different story. Even so, she went through her standard spiel smoothly enough.

'There you go sir. Can I get you anything else?'

Kyle slid his hand under the baseball cap and located, by touch, the far right-hand key on the device, pressing it once. 'I'm good, thanks,' he said.

She turned to leave; that was no good – he needed her stay close for at least a minute or so.

'Say,' he said, touching her arm – she stopped and turned back – 'I'm sorry about earlier. I never meant to upset you.'

'It's OK,' she replied – although the way she struggled to maintain eye contact suggested otherwise – 'it was just a bit of a shock to hear what happened to your girlfriend. Anyway, I hope you—'

'Thing is,' he said, anxious to keep her there a little longer, 'you were my last hope, and now … well I don't know what I'm going to do.'

'I'm sorry … really I am … but I just can't help you. Now, I really gotta get on.' She made as if to turn away again.

No, just a few more seconds, he thought.

'Uh, before you go …'

She looked at him, enquiringly.

'I appreciate that you don't know how to get in contact with Carla, but is there anyone else who might? Another girlfriend? Maybe a relative? I'm really desperate here.'

Now, Kyle thought he detected genuine sympathy in her eyes, but her response was just the same.

She shook her head. 'Look, I'm real sorry, but I don't know where she is, and I don't know of anyone else who might.'

He couldn't string this out any longer without either pissing her off or arousing suspicion that he had an ulterior motive. He hoped he had kept her there long enough.

'OK … I understand. Thanks anyway, for your understanding.'

'Sure,' she said. 'Now I really must—'

'Yeah, of course,' he said, smiling. 'I've already taken up too much of your time. Look, if by any chance Carla should get in touch with you in the future, will you let me know?' He handed her a card. 'Here's my number.'

Again, he picked up that look of compassion in her eyes, as she took the card and slipped it into her pocket.

'Enjoy your burger,' she said. And then she was gone.

Kyle lifted his baseball cap and stole a glance at the apparatus on the chair alongside him. The message on the screen read 'Scan complete – 5 devices captured'. He managed a grim smile: he had succeeded in illegally cloning María's cell phone and, apparently, those of four nearby diners too. If she had been lying to him and she *was* in contact with Carla, now he would know.

Chapter 9

James and Juanita made it back to their hotel without incident.

'I guess I screwed up pretty badly,' said Juanita, flinging the part-copied report down onto the bed and pacing over towards the window, clasping her hands together behind her neck, stretching her arms and shoulders.

'No,' said James, coming up behind her and encircling her waist with his arms. 'It was always going to be a tricky job; you did amazingly well to even get half of the report.'

She turned around and buried her head in his chest, pulling him to her. 'But now the cops are going to be looking for me, and they have my photo.' She stifled a sob.

'Shhh … it's OK. We'll work something out.'

She eased herself away from him and looked into his eyes. 'Like what?'

'Well, for a start,' he said, eying her long, glossy, black hair, 'you can change your appearance quite a bit just with a new hairdo.'

She took a lock of her own hair between thumb and forefinger, bringing it round in front of her face to look at it. 'You mean like …'

'Yeah … like when we had to quit Miami. You had it cut shorter and coloured a sort of medium blonde colour, with those darker streaks. It gave you a completely different look.'

She tipped her head to one side, a slight frown crossing her brow as she contemplated the strand of hair she was holding. 'Well, I suppose …'

'And what's more,' he continued, 'that's the look you have in your "official" passport – Juanita's passport.'

'OK,' she said, quickly making her mind up, 'I'll try and find somewhere to get it done tomorrow.'

'Good,' said James, planting a kiss on her cheek.

'But,' she said, 'if the cops are seriously looking for me, I don't think a change of hairstyle will keep me out of trouble for long.'

'I'm not so sure,' opined James. 'All they have is a very small lo-res photo and a completely fictitious name. As long as we're careful we should be able to stay under the radar for a while. Once we get out of New York City and back to Toronto I reckon we should be safe enough.'

'I guess,' she said, not sounding entirely convinced. 'How long do you think we'll need to stay in New York?'

'Depends … If I'm on the wrong track, and this murder was nothing to do with the guy I have in mind, then I'll drop the whole thing and we can get out of here pronto.'

'But how will you know for sure?'

He didn't answer her question directly. 'Let's take a look at what you've managed to copy,' he said, moving over to sit on the bed and picking up the papers, shuffling them into a more orderly pile. Juanita sat down alongside him as he began working through the sheets, reading out loud.

The first page used a lot of words but, in essence, just stated that the victim was female, of Hispanic appearance, aged in her twenties, and well nourished.

The second page described the two gunshot wounds: one to the chest and one inside the left ear. There was no exit wound from the chest shot, but the shot into the ear had emerged from the opposite temple, taking with it a large piece of the girl's skull.

The next two pages contained close-up photographs of the horrific wounds which the victim had suffered. Juanita's hand flew to her mouth to stifle a gasp.

'You don't have to look at the rest of this,' said James, placing a comforting arm around her shoulder.

'I'm OK,' she whispered, looking anything but.

'Sure?'

'Yes – carry on.'

James turned his attention back to the report. The next page speculated on the type of weapon used: the calibre of the bullets could not be accurately determined until the body was opened up and the slug retrieved, but the size of the entry wound in the chest suggested perhaps .38 inch or 9mm.

He paused for a moment, staring at the page. Both were fairly common sizes of bullet, so no real conclusions could be drawn, but he did know that the preferred handgun of his suspect was a 9mm Glock.

'What is it?' prompted Juanita, evidently sensing his disquiet.

'Nothing really – it's just … let's press on.'

He turned the page again: this part of the report detailed an external visual examination of the body. There were no signs of any physical struggle: no scratches or bruises; no traces of skin or fabric under the victim's fingernails, but then …

James froze, silent for several seconds before turning to Juanita and declaring, 'It's him.'

Chapter 10

Juanita's eyes widened. 'How do you know?' she gasped.

'Take a look at this.'

She looked at the photograph he was pointing out: it depicted a small piece of card, creased and heavily bloodstained. 'It looks like a business card, but I can't see any text at all on it … only some sort of image or logo. But with all that bloodstain it's hard to make out what it is.'

'It was rolled up and pushed into her throat, which was probably full of blood from one or both of the wounds,' he explained.

Juanita clapped her hand over her mouth as she tried to stifle the horrified gasp which escaped her lips. 'How could anyone …?' Her voice tailed off.

James didn't try to answer her unfinished question. 'If you look closely, it's just possible to make out what's on the card.'

He passed the report to her; she took it and leaned forward, peering intently at the photograph. 'It looks like … a scorpion.' She looked up at him, searching his eyes.

He nodded slowly, his mouth set in a grim, straight line. 'That's what this man calls himself: "The Scorpion". I don't know what his real name is. As I told you before, he's such an arrogant bastard that he actually advertises who carried out his hits. Not only does he stick to his trademark killing shot through the ear, but he also places one of his calling cards on – or, as in this case, inside – his victims. He seems to want to create an aura of notoriety and fear around his own legend and, in his own mind, he's too damned clever to ever get caught.'

Juanita's mouth hung open for several seconds as she digested James's words. When she finally spoke, there was trepidation in her tone.

'So what do we do now?'

'*We* don't do anything … I need to take it from here on my own. You've already done more than enough, and I can't risk getting you involved any further. The cops have your photo, and the man who carried out this murder is more dangerous than you can possibly imagine. It will be best if you go back to Toronto now, and wait for me there.'

When he looked into her eyes, they were filled with a fierce determination. 'Not a chance,' she insisted. 'We're in this together, and if you think I'm going to just sit at home waiting to hear from you, I'm afraid you'd better think again.'

He sighed heavily; he knew there was no arguing with her when she was like this. 'Well OK, you can stay here in New York but you have to keep a low profile and stay out of trouble.'

She gave a small smile. 'So,' she repeated, 'what do we do now?'

'OK,' said James taking the report from her and putting it aside, 'we need to try to find out what this girl was working on – like I said, it must be something big for anyone to pay this guy's fees to eliminate her.'

Juanita nodded, thoughtfully. 'And if we can find out … what then?'

'That depends on what it is that she was investigating, I guess. We obviously can't go to the police directly, given that we're both living under false identities and wanted by the authorities in Florida. And not only that: the NYPD will also be looking for you in connection with the attempted theft of the autopsy report here in New York.'

'But,' she said, 'if innocent lives are at stake, we have to do *something*. Maybe we could just give an anonymous tip-off to the police,' she suggested.

'Maybe, but we would need some evidence so that the police don't just dismiss it as a crank call.'

'Hmm,' she mused 'maybe we could—'

He shook his head, raising a hand to interrupt her. 'We're getting way ahead of ourselves here. Right now, we have absolutely no idea of what she might have been working on or why she had to be silenced, let alone what to do about it. Let's just take it one step at a time.'

'You're right,' she agreed, 'our first step has to be to find out what she was working on.'

'And right now,' he said, 'I'm not sure how we're going to do that.'

'Nor me,' she sighed. 'Let's sleep on it and see if we can come up with a plan in the morning.'

'Agreed,' he said, 'right now, I'm totally bushed.'

'There is one other thing I need to do in the morning,' said Juanita.

He raised an inquisitive eyebrow, inclining his head as he met her gaze. 'What's that?'

'I need to get that new hairdo. I'll start phoning around right now to see if I can get an early hair appointment somewhere nearby.'

He smiled, drawing her to him and taking a lock of her lustrous, long, black hair between his thumb and forefinger, stroking it tenderly. 'Just when I was getting used to this.'

'Needs must,' she replied pulling away from him. 'Now, let's check out all the hairdressers in the area and see if any of them can fit me in tomorrow.'

***

When the report of the attempted theft of Julia Turner's autopsy report reached the police, Mark Bowman's heart skipped a beat. If this woman had been snooping around using a false name to gain access to Julia's autopsy report, she must surely have been involved in her murder. He had, until now, assumed that the killer must be a man, but why couldn't it be a woman? Although his own sensibilities found the prospect of a woman carrying out such a brutal killing distasteful and repellent, that was no reason why it couldn't be so; God knows, he'd seen some pretty hideous crimes committed by women during his time with the NYPD. But why would she need to see the report? At this stage, he had no answers.

He still had no idea what Julia might have done to provoke her vicious murder on the very day he had planned to propose to her, but maybe there was a lead somewhere here which could guide him to those answers and make sure the perpetrator paid. He immediately asked to be assigned to the investigation, but his boss refused, saying he was too emotionally involved and would not be objective. The case would be assigned to one of his colleagues; Mark was to stay well out of it.

Fuck that! Sure, he was emotionally involved, but what he might lack in objectivity he sure as hell made up for in determination. Whatever his superiors said, he was damned well going to find Julia's murderer. If his insubordination cost him his job, then so be it.

I'm coming for you, you murdering bitch.

Chapter 11

María García Ruiz had finished her shift and was now sitting on her couch in front of the TV, with a home-delivered pizza, still in its box, on her lap.

She wasn't especially hungry, and her attention kept wandering from the – admittedly pretty dire – chat show. The truth was, all she could really think about was the visit from that guy looking for Carla; she had been genuinely moved by his obvious distress. What must it be like to lose a lover under such horrendous circumstances and never know why? How gut-wrenching must it be for him to know her killer still walked free? He was obviously desperate to achieve some sort of closure, and maybe Carla really did have some answers. She had been so secretive about what had happened to make her run like that, just over a year ago, leaving no clue about where she was going, or with whom.

When Carla had left that cell phone number before fleeing Miami, she had insisted that it could only be used to contact her in situations of absolute emergency: say, if the cops were asking questions about her for instance. She had also told María that she must not enter the contact details in her own cell phone for fear that someone, at some time, might discover them. Instead she was to memorise the details and then destroy any paper copy she had. The number, Carla had explained, was not that of her regular cell but of an untraceable pay-as-you-go phone which she could discard at any moment if she needed to. She had, however, promised to keep it always switched on and charged until that moment arrived … if it ever did. María had never once called or texted that number in over a year.

Now, though, she faced a dilemma: was this an emergency sufficient to warrant breaking her silence and calling that number?

Probably not ... and yet, she just could not shake off the image of that poor guy in the diner, utterly distraught, and desperate for answers.

She gave up on the banal chat show and surfed through the other channels, trying to find something more engaging to take her mind off the desperate stranger who had come to see her, seeking her help. She eventually settled for a news channel, but still she could not focus.

She reached for her purse and found the card which this guy had given her. He had not actually mentioned his name when he had spoken to her, but now she read it out loud: 'Kyle Richards'.

She gazed at the card; should she, or shouldn't she?

***

Just a few miles away, Kyle was busy trawling through the contents of María's phone, which he had illegally cloned back at Eduardo's Restaurant.

Her contacts list contained a hundred and ninety-four names, around three-quarters of which sounded like women's names. Not one of them was a 'Carla', however. It was possible, of course, that her details had been entered under some other name, but Kyle quickly dismissed the idea of phoning all the women's names in the list at random in the hope of stumbling across Carla: it would almost certainly get back to María that he was doing so, and as she had *his* contact details this could land him in all kinds of trouble. It was also possible, of course, that Carla's details were not in the contacts list at all.

He decided to go through all María's social media accounts in the hope that she might perhaps be in contact with Carla through one of these.

Facebook: nothing.

Twitter: nothing.

Instagram: nothing.

These appeared to be the only social media platforms that María used.

He slammed his hand on the arm of his chair in frustration; the next step was one he'd hoped to avoid, as it would be agonisingly slow and laborious. There was, however, nothing else for it: he would have to start ploughing through María's emails. Although

Carla didn't appear to be in her contacts list, it was still possible that the two of them could have exchanged emails. And if she was in the contacts list under some other name, it might just be possible to figure it out from the contents of any emails exchanged between the two of them. But this was going to be one hell of a tedious slog, with only a slim chance of yielding a result.

He made himself some strong, black coffee as he prepared to settle to his task; it was going to be a long night.

***

Kyle awoke at 5.40 a.m. still fully clothed; still in his armchair. The handset containing María's cloned phone had fallen to the floor. His throat felt like sandpaper. He had spent hours painfully scouring her emails, refuelling with copious amounts of black coffee to try to stay alert. In the end, though, sleep had overtaken him, and he was still no closer to finding any communication which might have been with Carla. All he had succeeded in doing was to make himself feel like some sort of grubby voyeur as he had probed every detail of María's private life – or at least, every detail that could be revealed from her email traffic. And all for nothing.

With a sigh, he levered himself out of his armchair and staggered through to the kitchen, pouring himself a large glass of water to soothe his parched throat. He made his way through to the bathroom, stripping off his crumpled clothes and letting them fall to the floor. After a quick shower and a change of clothes, he began to feel more human once again, but no less despondent about his chances of locating Carla.

Returning to the kitchen, he loaded the filter machine with yet another couple of spoonfuls of ground coffee and topped up the water reservoir, flipping the power switch on and then popping a couple of slices of bread into the toaster. He wasn't into cooking and had very little food in the fridge, so the toast, together with an apple he grabbed from the glass bowl on the counter top, would have to serve as breakfast.

As he sat down to consume his makeshift breakfast, he contemplated his next move. Try as he might, though, he couldn't think of anything else he could do.

But maybe, just maybe, he had already done enough. His last hope depended on two things: firstly, whether María had been lying about not being able to contact Carla: and secondly, just how good a job he had done at evoking her sympathy and compassion.

All he could do now was wait.

Chapter 12

Juanita had been lucky: she had managed to find a hairdresser that could fit her in at 9 a.m. the very next morning.

Although it wasn't very far, the walk from the hotel to the salon, in a brand-new pair of shoes, had made her feet pretty sore. When she sat down for her hairdo, she gratefully slipped her shoes off before the gown was fastened around her neck.

The girl who did her hair was way too chatty and inquisitive for Juanita's liking. What was she doing in New York? How long was she going to stay? Why was she going for such a radically different look? And many more probing questions.

Juanita guessed that she was just trying to be friendly, but under the circumstances she would much have preferred not to have to dream up plausible responses to all these questions. She just wanted the job done as quickly as possible so that she could get out of there and focus on the much more important question of how to learn what the murdered journalist had been working on.

She had to admit, though, that the girl had done a good job: the shorter style, in a medium-blonde tone with contrasting lowlights looked really good, reminding her of the look she had adopted when she and James had first fled Miami in search of a new life in Canada. More importantly, she now looked very different from the woman who had been photographed for the fake passport which would now be in the hands of the police.

'There,' chirped the girl, holding up a mirror behind Juanita's head, 'all done. Do you like it?'

Juanita tilted her head one way and then the other in order to get an all-round view. She nodded, approvingly.

'Yes … I do,' she said, truthfully.

The other girl removed the gown from Juanita's shoulders, and she stood up, wincing slightly as she levered her feet back into her shoes.

She picked up her purse, rummaging inside for her wallet. 'How much was it again?' she asked.

'It's two hundred and seventy dollars ... but there's no hurry; my next appointment's not for another half an hour. Why not stay for a coffee and a chat ...it's Gema isn't it? I'm Mandy by the way.'

Juanita had momentarily forgotten the false name she had used to book her appointment and stumbled slightly over her response. 'Er, yes ... Gema. Look, that's very kind, but I'm in a bit of a hurry.' She opened her purse and withdrew three $100 bills from a substantial stack within.

Mandy leaned forward and took a good look at the contents of Juanita's purse. 'Wow! You should be careful carrying that much cash about with you in the city ... there are some bad people out there.'

Juanita snapped the purse shut. 'Oh ... all my cards are back at my hotel, but yes, I will be careful ... thank you. Keep the change.'

'Thanks ... would you like me to call you a cab?'

'No, that's fine, thanks. I can walk. The hotel's not far.'

With that, she hurried out of the door, her heart racing: she had been disproportionally unsettled by this girl's constant prying. By the time she had walked a couple of blocks, though, she had regained her composure – the girl was surely just trying to be friendly.

As she passed the massive tower which housed the New York Times office, her thoughts turned to the young journalist who had worked there before being so brutally murdered. Why? Just what on earth *had* she been investigating?

Suddenly, she had an idea. Stopping in her tracks, she withdrew a small mirror from her purse and took a moment to check that her new hairdo had not been unduly disturbed by the gentle breeze blowing down 8th Avenue; it looked fine. She applied a little extra lipstick before turning around and marching towards the main entrance of the building.

***

'You did what?' exclaimed James.

'I've applied for a job as a temporary office assistant at the New York Times. I've got an interview tomorrow morning,' replied Juanita.

'Are you crazy? You're supposed to be keeping a low profile.'

'Look,' she said, sounding oh-so-reasonable, 'we need to find out what that journalist was working on. If I can get this job – it would only be for a week – I might well be able to get some information.'

He shook his head, avoiding responding directly to her assertion. 'How did you even know there was a vacancy?'

'I didn't. I just figured a huge outfit like the New York Times must rely on temps quite a lot, you know, for vacation cover, maternity leave cover and so on, so I just went inside and asked. Turns out one of their secretaries has recently left unexpectedly and they need some temporary cover until her replacement starts. Seems I turned up at just the right moment.'

James was exasperated by her impetuous action but, at the same time, full of admiration for her initiative and determination. He sighed heavily. 'What name did you give them?'

'"Gema López" … same as I used at the hairdressers.'

'Hmm … you don't need to do this, you know. You can just not show up for the interview. We can think of some other way to find out what she was investigating.'

The determined look on her face, as she tilted her head and fixed him with a steady stare, conveyed her response as clearly as any words would have done.

He sighed heavily. 'I guess that's a "no" then.'

She smiled. 'We've got work to do before my interview tomorrow: I need to write a suitable résumé, and you,' she said, 'need to make me another I.D.'

He gave a wry smile. 'You are utterly incorrigible.'

She gave him a peck on the cheek. 'It's what you love about me.'

Which, he had to admit, was true – amongst the many other things about her which captivated him. 'I guess you'll need to get another photo done – with your new hairstyle.'

She smiled, reaching for her purse and withdrawing a thin, glossy sheet of card with four images on it. 'Got it done on the way back to the hotel.'

'Why, you didn't even wait to—'

He was interrupted by an electronic beeping sound emanating from Juanita's purse. He didn't recognise the ringtone. She was evidently disoriented, too, for at the sound, her eyes widened in surprise, and her hand flew to her mouth.

'That's not my regular cell,' she breathed, reaching into her purse.

'You mean ...?'

She nodded, withdrawing the emergency pay-as-you-go phone, holding it at arm's length as though it might bite her. She made a couple of taps and swipes before staring intently at the screen for around twenty seconds.

'Well?' enquired James, unable to contain himself any longer, his heart filled with trepidation.

'It's a text ... from María.'

'Your friend at the diner back in Miami?'

'Uh, huh ... I'll read it out.'

Carla,

Sorry to contact you on this number, but there's something I thought you should know. I got a visit from a guy called Kyle Richards – says his girlfriend, Sylvia, was murdered, yes MURDERED, a year or so ago. He claims she was a good friend of yours and he thinks you may know something about what happened. I know it all sounds crazy, but this guy looked SO upset – he really seemed genuine.

I don't know what you might have gotten mixed up in just before you left so suddenly – and I don't want to know, but the question is – do you want to talk to this guy? Should I give him your number? Or, if it's better, I can give you his number.

All my love,
María.

When she looked up at James, her eyes were moist. 'Oh, poor Kyle. This must have been eating him up for over a year.'

James was firm in his reply. 'You can't contact him, Juanita ... absolutely not. It's terrible what happened to Sylvia, but what's done is done. Letting anyone know what happened, or where we are, or what names we're using, can only lead to trouble. I wasn't too happy about your even leaving that phone number with María, but it absolutely must not go any further.'

The tears she had been holding back welled from the corners of her eyes and trickled down her cheeks. 'I know … I know you're right, but—'

'Shhh,' he whispered, pulling her to him and encircling her in his arms.

They clung together for several long seconds, before she pulled away and wiped her eyes with the back of her hand, leaving dark streaks of mascara across her cheeks. 'I'll reply right now.'

He nodded. 'Don't reply as Juanita – use your old name.'

She nodded, sniffing and wiping her cheeks again before hitting the 'reply' button. Her reply was short and to the point.

María,

No, I cannot talk to him, and you must not give him my number. Sorry, I can't explain, but there are good reasons for this, which I'm afraid I cannot go into.

Carla x

Chapter 13

Kyle Richards smiled; his plan had worked. He had picked up both María's original message and Carla's cryptic reply.

He sat down in front of his laptop and, with a few clicks on the trackpad called up a page displaying the full details of the phone which had sent the reply to María. What he was hoping to find, was that the GPS tracking function on this phone was switched on. Unfortunately, it wasn't. This would make his task rather more difficult. But he did have a possible way to get around this obstacle.

He composed a very short and simple text message, purporting to come from María.

Carla,

OK – I understand. Good luck.

María x

His plan now relied on Carla believing that the message had, indeed come from María. He hit 'send' and settled back to wait.

He didn't have to wait long: it was just two minutes later that an electronic bleep from his laptop indicated that the recipient of his text message had clicked to open it. He waited a few more minutes to see if there was any reply, but there was none. It didn't matter: the moment that text message had been opened, the bug he had attached to it would have been installed on Carla's phone. A few more swipes and clicks on the trackpad of his laptop brought up a new screen: a world map with a single red dot on the east coast of the USA pulsing brightly. He zoomed in to reveal that the location of the dot was

New York City. Zooming in further revealed that the exact location of the phone was The Manhattan at Times Square hotel.

Now that he had finally succeeded in finding out where Carla was, Kyle felt strangely conflicted. His euphoria at tracking her down was tempered by feelings of guilt and betrayal at the deception he had employed to do so: Carla, after all, had been Sylvia's best friend. He shook his head, trying to dispel the negative vibe as he set about booking a flight to New York City.

***

'That's odd,' said Juanita.

'Hmm?' murmured James, evidently totally engrossed in the task of creating a new false I.D. for Juanita's forthcoming interview.

'It's another text from María.'

James looked up, now paying full attention. 'What does it say?'

'Much the same as the last one, really: "OK – I won't say anything to him. Love, María".'

'I wonder why she sent another message?' said James.

Juanita pondered this thought. 'Maybe the fact that I didn't reply to the last one made her think I hadn't received it.'

'Could be,' agreed James. 'Why don't you just acknowledge this one be sure she knows you've seen it?'

'OK.'

Juanita sent a brief reply.

María,

Thanks. Sorry I can't tell you any more.

Carla x

James returned his attention to his laptop while Juanita fired up hers. She typed the following title.

Résumé – Gema López Arteaga

She sat back to consider just how to pitch this work of fiction. It needed to be convincing enough to help secure her the job, without claiming skills which she patently did not have, for to do so might see her cover blown within days or even hours. Hopefully, her prospective employer would be somewhat desperate to fill the hole created by the unexpected departure of the secretary and wouldn't probe too much.

She began to type …

Chapter 14

Mark Bowman sat at his desk in the NYPD reading through the report about the woman who had attempted to steal Julia's autopsy report. His concentration was rudely interrupted by the booming voice of Sergeant Sean O'Reilly.

'How're you getting on with the Patterson case, Detective?'

Scott Patterson was a media tycoon, and a big name in New York society. He was a vociferous advocate of a tough line on law and order and hobnobbed with those at the most senior levels in the NYPD. In spite of, or perhaps because of, his outspoken views on crime and law enforcement, his home had been targeted by thieves, who had gotten away with most of his wife's jewellery, two of his Rolex watches, and his cherished vintage Jaguar car. In the process of the robbery, they had been disturbed by Patterson's wife, Martha, who, for her trouble, had received a blow to the head which rendered her temporarily unconscious. She had been unable to identify her attacker, who had been wearing a balaclava.

When Mark had been assigned to the case, he protested that, in spite of the assault, the lady had eventually made a full recovery, and that this was hardly a case for Homicide. O'Reilly's reply was that Scott Patterson was a very important man and that the powers-that-be had declared this to be not just any old burglary, but a case of attempted murder. Homicide had to take the case, whether they liked it or not. Mark knew full well that this was a case his superiors wanted solved quickly: the fallout if the NYPD failed on this one would be considerable.

'Uh, well, I don't have anything concrete yet,' replied Mark, in answer to O'Reilly's question, surreptitiously sliding the report he had been reading to one side and nudging the mouse on the desk to wake up his computer, 'but I've got a promising lead to follow up.'

O'Reilly was a big man, and Mark could not help but feel intimidated as he came around the desk to look over Mark's shoulder. 'Like what?' he said, leaning forward until his jowly chin was right alongside Mark's cheek.

The computer screen was showing CCTV footage of the opulent mansion owned by the influential billionaire.

'See the jacket that guy's wearing?' said Mark; he zoomed in on a blurry image of one of the two presumed perpetrators.

'Yeah ... what of it?'

'Well that logo on the back is very rare ... and it matches one on a jacket stolen in another robbery last month over in Staten Island.'

'So, you sayin' this guy wore a stolen jacket to commit another robbery?'

'It's a possibility,' replied Mark. 'I'm going to go and talk to the guys investigating the other robbery and see what we can come up with.'

O'Reilly seemed satisfied, for the time being at least. 'OK, but don't take too long about it – the big guns want this case solved ASAP.'

'On it,' Mark confirmed.

Sergeant O'Reilly moved away, with his familiar rolling gait, no doubt ready to make some other poor bastard's life a misery. But Mark knew this could only be a temporary reprieve. He returned to his scrutiny of the report concerning the attempted theft of Julia's autopsy report from the pathology lab by the woman who had claimed to be her sister.

The whole thing about the jacket being potentially linked to another burglary had been a complete fabrication, designed to keep O'Reilly off his back while he concentrated on the much more important task of tracking down his girlfriend's murderer.

He decided to start his enquiry with a visit to the Edward Mason Pathology Lab.

***

'How can I help you, Detective?' said the receptionist. 'I already told the other police officer everything I know.'

'Oh, just a few additional questions,' said Mark, '... any little thing you can tell us Miss ...' He glanced at his notebook, having already forgotten her name.

'Oh, you can call me Mary-Jane,' she cooed. 'We can sit down over there.' She indicated the two white couches flanking the corner of the room.

She stood up and came around the desk, revealing that she was wearing a knee-length, figure-hugging, grey skirt, teamed with a close-fitting, white shirt cinched in by a black patent belt. She ushered Mark over to one of the couches and sat down half-facing him on the other one, hitching up her skirt to show just a little more thigh than was really necessary. She crossed her legs and leaned towards him slightly, flicking a tress of blonde, wavy hair from her cheek.

Mark was used to this sort of reaction from women: he was a good-looking guy, and his deep, mellifluous voice seemed to make many go weak at the knees. It wasn't something he purposely exploited – well, usually at least – for Julia was the only woman he had ever truly cared for. However, the receptionist would have no knowledge of his relationship with Julia; otherwise she would surely have been more respectful.

On this occasion, though, he figured a little flirting might just help his cause.

'Well, thank you Mary-Jane … and you can call me Mark.'

She flashed him a radiant smile, revealing two perfectly even rows of dazzling white teeth. 'So how can I help?'

'I understand this woman claimed to be Julia Turner's sister?'

'Yeah … said her name was Susan Turner.'

'But your records didn't indicate that Julia even had a sister?' He knew full well that they did not.

'That's right … but this woman said she'd been living over on the west coast for years, having been more or less disowned by her parents. She knew the names of both of the deceased's parents and, actually, sounded pretty genuine.'

'But you weren't completely convinced, right?'

She shook her head, placing a hand on Mark's arm as she leaned in a little closer, now speaking in a conspiratorial whisper. 'The thing is … Mark … I have this kind of inbuilt intuition thing going for me.'

He nodded, making no attempt to shrug free of her hand.

'I have an instinct for when someone's lying. Even though the passport looked legit and she said all the right things, I just didn't feel comfortable about her, particularly as the deceased was a murder victim.'

'So, what did you do?'

'I went to see my boss. I took her passport and explained the situation to him.'

'And?'

'Well, I told him I was a bit suspicious, and he said he wanted to see her himself. You see, Mr Marzetti – that's my boss – knows how good my instincts are, and he trusts my judgement completely.' She preened, removing her hand from Mark's arm to flick away the errant tress of hair once more, this time running her fingers through it, before tucking it behind her ear.

'So, what happened next?' said Mark, now starting to get slightly irritated with the constant prompting which this woman seemed to need in order to get her to tell her story.

'Well,' she said, placing her hand on his arm once more as she lowered her voice, 'just as we were coming back into the reception area, we saw her running out of the door … right there.' She raised her hand to point at the door – a somewhat superfluous gesture, since it was blindingly obvious where the door was.

'Did you follow her out?'

'We called after her, but by the time we got to the door, she was nowhere to be seen; she must have run like the wind. I knew, right there and then, that I was right to be suspicious of her.'

'And how did you discover that she'd gotten away with a copy of Miss Turner's autopsy report?'

'Well, you see that room over there?' she pointed to the filing room, waiting for Mark to offer a nod of his head. 'The door was wide open and the report was open, face-down, on the photocopier glass.'

'Can I take a look in the room?'

'Oh sure.'

She stood up, smoothing down her skirt and making her way over to her desk, adopting a slightly exaggerated sway to her hips. Although Mark wasn't even slightly interested in this woman's too-obvious overtures, he did have to admit she had a damned good figure, an asset which she was clearly well-skilled in using to maximum advantage.

'I always keep the room locked and the key right here,' she said opening her desk drawer and withdrawing the key, holding it aloft with a flourish.

'So she must have taken the key from your drawer when you left the room.'

'Yeah,' replied Mary-Jane, 'she must have seen me put the key back in the drawer after I locked up the room.'

'The room was unlocked before that?'

'Oh no ... I just unlocked it to get the deceased's file. But I put the file back and locked the room again before going to see my boss. Strict rules you see.'

Mark nodded. 'So, can we go in please?'

'Oh, sure.' She stepped over and unlocked the room, standing to one side to allow Mark through, but only so far that he could not avoid brushing very lightly against her breast and inhaling her perfume as he passed her. She really was deploying all her feminine weapons now.

She followed him in. 'That's the filing cabinet where the deceased's file was kept,' she said, pointing.

The one she was indicating was the second of four identical cabinets.

'So how would she have known where to look?'

The woman shrugged and spread her hands, somehow using the gesture to push her breasts forward at the same time. 'I guess she must have watched me, through the open door, getting the file out or putting it back.'

'Hmm,' mused Mark. All of this suggested that the mystery woman was a seasoned professional: that she had planned every move ahead of time. 'And this,' he said, placing a hand on the machine alongside them, 'is, I assume, the photocopier she used to copy the report?'

'Uh, huh ... but I don't think she managed to copy the whole thing: it was open at a page about half way through. My guess is that she'd only copied about half before she heard us coming back and ran.'

'You're probably right,' said Mark. 'So, is there anything else ... anything at all which you can remember which might help us identify this woman?'

'Well, she had a slight accent ... I'd say Central or South American.'

Hardly surprising, thought Mark, given her obviously Hispanic appearance in her passport photograph, but then again, many second and third generation Hispanics had no discernible accent, so this observation might indicate that she had been born and brought up outside the USA. It wasn't definite of course, but it was a clue which might just help his investigation at some point.

'Well, thank you Miss ...'

'Mary-Jane,' she reminded him.

'Yes, of course ... Mary-Jane. You've been most helpful.'

Actually, she really hadn't told him anything he didn't already know, but it was always a good idea to give any witness the impression that their input had been genuinely useful.

They stepped out of the room. She dutifully locked up and replaced the key in her desk drawer.

'Are you sure there's nothing else I can do for you?' she purred, with barely concealed innuendo.

He smiled. 'I don't think so ... not right now. Like I said, you've been very helpful.'

'Well, before you go, Detective Bowman ... I mean Mark,' she said, reaching towards a box of business cards on her desk, 'here's my card ... you know, if you need go over any more details or anything.' She grabbed a pen and scribbled something on the back. 'That's my cell number ... just in case it's out of office hours. I live on my own, so you can call any time. I want to help the police in any way that I can; you guys do *such* a fantastic job.'

'Thank you, ma'am.'

'Mary-Jane,' she reminded him again.

'Yes ... thank you, Mary-Jane. I'll be in touch if necessary.'

'Oh, don't hesitate,' she cooed.

He beat a hasty retreat.

***

Back at the station, Mark reflected on what he had learned – which, in all honesty, amounted to precious little.

The woman claiming to be Julia's non-existent sister had obviously gone to the pathology lab with the clear intention of obtaining a copy of the autopsy report. But why? What was she looking for?

Assuming she was the murderer, or at least an accomplice of the murderer, she would know precisely how Julia had been killed. What could there possibly be in that autopsy report which she didn't already know? And then a thought struck him: perhaps it wasn't something *she* needed to know; perhaps she was looking for anything in the report which might give the police some clue as to who she was.

He thought about the mysterious matter of the card with the scorpion image. His research had revealed that such cards had been left at the scenes of a number of other assassinations in the UK and the USA, all of high-profile figures, and all unsolved. The working assumption of the various police forces involved was that the same man – or woman – was responsible for all these hits. A professional assassin who, for whatever reason, liked to advertise himself – or herself. Incredibly there was absolutely no information about this shadowy figure's likely identity.

Could the woman he was hunting be this mysterious assassin? And if so, why would she have targeted a junior journalist, when all of the other victims had been such prominent figures? If it *was* her, then perhaps she had been looking for something in the autopsy report which might blow her cover.

He decided to go through the report yet again to see if he could find something – anything – which the killer could have been looking for.

He steeled himself for what was to come. He knew about the horrific wounds which his girlfriend had suffered, but he needed to try to stay detached, analytical, if he was to discover the crucial clue which might help him nail the murdering bitch responsible for her death.

It didn't work. He managed to stay strong for the first two pages, which described the details of the victim and the two gunshot wounds she had sustained. He even held it together when he turned to the third page which showed close-up photographs of the gunshot wound to the chest. When he turned to the fourth page, however, the breath was literally sucked from him. There, laid bare, was a graphic colour photograph of Julia's face and head, with a large piece of her skull detached, exposing a bloody mess of red and grey.

A dark veil began to descend as his lungs were seized by an invisible iron fist. Yet, somehow, he couldn't tear his gaze away from the obscene image, even as he felt his consciousness slipping away.

'Hey Mark ... what is it? Are you OK?' The voice of his colleague and good friend, Alexis Miller, penetrated his state of paralysis.

Alex had joined the force on the very same day as Mark; they had hit it off immediately. She was smart, pretty – with her button nose, big brown eyes, and dimpled cheeks – and a great sounding-board when one was needed. She and Mark had often shared a beer or two when off duty and, on one occasion, indulged in a drunken kiss and fumble at her doorstep. It might have gone much further in due course but, when Mark met Julia, he just knew that she was 'the one' – and Alex knew it too. They remained good friends, and always watched each other's backs, but the budding romance was never to be.

Mark snapped the report shut, looking up her. 'I ... uh ... no, not really.'

Alex came over to his desk, placing her arm around his shoulders. 'What's the ...' Her voice tailed off as she read the title on the cover of the report on his desk.

'Hey, you two ... get a room will you?' came an uninvited voice from behind them.

The intrusive comment had come from Chuck Bronsky, one of the older detectives who shared the office. Tact and diplomacy were not his strengths at the best of times ... and this was definitely not the best of times.

'Go fuck yourself, Chuck,' hissed Alex, adding, ''cause you sure won't find a woman to do it.'

Bronsky raised both hands in a defensive gesture. 'Ok, ok ...just trying to inject a bit of levity into this humorless joint.' He shrugged, turning away to return to whatever he had been doing before his interjection.

Mark had barely registered the fractious exchange: the hideous image of Julia's ruined face was burned into his brain and he could not shake it.

Alex placed her hand on top of the report, craning around Mark to make eye contact. 'Mark, you have to stop torturing yourself like this; it's doing you no good. Let the other guys handle the investigation.'

He could feel the tears welling up; he fought to hold them back. 'How can I just stand back and do nothing? She was everything to me … she was …' His voice tailed off.

'I know,' said Alex, placing a hand on the side of his cheek, 'but you have to stand back from this. Quite apart from the way it's tearing you apart, O'Reilly'll kill you if he finds out you're working on this.'

Mark felt physically sick; his stomach was churning, and he could feel rivulets of perspiration coursing down his temples and forehead, stinging his eyes. 'I'm sorry Alex, I can't think straight right now, and I don't feel …'

'Go home Mark. I'll cover for you – I'll tell O'Reilly you've come down with food poisoning or something.'

He looked her directly in the eyes. 'Maybe you're right.' He forced a small smile as he closed the report. 'Thanks, Alex.'

She didn't see him slip the autopsy report inside his jacket as he left the office.

Chapter 15

Juanita got the job.

Her first day had been uneventful, verging on tedious. There had been something of a backlog of regular filing to do, a pile of letters to be franked and sent for mailing, and a couple of boxes of documents to be shredded. Still, she could hardly have expected that a temp hired for just a week would be given interesting and challenging tasks. In any case, that was hardly the point of being there: she needed to find out where the murdered journalist had been working and, more importantly, what she had been working on.

It was now just twenty-five minutes before the end of her working day. Juanita had completed all the tasks she had been assigned, so she went over to the Managing Editor, Cynthia Newman. Cynthia was a pleasant, round-faced, bespectacled woman in her fifties, with an unruly shock of curly red hair – improbably red, to be honest, but it sort of suited her. Juanita had warmed to her immediately. At Juanita's approach she looked up from her desk; a tense frown creasing her features. The expression was only fleeting, but it spoke of a woman under far greater stress than she normally showed. Within a second or so, though, her face resumed its usual friendly, welcoming manner.

'Hi,' she said, laying down her pen, 'how's it going? Any problems?'

'No ... no problems; I just came over to let you know I've finished the jobs you gave me.'

Cynthia's eyebrows rose. 'What ... all of them?'

'Uh huh.'

'Well, aren't you a find then? I thought that stuff would keep you busy for all of today ... and a fair chunk of tomorrow, too.'

Juanita smiled. 'I like to keep busy.'

Cynthia nodded, appreciatively. Glancing at her watch, she said, 'It's probably not worth starting on anything else now, but if you come and see me first thing tomorrow—'

'I don't mind staying late if that helps.'

'Wow, that's the first time I've ever heard one of our temps say that.'

Juanita smiled. 'If there's more of the sort of stuff I've been doing today, I'm happy to work as long as necessary to get on top of it, but ...'

'But what?' enquired Cynthia, inclining her head.

'I just wanted to say, that I can handle more ... well ... demanding tasks, if that would be helpful.'

The older woman's face broke into a beaming smile. 'It sure would, honey. You really are a find ... most of the temps I've had in here just want to do the minimum they can get away with to collect their pay check.'

Juanita shrugged. 'Just trying to help as much as possible, Mrs Newman.'

'Oh, call me Cynthia.' She paused for a few moments, looking thoughtful as she cupped her chin between thumb and forefinger. After some seconds she stood up.

'Come with me,' she said, beckoning.

She led Juanita to a desk just a few yards away. It was piled high with chaotically placed papers.

'This desk was occupied by my secretary, Penny. She left in a bit of a hurry and, as you can see, didn't exactly leave everything in good order. I haven't yet had a chance to go through all this and find out how she's left things.'

'You want me to sort this lot out ... find out what's here and put it into some sort of order?'

'If you think you can. I mean I've really no idea what she's left outstanding.'

'I'll give it my best shot,' said Juanita, smiling. 'Anything I don't understand, I can always come and ask.'

'Great. Well, that's your task for tomorrow then.'

'And, as you're short of a secretary right now, maybe I can help with some of the other things she used to do. I'm pretty good on spreadsheets and word processing, and maybe I can take phone calls for you?'

Cynthia pursed her lips and exhaled a small sigh of relief. 'Amazing. Gema ... you're on.'

Juanita was momentarily thrown by this remark – until she remembered that Gema was her latest false identity. It was getting kind of hard to keep up.

'I'll make a start on this stuff right now and let you know where I've got to tomorrow.'

'Fantastic!' said Cynthia, stepping away to return to her own desk.

Juanita smiled. She had so far learned nothing about the murdered journalist, or what she had been working on, but she felt sure she had succeeded in gaining the confidence of her manager. That was surely a good first step from which to launch her investigation.

***

'So how was your first day?' said James, that evening, pouring two glasses from the bottle of Chardonnay he had had sent up to the room while anxiously awaiting Juanita's return.

She took a grateful sip of the cool, fragrant liquid. 'Pretty good, I think. It's far too soon to have found any opportunity to dig into what the murdered journalist had been working on, but my new boss, Cynthia, seems to have sort of taken to me. Although I spent most of today on pretty mind-numbing tasks, she seemed quite impressed.'

'Who wouldn't be?' said James, holding forth his glass, 'by someone like you?'

'Charmer,' she replied, clinking glasses with him. 'Anyway,' she continued, 'tomorrow, I have some more interesting tasks to do. If I can do a good job on that stuff and gain more of her confidence, maybe she'll give me enough free rein to find some opportunity to go looking for the information we need.'

'You really are quite something,' said James.

'Funny you should say that ... I believe Cynthia said something similar.' She took another sip of her wine, before breaking into peals of laughter.

James offered his glass, once again, for Juanita to clink. 'But be careful,' he said, his tone more serious now, 'don't take any unnecessary chances.'

'When would I ever do anything like that?' she said, tilting her head and giving an impish grin.

'No, I mean it. If anyone there gets the idea that you're anything more than just a temp looking for a week's work, there's every chance that they might involve the police. If that happens, who knows what—?'

She cut him off. 'Shhh … I get it … I'll be careful.'

And she knew that she had to be. As yet, she had no idea how she would be able to find out what Julia Turner had been working on, but she had to find a way to do so without arousing any suspicions.

Right now, though, she just wanted to enjoy another glass of Chardonnay with the man she loved.

***

Kyle Richards checked his watch: 3.50 p.m. He should be on the ground at JFK airport in less than an hour. He folded up the magazine he had been absently browsing and tucked it into the seat pocket before draining the last of his beer, crushing the plastic tumbler and jamming that, too, into the seat pocket before folding away his tray table.

He gazed out of the window at the white carpet of cloud below. It was completely unbroken, looking almost solid enough to walk on. The forecast of a wet and gloomy day down below looked about right. Not as gloomy as his mood though.

The initial euphoria he had felt at the prospect of tracking Carla down and, perhaps, at last getting some answers about what lay behind Sylvia's untimely death, had long since faded. It had been replaced by a deep sense of guilt about the tactics he had used, overlaid with a crushing trepidation about how he should approach Carla when they finally met.

Although Carla had been Sylvia's best friend, he had only actually met her once. He had heard so much about her from Sylvia, but he didn't really know her personally, and he was desperately unsure how to handle the situation. How would she react? Would she be furious with him, and refuse outright to speak to him? He just had to hope that if Carla was the kind, caring person that Sylvia had described, she would appreciate the deep despair which had driven him to the subterfuge and deception he had employed and forgive him for it.

His thoughts were interrupted by a sudden easing of the monotonous drone of the engines, accompanied by a familiar weightlessness in his stomach: they were beginning their descent. It wouldn't be long now.

Chapter 16

Juanita had spent most of the following morning sorting through the mess left by the previous secretary. Now she was updating Cynthia on the progress she had made.

'Quite a lot of it looked like stuff she had dealt with but just not got around to filing or putting away, so I've done that now.'

Cynthia nodded. 'Good - what else did you find?'

'There were a number of letters which had been signed and were just waiting to be sent out. I've put them in envelopes and mailed them.'

'Great – anything else?'

'Yes – there were a number of letters addressed to you. Most of them were just speculative enquiries which I guess you won't want to be bothered with. I've taken the liberty of typing brief replies on your behalf, which are here' – she held forward a cardboard folder – 'together with the original enquiries. If you can just check you're happy with my replies, you can sign them, and I'll get them sent off.'

'Fantastic.'

'But there are three here which I believe will probably need your personal attention.' She held forward another folder. 'If you'd like to take a look at them and record your replies, I'll take care of them.'

Juanita had previously noted the small dictation recorder lying on Cynthia's desk. It was fortunate that Cynthia used such a device, for if she had wanted to dictate her replies directly, it would have exposed the fact that the shorthand skills claimed in Juanita's – or rather Gema's – résumé were, in fact, non-existent.

'I'll do that,' said Cynthia. 'Thank you.'

'And finally,' said Juanita, 'there are these documents' – she proffered a third folder – 'which I don't really know what to do with.'

Cynthia opened the folder and flipped briefly through the few documents inside it. 'These are the only ones you haven't dealt with?'

'Uh huh.'

'Out of that whole pile of stuff on Penny's desk?'

'Well yes ... I mean there's nothing else there. Her desk is clear now.'

'Wow ... that's great work Gema.'

'Thanks. Er ... if you don't mind me asking ... why did your secretary leave so suddenly?'

A dark cloud flitted across Cynthia's face. 'I suppose you might as well know, but please don't go discussing this with anyone else who works here.'

Juanita's interest was immediately piqued. 'No, of course not. I would never repeat anything that you choose to tell me in confidence.'

'OK then ... you heard about the murder?'

Juanita figured it was best to feign ignorance. 'What murder?' she said.

'The journalist murdered in Central Park.'

Juanita frowned and tilted her head backwards a little, as though trying to recall something. 'Oh, yes ... I think I saw a piece about it on TV a few days ago, but what does that have to do with your secretary leaving?'

Cynthia lowered her voice. 'The murdered girl worked for this newspaper.'

Juanita let out a gasp. 'Oh God! That's awful.'

'Yeah, it is ... and the cops apparently don't know what the motive for her murder was. And you know how people are: as the cops can't come up with a motive, then folk will soon come up with their own ideas. So now there's a theory going around the office that the murderer might have a grudge against this newspaper. There's absolutely no evidence that that could be the case, but the idea's really spooked some of our employees; they're whispering "who's next?". Penny was so freaked out by the whole thing she just left without giving any notice. I gather there may be others also thinking of leaving.'

Juanita listened intently to this explanation before replying, 'Seems a bit drastic: quitting your job on the strength of a completely unsubstantiated theory. I mean, obviously, it's a real shock when something like this happens so close to home but, in all honesty, there are murders happening all the time in New York City, and a lot of them are just muggings gone wrong, or something like that. It's quite a stretch to imagine someone with a grudge against this newspaper would just start murdering its employees at random to get back at the paper.'

'I agree, but there it is. Anyway, it's best you heard it from me first rather than through the office grapevine. So, I hope I haven't scared *you* off now.'

Juanita laughed. 'I don't scare easy. To me, the whole idea seems ridiculous when—'

Their conversation was interrupted by the unexpected arrival of a breathless, somewhat overweight, red-faced man in an ill-fitting grey suit.

'Hey, Cynthia, I need to talk to you urgently,' he blurted.

Cynthia was clearly irritated by his blunt interruption. 'Gema, this is Joe Goldsmith, Assignment Editor from the floor above; Joe, this is Gema, my new temp.'

She had succeeded in taking the wind from his sails. 'Oh, I … uh … real sorry to interrupt like that, Cynthia. Pleased to meet you, Gema.'

'Likewise,' she replied. 'We were just finishing up anyway, so I'll get out of the way and leave you to it.' She turned to Cynthia. 'I'll just be at Penny's desk if you want me; I'll take your calls while you guys are talking.'

'Thanks, Gema,' said Cynthia.

Juanita retreated to what was now *her* desk, appearing to become engaged with something on her computer screen, while actually listening intently to the conversation between Cynthia and the guy from upstairs.

'I got a problem, Cynthia.'

'*I* could have told *you* that,' she fired back, quick as a flash.

'Oh, very funny … but look, I'm serious. The cops have been on the phone. They still don't seem to know why Julia was killed, so now they want to know exactly what she had been working on before she died. Thing is, I don't really know myself. She had been acting kind of secretive lately; I think she may have been onto something big and not wanted to share it yet.'

'So what does this have to do with me?'

'They're coming here tomorrow morning and they want to take away all her papers, her computer, and anything else which might shed some light on what she was working on.'

A leaden boulder descended in Juanita's stomach: once the police had taken away all of Julia's things there would be no hope of finding what she was looking for. *Shit.*

'Like I said,' continued Cynthia, 'what does this have to do with me?'

'I haven't got anyone to sort through it all and get it organised for them to collect: my admin assistant quit yesterday – she's bought this damned conspiracy theory going around – and my secretary called in sick this morning. I was wondering if you could spare anyone?'

'Well, it may have escaped your notice, but I'm short-staffed too.'

Oh no! This was the perfect opportunity to rescue the situation, but Cynthia was about to scupper it. She couldn't let that happen. She took a deep breath, stood up, and walked over to where the other two were talking.

'Excuse me Cynthia, but I couldn't help overhearing your conversation.'

Cynthia drew her eyebrows together in a frown. 'Oh really?' She sounded a little irritated.

'I just thought maybe I could help. I'm pretty much on top of things for today and I could probably spare a few hours this afternoon to help Mr Goldsmith.'

Cynthia's frown deepened: Juanita had the distinct impression that there was no love lost between the other two.

'Hey, that'd be great,' piped up Goldsmith.

Juanita was acutely aware that diving in like this without Cynthia's say-so risked undoing much of the goodwill she had built up with her boss; in fact, Cynthia's tone suggested she may have already done so. But there was no alternative: once those papers and files were gone there would be no means of finding out what the murdered journalist had been working on.

Cynthia sighed. 'OK then, but I need you back here first thing in the morning.'

Goldsmith visibly relaxed. 'Thanks Cynthia … you're a doll. And thank *you* er …'

'Gema.'

'Yes, thanks Gema.' He turned back to Cynthia. 'OK if I swing by just after lunch to show Gema where Julia's things are? Say about one?'

'Yeah, I guess so.'

As the man walked off, looking a lot happier than when he had arrived, Juanita took the opportunity to avoid the awkward conversation with her boss which she sensed was coming.

Glancing at her watch, she said, 'I guess I'd better go for lunch now then, to make sure I'm back by one.'

She stepped back to her own desk, picked up her purse and slipped away, before Cynthia had a chance to say anything further.

***

Juanita was glad to escape from the office for a while, following the fractious exchange between Cynthia and the guy from upstairs: it gave her the chance to avoid, temporarily at least, what she assumed would be a rather difficult conversation with her boss.

But she didn't have any lunch that day: she used her lunch break to find an electronics store and purchase a portable hard drive. The largest capacity model they had was two terabytes; she figured that should be enough to copy the entire contents of the dead journalist's computer, assuming she could do so without someone realising what she was doing.

She arrived back in the New York Times building at around 12.45 p.m. Five minutes later she was back at the entrance to the office. To her dismay, Cynthia was still at her desk; she must have worked through lunch or decided to wait for Juanita's return before going for a late lunch, in order to remonstrate with her. Juanita really didn't want that conversation right then: at best it would be awkward, and at worst Cynthia might just have changed her mind about allowing her to help out upstairs. She couldn't risk that happening.

What to do? There was, as yet, no sign of Joe Goldsmith, so maybe she could hang back outside the office, staying discreetly out of sight until he showed up and went over to Cynthia's desk; he should be arriving any time now. Juanita could then follow him in just seconds later, pretending to have only just returned from lunch. She doubted that Cynthia would give her a dressing down in front of Goldsmith, but there was still a risk she could rescind her decision and prevent her from going upstairs. She decided on a different strategy.

She located the elevator and rode up one floor. Stepping out, she stopped the first person she saw in the corridor: a flustered-looking young woman hurrying along clutching an armful of papers.

'Excuse me,' called out Juanita. The woman stopped in her tracks, eying Juanita up and down. 'I'm looking for Joe Goldsmith. Do you know where I can find him? I'm new here,' she added, by way of explanation.

'Oh, sure,' replied the woman. 'In that office.' As her arms were completely overloaded with papers, she resorted to indicating where she meant by inclining her head in the direction of the entrance. 'Joe's desk is right over at the far side.'

'Thanks.'

The woman hurried on, shifting her grip on the pile of papers to prevent them slipping from her grasp.

Juanita entered the office, which proved to be a large open-plan room, similar to the one below, except that it was more densely populated, with most of the desks arranged in long, closely packed rows. It wasn't going to be easy to do anything without being observed by others.

She made her way across the office and quickly spotted the man who had come to see Cynthia earlier. He had his head down, apparently engrossed in the file open on his desk. He looked up, however, as Juanita approached, glancing at his watch.

'Oh, hello there, uh ...'

'Gema,' she reminded him. She was finally getting used to her adopted name.

'Yes, of course ... Gema. Sorry, I meant to come down and collect you ten minutes ago, but I got kinda ... snowed under.' He indicated, with a sweep of his upturned palm, the unruly piles of papers spread haphazardly across his desk.

'Oh, that's OK, Mr Goldsmith; I can see you're really busy. It was no problem finding you.' She flashed him her most winning smile.

'Please,' he said, gesturing towards the chair in front of his desk, 'do take as seat.'

She was dressed conservatively, in a grey business suit, but his attempt to disguise the involuntary scan which his eyes performed up and down her slim, shapely body before she sat down failed miserably. That was OK - his interest could only help her cause. She maintained the smile, widening her eyes ever so slightly. 'If you'd like to show me what I can do for you' – the *double entendre* was unintentional, but the way Goldsmith ran his tongue along his upper lip clearly indicated it had not been lost on him – 'then I'll get started and let you get on.'

'Sure,' he said, smiling. 'I'll just let Cynthia know that you're up here.' He picked up the phone and punched a couple of keys. 'Hi, Cynthia. Just thought I'd let you know that your charming assistant' – he shot Juanita a knowing glance – 'is already up here. Thanks so much for—' He fell silent, apparently having been interrupted by the voice on the other end of the line. After about ten seconds he put down the handset. 'I guess Cynthia must have got out of bed on the wrong side this morning.' He rose from his chair, beckoning. 'Come on, follow me.'

He led her over to an unoccupied desk, a few rows away. To Juanita's dismay, the desks either side were occupied: on one side by a young girl, probably barely out of college, and on the other by a tired-looking, middle-aged man with a hopelessly unsuccessful combover. Goldsmith introduced her to both of them.

'Guys ... got a moment?' They both looked up. 'Gema, this is Emily, and this is Scott.'

'Pleased to meet you both,' she replied shaking each of their hands in turn. Emily's was small and feminine; Scott's cold, damp, and limp.

'Gema's helping out this afternoon by sorting out and boxing up all Julia's things. The police want to take them away tomorrow morning.'

Juanita noticed a fearful shadow flit across the other girl's eyes as she gave a tremulous intake of breath. As Cynthia had already told her, Julia's murder had evidently unsettled some of the other staff.

'I'll try not to get in your way too much,' said Juanita.

Introductions over, Goldsmith turned his attention back to Juanita. 'OK,' he said, 'Julia was using these three filing cabinets.' He slapped his hand on top of each in turn. 'You'll need to box up everything inside them, and everything from inside her desk drawers; you'll find some suitable boxes in that room over there.' He pointed at an open door at the side of the office. 'They'll also need her laptop and any flash drives, discs and so on which she may have been using.' He paused for a moment. 'You OK with all that?'

'Sure – that's fine.'

'Anyway, if you need anything else, I'm sure Emily or Scott will be able to help you.'

Emily nodded; Scott just grunted.

Goldsmith patted her on the arm, letting his hand linger rather longer than was necessary, before turning and heading back to his own desk.

So far, so good; but how the hell am I going to copy any documents or computer files with these two sitting right alongside me?

Chapter 17

Mark Bowman was back at his desk, supposedly recovered from his fictitious stomach bug.

Sergeant O'Reilly was his usual sympathetic self. 'You're back, I see. How's progress on the Patterson case?'

'Yeah, I'm OK now, thanks,' retorted Mark. 'Must have been something I'd eaten.'

O'Reilly ignored the sarcastic reply. 'And the Patterson case?' he persisted.

'Well,' began Mark, taking a deep breath as he prepared to deliver another pack of lies to his superior, 'I think we're onto something with the link to the jacket I told you about.'

'Yeah?' grunted O'Reilly. 'What you got?'

'Turns out the stolen jacket turned up in a dumpster two days after the Patterson burglary; the owner has confirmed it's his. I've seen the jacket for myself and I'm almost certain it's the same one that guy who got caught on CCTV at the Patterson spread was wearing.'

Mark was really sweating now. It would be the easiest thing in the world for O'Reilly to check out his story; Mark just had to hope he wouldn't have any reason to do so.

'So why'd this guy dump the jacket after going to the trouble of stealing it?'

'My guess,' said Mark, 'is that he realised he'd been caught on camera and figured that hanging on to the jacket might make it easier to track him down.'

'Hmm,' said O'Reilly, stroking his chin, 'could be, I guess. Anyhow, we gotta nail this guy and find the stolen stuff – especially that Jaguar. Apparently, Patterson's going completely apeshit about that: seems he cares more about that damned car than his wife getting whacked over the head.'

'I'm on it Sarge – I'll work with the guys investigating the other burglary over at Staten Island. I'm also going to put out the word with a couple of my informants. Trust me - we'll get these guys.'

'You'd better,' growled O'Reilly, 'the chief's right on my ass over this.'

Yeah, and you're right on mine, thought Mark. 'Sure thing Sarge,' he said.

As O'Reilly lumbered away from his desk, Mark exhaled a long, slow sigh of relief. His heart was racing and his shirt drenched in perspiration.

Alexis, sitting at her desk nearby, had obviously overheard much of the conversation. She shook her head, slowly, before standing up and coming over.

'Mark, you gotta be careful,' she whispered. 'If you're bullshitting him, he's gonna find out eventually.'

'I guess,' acknowledged Mark, 'but I've got to keep him off my back until I can find Julia's killer.'

'Oh, Mark, you have to leave it to Don: he's the detective in charge of Julia's case. You'll be in all sorts of shit if O'Reilly finds out you've been working on it too.'

'I know, but …'

'Let it go, Mark.'

He hung his head for a few seconds, before raising his gaze to meet hers. 'I guess you're right.'

'I am,' she insisted. 'Now get on that Patterson case, before O'Reilly skins you alive.'

He gave a weak smile; she patted his arm and returned to her desk.

But Mark couldn't just let it go. Don Lister had been in the force for almost thirty years, and he was due to retire in a few months' time. He'd never exactly been the sharpest tool in the box, and it was no surprise to Mark that he'd never progressed beyond the rank of detective. He had very little confidence that, with retirement beckoning, Don would solve Julia's murder and bring her killer to justice. But then, he had to admit that he wasn't getting anywhere himself, either.

He clicked the mouse alongside his computer and brought up, once again, the CCTV clip which he had been studying before

O'Reilly had interrupted him. For the seventh or eighth time, he watched the young woman come rushing out of the front door of the Edward Mason Pathology Laboratory, clutching a sheaf of papers. As she broke into a run, her long, dark hair streaming behind her, he hit 'pause'. Frustratingly, he couldn't get a clear view of her face, but there could be no doubt that this was the woman who had attempted to copy the autopsy report. How much she had succeeded in copying was difficult to determine, but from the page at which the original report had been left open on the photocopier, he guessed about half.

He hit 'play' and slowed the playback down to one quarter speed, watching as the woman sprinted, in slow motion, towards the corner of the next street, wheeling around to the right while barely breaking stride. Still he could not see her face clearly or glean any clue as to her identity. At least they had the passport photo, but it was small, and of poor resolution. When blown up to a larger size it was blurry and pixelated.

Once again, he flipped to the recording from the next camera, around the corner; once again, there was no sign of the running woman. He had already determined that there was a blind spot spanning the first thirty yards of that street before that camera's field of vision kicked in. His quarry had managed to disappear somewhere within that blind spot; she must have either dived into a building within that first thirty yards, or into a waiting car. Mark had already checked the area and there were only three businesses with a door directly onto the street in that zone, and all three had numerical keypads to afford entry. Unless this woman knew the code of one of them – unlikely, in Mark's view – then she had to have gotten away in a car. He assumed that, as she was in such a hurry, she would have set off immediately in the car: he estimated that there was a window of perhaps forty seconds during which time the car would have entered the camera's field of vision.

He scrolled through the recording in slow motion, paying careful attention to the time stamp. There were four possible vehicles in which the suspect could have escaped: a black Ford Edge SUV, a silver Toyota Camry sedan, a dark blue GMC Sierra Pickup, and a white Ford Transit Connect van. Frustratingly, the location of the camera did not afford a view of the licence plates, but it was possible to get a view of the front passenger seat of each vehicle. Mark figured it unlikely that the woman would be driving; leaving her car on a yellow for any length of time in New York's busy streets would have been just asking for it to be towed away. No, she most likely had an accomplice waiting for her.

Only two of the cars had a front seat passenger: The Camry and the Sierra. Both were women, but only the Camry's occupant had long, dark hair. So now he knew, with near certainty, that the suspect had escaped in a silver Toyota Camry. Without the licence number, it didn't exactly narrow the field too much: there were probably hundreds, perhaps thousands, of such vehicles in the New York City area. But it was a start, however small; if he could get some other clues to put together with this snippet of information then maybe, just maybe, he could get on her trail.

Chapter 18

'Guess I'll get started right away,' said Juanita, addressing her remark to the young girl, Emily, rather than Scott, who seemed altogether less friendly.

'Sure,' she said, smiling. 'Anything we can help you with, just ask.'

'Thanks. First off, I guess I'll go and get some of those boxes.'

The room Goldsmith had indicated was about fifteen feet square and, judging by the tired décor and copious amount of clutter, was evidently treated as a sort of general dumping ground. The wall to the left was lined with several teetering stacks of box files and yellowing piles of papers. At the back of the room, below the single small window, were the boxes to which Goldsmith had referred: dozens of them. But the most important thing of all was located to the right of the door: a photocopier. Perhaps, if this room was not visited by other employees too frequently, she might be able to snatch enough privacy to copy some of the papers.

She had made sure her cell phone was fully charged this time, having well and truly learned her lesson from her stupid mistake at the path lab, but given the substantial volume of material she might need to copy now, the automatic document feeder of the photocopier would be far quicker than photographing individual pages. Even so, with the contents of three large filing cabinets, and Julia's desk, to deal with, she would still need to be very selective about what she chose to copy. There was also the consideration of just how she would smuggle out the copied documents if she attempted to copy too much.

She grabbed two of the boxes and headed back to Julia's desk.

'I'll make a start then,' she said to Emily, who smiled and nodded in return.

There were several piles of papers on the desk. Juanita guessed that these were more likely to relate to what Julia had been working on recently than the huge amount of material in the filing cabinets, so she decided she'd concentrate her efforts on those. However, she was acutely conscious of the frequent furtive sidelong glances from Scott, seated alongside; he was bound to notice if she was examining these papers in any detail. She decided to start with the filing cabinets; hopefully, by the time she started sifting through the papers on the desk, he'd have lost interest in what she was doing.

***

An hour had passed, and Scott never did lose interest: he seemed to be paying more attention to what Juanita was doing than to his own work. Every time she stopped to take a look at some of the papers that she removed from the filing cabinets, his head swivelled towards her. Even when she had her back turned, she could feel his eyes boring into it. This was hopeless; she'd already more or less given up on gleaning much useful from the material in the filing cabinets, but when it came to sorting through the – hopefully more significant – papers on the desk, she'd have to get them away from under Scott's watchful gaze.

She had an idea.

'Uh, Emily,' – the young girl turned towards her – 'I'm kind of tripping over myself with all these boxes under my feet, and I've still got one more filing cabinet to unload. D'you think it'd be OK if I moved them over to the room where I got the empty boxes from and put everything together there for the police to collect tomorrow?'

'Oh, sure … no-one cares about that room. There's stuff in there dating back to the dark ages,' she laughed.

All the time Juanita had been engaged in boxing up the papers, she had also been keeping an eye on the door to the room. Given that it contained the only photocopier in the office, it was not surprising that quite a few people were in and out of the room all the time. The intervals were, of course, quite random: sometimes no-one would enter or leave for around fifteen minutes; other times there would be an almost constant stream of people entering and leaving. Still, it was her best hope; at least she could sift through some of the papers away from Scott's prying gaze. Furthermore, most people in the office appeared to be super-busy – unlike the slothful Scott. She hoped no-one would be too interested in why a temp was doing some photocopying.

'Thanks,' said Juanita, bending down to try to lift one of the boxes; it was way too heavy.

'Oh, don't try to do that,' said Emily, rising from her chair. 'There's a sack truck in the room over there. Come with me ... I'll show you.'

The two of them went over to the photocopier room, returning a minute or two later with the truck. Emily tried in vain to lift the first box onto the truck.

'Scott,' she chided, 'are you gonna help here, or not?'

The big man exhaled noisily as he levered himself to his feet. 'Shoulda thought about that before loading up them boxes so full,' he muttered.

'Thanks a bunch for the advice,' she replied, a sharp edge to her voice. 'So, you gonna make her unpack the boxes, or you gonna help?'

'Yeah, yeah,' he grunted as he bent down and heaved the first box onto the sack truck. He stood back, evidently not expecting to actually wheel the truck over to the photocopier room.

'Thanks,' said Juanita, trying not to let the sarcasm show in her voice, 'I guess I can manage this bit on my own.' She placed a foot on the base of the truck and heaved backwards, tipping it until it felt balanced, before setting off with it.

'You're such a shmuck, Scott,' she heard the young girl hiss at him from behind her.

Juanita didn't know what else Emily might have said to him in the minute or two she was away, but it must have had some effect because he then offered to move the rest of the boxes himself, though he barely uttered a word while doing so.

When he had finished, in spite of his somewhat surly demeanour, Juanita treated him to her most winning smile, touching him lightly on the arm. 'Thanks *so* much Scott ... it's good to have a strong man around to help.'

His expression softened; there was even a hint of a smile. 'Oh, that's OK,' he murmured, before turning back to sit at his desk.

Emily and Juanita exchanged a knowing glance. *Men,* Emily mouthed silently, before returning to her work.

OK, so far so good. What next? thought Juanita. For once, Scott seemed now to be actually paying attention to his own work. This could be a good time to attempt to copy the contents of the laptop onto the hard drive. She opened the lid of the laptop and pressed the power button. After a few seconds the screen lit up with a stunning view of snow-covered mountains, infused with a golden glow by the setting sun. In the centre was Julia Turner's name and photograph: the contrast between this beautiful, vivacious-looking girl and the shockingly mutilated face she had seen in the autopsy report elicited from Juanita an involuntary gasp. But it was what lay below Julia's name that made her heart skip a beat: a white box containing the single word, 'Password'.

Shit!

Chapter 19

Juanita's heart began to race as she tried to figure out what to do. She had been counting on the computer to provide the best evidence of what Julia had been working on – it would be impossible, in the time she had available, to sift through the entire contents of those boxes of files. There were, of course still those piles of papers out on the desk, but it was the computer which was most likely to hold the key.

She sat for a few minutes, going through the motions of reorganising the piles of papers while she tried to compose herself and come up with some plan. Should she risk actually stealing the laptop? Even if she did, how would she and James get past the password barrier, no matter how much time they had? Furthermore, once the police realised the machine had been stolen, they would know, straightaway, that she was probably the one responsible and it was more than likely that they'd eventually make the link with the copying of the autopsy report. Then she'd really be in their crosshairs. This was all getting far too dangerous: maybe she should just abandon this mission completely and try to convince James to do likewise.

Her introspective pondering was interrupted by a loud creaking noise as Scott levered his considerable bulk from his protesting swivel chair. 'Gotta use the men's room,' he informed her, somewhat unnecessarily.

With most of her options now closed off, Juanita decided she'd use the few minutes while Scott was away to see if Emily knew anything. 'Nearly done,' she said, as a means of opening the conversation. She tried to keep her voice as calm and casual as possible.

Emily managed a small smile, but there was something about her demeanour that made it clear she wasn't in a smiling mood. It didn't take long for her to reveal why.

'I still can't believe that Julia's gone. I was so used to her sitting right there, alongside me. Seeing all her work reduced to a just a few boxes of papers like that ... it kind of brings it all back. It's all just so ...' her voice tailed off as she fought back the tears which threatened to burst forth.

Juanita placed a comforting arm around her shoulders. 'Yes, it's a terrible, terrible thing.'

The moment passed, and the tears never came, but once again, fear showed in the young girl's eyes as she visibly shuddered. 'I know ... it's absolutely awful.'

'Why on earth would anyone do that?' said Juanita.

'I don't know,' said Emily, 'but everyone's really scared that there could be a serial killer out there with a grudge against the newspaper.'

'Seems unlikely to me,' said Juanita. 'It could just be a random attack ... or maybe she'd upset someone with an investigation she was working on.'

'Maybe,' conceded Emily, 'but ... oh, I don't know.'

This was the moment: Juanita needed to sound as casual as possible. 'What *was* she working on, anyway?'

'Oh, she was doing a feature on companies employing illegal immigrants as cheap labour. She was homing in on the building industry ... apparently, in New York alone, they use thousands of illegals, mostly from Mexico.'

Ironic, thought Juanita, that Emily was telling her this when she was an illegal immigrant from Mexico herself. But there was no time to dwell on this; she needed to get to the point as quickly as possible, before Scott returned. Although Emily seemed completely credulous that her questions were born merely out of curiosity, she doubted that Scott would be as accommodating.

'D'you think that, during her investigation, she could have trodden on enough toes to bring about her murder? I mean it's not exactly headline news that there are a lot of workers in the building trade who shouldn't really be here in the USA.'

'I don't know,' whispered Emily, leaning in as she lowered her voice, 'but I think she might have stumbled across something else: something bigger.'

Now she had Juanita's full attention. 'Do you know what it was?'

'No, I don't, but Julia always used to chat with me and tell me everything about how her investigation was going, but then, all of a sudden, she seemed to go all secretive. I think she'd discovered something important and wanted to keep it to herself for some reason.'

'But you don't know—?' She abruptly abandoned the question when she saw Scott's bulky frame lumbering towards them. 'Anyway,' she said, wrapping up the conversation, 'I'm sure you don't need to worry that her killer will be targeting any of the rest of you.'

Emily still looked doubtful.

'That's better,' declared Scott – information which neither of the women really needed to hear. 'Do you need any more help, before I sit down er ...?'

'Gema,' she reminded him. 'No, I've only got these papers on the desk to sort out now.' Again, she smiled broadly: in spite of her initial distaste for the man, she had to admit his attitude did seem to have softened considerably.

She took her time over boxing up the remaining papers, scanning the headings to try to identify any documents which looked as though they were worth copying. One, in particular, caught her eye: the heading read, 'Employment of Illegals by Johnson Brothers'. Evidently Emily had been right about what Julia had been working on. She found a couple more documents which seemed to be related and put them to one side as she packed what seemed to be the less interesting stuff into the box. Finally, she put the documents she intended to copy on the top, before placing the box – much lighter than the others – on the sack truck and heading towards the photocopier room.

Her interest had now been well and truly piqued by Emily's suggestion that her dead co-worker's investigation may have led her to discover something bigger; this chimed with James's assertion that the suspected assassin would only have been contracted to eliminate a junior journalist if she was about to reveal something *very* important.

She set about copying the relevant documents and was only interrupted twice by others coming in to use the machine. On both occasions they only had a single sheet to copy, so she readily stood aside long enough for them to do so. Neither showed any interest in what she was doing; they both looked too busy and too harassed. On both occasions they thanked her for letting them interrupt her and hurried back to work. When she had finished, she took one of the old box files that were heaped alongside the wall, tipped out its contents, and replaced them with her own papers. She would have to hope that, at the end of the day, she could smuggle it out without being noticed.

By the time she had finished her copying task, she had managed to banish all her earlier self-doubts; now she was fired with renewed determination. She decided that, somehow, she *had* to get access to that computer. She chose a high-risk strategy.

Chapter 20

Juanita made her way over to Joe Goldsmith's desk, her heart rate steadily rising and her palms sweating as she prepared for the biggest gamble of the whole mission.

'Excuse me Mr Goldsmith.'

He looked up, smiling as he laid down his pen and gave her his full attention – actually, a bit too much attention, as his eyes flitted between her face and her breasts, in spite of the sober jacket she was wearing.

'How's it going?' he enquired.

'Oh, I'm almost finished, but there's one thing I wanted to ask your advice about.'

'Sure,' he said gesturing for her to sit down on the chair opposite him, 'fire away.'

'Well,' she said, smiling as she sat down, desperately hoping that her fear would not show in her face or her voice, 'I think you said the police would want to take her computer as well as all her papers.'

'Uh-huh.'

'So, I thought I'd power the machine up … just to check everything was OK.'

Goldsmith narrowed his eyes slightly as his forehead creased in a puzzled frown. 'How d'you mean, "OK"?'

Fighting to control her rising panic, Juanita looked directly into his eyes with what she hoped was an innocent, wide-eyed gaze. 'I just wanted to make sure the police wouldn't have any problems accessing the information they need.'

He shrugged, 'Why should they?'

'Well, it looks like the machine is password protected.'

'Ah, I see,' he said. 'Of course.'

'I wondered if we should give them the password … you know, just to make their job easier.'

Goldsmith cradled his chin between thumb and forefinger as he considered this request. 'Hmm … thing is, our employees choose their own passwords. I've no idea what password Julia would have used.'

Juanita had guessed this was probably the case but was hoping against hope that Goldsmith would come up with some solution. She decided to employ a little gentle prompting. 'Oh, well I guess the police must have I.T. people who might be able to get past the password somehow; it's just a shame that we can't make their job less difficult.'

He took the bait.

After pausing for a few moments, with furrowed brow and pursed lips, his expression relaxed as he raised a forefinger in the air. 'Wait, let's see what our own I.T. people can do.' He picked up his phone and punched a few keys. 'Hi George. Look, I've got a bit of an issue down here. The cops are coming tomorrow morning to pick up Julia's computer, but it's password protected. Any chance one of your guys could get around the password so they can access the machine?' He paused for a few moments, evidently listening to the reply from the other end of the line. 'Yeah,' he said, after around fifteen seconds, 'I know they'll have their own I.T. people, but I'll bet they're not as hot as your guys.' He winked at Juanita, who smiled back at him, her heart rate now starting to slow a little. 'And even if they were,' he continued, 'we should do our best to help New York's finest, shouldn't we?' He paused for some seconds. 'Well it really needs to be this afternoon.' Another pause. 'That's great, George. Just ask him to come over to my desk and I'll introduce him to the charming young lady who's sorting out Julia's things for me.' He put down the phone with a triumphant smile. 'Nothing like a bit of flattery to get things done,' he said. 'They're sending someone down right away.'

'That's great. Uh … shall I just go back over to finish off a few other bits and pieces while we're waiting?'

'Nah, they'll probably only be a few minutes. Why don't you just stay and chat 'til they get here.'

Juanita had no desire whatsoever to 'stay and chat', but she wanted to keep Goldsmith sweet, so she leaned forward placing both elbows on the desk, interlacing her fingers and placing her chin on the back of her hands. 'That's very kind of you, Mr Goldsmith,' she simpered.

'Oh, call me Joe.'

'OK, I will … Joe.' She flashed him another dazzling smile, but within moments she began to regret her foolishness in encouraging this man to engage her in further conversation.

'Where'd you work before Cynthia snapped you up?'

Her heart skipped a beat; she'd have to improvise now. 'Oh here and there; short term temping suits me just fine. Last place was a law firm in Brooklyn.'

'Oh really – what're they called? I might know of them.'

Oh Christ! After the risks she had taken to get this far, the last thing she wanted was to get tripped up on this casual chit-chat. But she'd just had to bluff it out now. 'Smith and Williams,' she replied, falling back on the two commonest surnames she could think of on the spur of the moment, 'd'you know them?'

As soon as she had uttered the words, she realised that her answer would not match the work history she had put in her fictitious résumé. Would he have read it and, if so, would he remember what was in it? Her heart began to race once more.

'Don't think so,' he said. 'Never mind. Where d'you come from … originally I mean?'

This was getting really tricky now; she hadn't expected to have to memorise every detail of her résumé once she had actually landed the job. 'Well,' she said, stalling for time as she desperately tried to decide on an answer, 'I've been here, in the Big Apple, most of my life but—'

She was saved by Goldsmith abruptly looking up and cutting off her faltering reply. 'Ah!' he said, 'here's Rick, from I.T.'

Juanita let out a massive sigh of relief at this timely respite. She turned to see a young guy, who looked as though he was barely out of high school. His ripped jeans and Guns 'n' Roses tee-shirt contrasted sharply with the 'business casual' dress code adopted by most in the office. *Christ, this kid wouldn't even have been born when Guns 'n' Roses were at their peak*, she mused. His long, scruffy hair also seemed incongruous in the office environment. No matter; the only thing that mattered right now was his technical expertise.

'Thanks for coming down at short notice, Rick. This is Gema. Gema … Rick.'

Juanita offered her hand which the youth shook, limply.

He didn't bother with pleasantries. 'You got a computer you want unlocked?'

'That's right,' interjected Goldsmith … 'Gema will show you.'

'OK,' he grunted. And that was the extent of the conversation before Juanita led him over to Julia's desk. Scott looked up, enquiringly.

'Rick has come down to unlock Julia's computer so that the police can access her files,' she explained.

Scott didn't reply; he just nodded, before turning back to the folder he had open on his desk. She turned her attention back to the scruffy youth whose expertise – or otherwise – was the only thing standing between her and the information she sought.

'Do you think you'll be able to do it?' she asked.

'Might do,' was the cryptic reply.

He took from the bag he was carrying a small, rectangular, plastic box which he connected, with a cable, to the computer. He punched a few keys on the device, and its display lit up, accompanied by an electronic bleeping sound.

'OK, here we go,' he announced.

He pressed one more key and immediately the display sprang to life, letters and numbers scrolling through at breakneck speed, forming an indistinguishable blur.

'What does that box actually do?' asked Juanita.

'It's kinda complicated.'

'I guess,' she conceded. 'Well, how long do you think it will take?'

'Dunno … depends.'

She concluded that any further attempt at conversation with this geeky-looking young man would be futile.

'Guess I'll leave you to it, then. I've still got a bit of work to do over in the room over there' – she pointed her finger – 'so if you manage to—'

'Result!' interrupted the youth, jumping to his feet and punching the air.

Scott and Emily both spun round at this sudden and unexpected display of enthusiasm from the young man.

Juanita was also taken aback to see him looking so animated. 'You've done it?' she said.

He nodded. 'Real weak password,' he declared. 'That's why it didn't take long to crack.' He tapped a few keys on the computer, which, after a few seconds lit up, finally settling on a familiar-looking Windows home screen. 'I'll just reset the password for you … something nice and simple.' After a few more taps and clicks, he grabbed a notepad and pen from the desk and scribbled something down. 'OK, that's your new password – "Admin1" – upper case "A".'

'Wow!' exclaimed Juanita, genuinely impressed. 'How did you do that?'

He tapped the side of his nose with his finger. 'It's not that hard when you know what you're doing.' With that, he unplugged his little box of tricks and departed.

Juanita could hardly believe her luck: the trickiest bit of the whole mission had been overcome without a hitch. Now all she needed to do was find a way to copy the contents of the computer to her own hard drive without being detected. Clearly, though, she couldn't do it right there, under the watchful gaze of the inquisitive Scott.

She powered the machine down and closed the lid. 'Right,' she said, addressing herself to both Scott and Emily simultaneously, 'that's me just about done. I'll take the laptop and put it with all the other stuff that the police have to collect in the morning. Then,' she said, looking at her watch, 'it'll be about time to go home. Thanks to both of you for all your help.'

'Oh, you're welcome,' said Emily, 'it was nice chatting to you, Gema.'

'Sure,' grunted Scott.

When she returned to the storage room, she looked around for a power socket; she didn't want to risk the laptop's battery dying on her in the middle of the copying process. When she found one, she set the computer down on the floor, connected her hard drive and switched the machine on. After typing in the new password, she quickly started the copy process. The estimated time to complete the process was sixteen minutes. She pulled a few boxes in front of the computer to conceal it from anyone who might come in and settled down to wait.

After about ten minutes a young woman of Afro-Caribbean appearance, with an abundant mass of frizzy black hair, entered the room. Juanita pretended to be reorganising the papers in one of the boxes she'd packed.

'Oh hi,' said the woman, 'I just need to grab a couple of those empty boxes.'

To Juanita's dismay she headed straight for those which she had placed in front of the computer. *Damn!*

Chapter 21

Before Juanita could even begin to think of a way to stop her, the woman had covered the two or three paces to where the boxes had been placed. She stopped for a moment, surveying the boxes as though trying to decide which ones to take. To Juanita's horror, the woman's gaze seemed to settle on one of those which was concealing the laptop and hard drive. She would have to act fast if she was to avoid being discovered.

'Why don't you try these?' blurted Juanita, rushing forward, almost tripping over her own feet in her haste to divert the woman's attention.

'Huh?' she muttered, turning her head, her expression puzzled.

Juanita pointed to some other boxes a few feet away. 'I've been boxing up papers all afternoon and those boxes weigh an absolute ton when they're loaded up.'

The woman shrugged, tilting her head. 'I guess.'

'These are smaller,' said Juanita, picking one up and holding it forward '– much easier to lift.'

The woman took a step towards her and took the box, tilting it back and forth as she appeared to be assessing its suitability. 'Yeah, I see what you mean. I might need three or four of these though … I've got quite a lot of stuff to box up.'

'Better that than wreck your back,' suggested Juanita trying hard to sound casual, despite her racing heartbeat.

'I guess you're right,' laughed the woman. 'My boyfriend put his back out last year ago by lifting a lawnmower into the back of his pickup … took months to recover.'

'Definitely not worth risking it,' agreed Juanita, laughing.

'I'll just take two for now and see how I get on. I'll come back later for any more I need. Thanks for the tip, er …'

'Gema.'

'Thanks, Gema; I'm Sue by the way. Say, you're new, aren't you ... you just started?'

Juanita just wanted to wrap this conversation up, retrieve her hard drive, and get out of there as soon as possible, but having seemingly averted any suspicion from this woman, she had to go along with the casual chat.

She nodded. 'I'm just temping for one week ... working for Cynthia, downstairs.'

'A week's enough ... working here for much longer's enough to drive you mad ... the pace is just crazy.'

For Christ's sake ... can't you just take the damned boxes and go?

It was as if she had somehow picked up Juanita's unspoken thoughts. 'Talking of which, I've got to rush.' She grabbed two boxes and turned to go. 'Anyway, nice talking to you, Gema. Enjoy your life outside of the madhouse.' She laughed at her own joke as she swept out of the door.

The release of tension was palpable; Juanita took several long, deep breaths, leaning against the photocopier, as her racing heart began to slow. But there was no time to waste now; she had to complete her task before any further risk of discovery arose. She glanced at her watch 5.47 p.m. It was past the end of her official working day, so once she had finished copying the files and shown Goldsmith where she'd left everything for the cops, she'd be able to leave straightaway.

She took a few paces towards the door, looking out to check that no-one was approaching. The office was still busy, but there was no-one heading in her direction. She rushed over to where the laptop was hidden, relieved to see that the copy process was complete. Unplugging the hard drive and slipping it into her purse, she shut down the laptop and placed it on top of the stack of boxes containing Julia's files. Now she just wanted to get out of there as soon as possible, but she still needed to check in with Goldsmith. She headed over towards his desk.

'Excuse me Mr Goldsmith.'

'Joe,' he reminded her, looking up as she approached. Once again, she noticed his appraising scan up and down her body.

'Yes, of course ... Joe. I've finished now – can I show you what I've done?'

'Sure … lead on.'

She could sense his eyes boring into her butt as he followed her towards the storage room. She quickened her pace a little, anxious to get this over with as soon as possible.

'So, all the papers from Julia's filing cabinets and desk are in these boxes. I've tried to separate them into logical categories to make things easier for the police. Her laptop's right there.'

'Oh yeah … did the I.T. guy manage to get past the password?'

'Yes,' she said, offering him a slip of paper. 'This is the new password.'

He nodded, approvingly. 'Great job, Gema.'

'Thanks. Now if that's everything you need me to do, I'll get ready to leave.'

'Say, I gather tomorrow's your last day with Cynthia.'

'Yes, why?'

'I'm real short-handed right now. How'd you like to come and work for me for a couple of weeks?'

'I … er, well under normal circumstances I'd love to, but I've already got another temporary post lined up for the next three weeks.'

'Well, I can give you three weeks' work. What are they paying you? I'll at least match it.'

This was getting tricky now. She paused for a moment as she tried to figure out a plausible response. 'That's really kind of you Mr Goldsmith, but—'

'Joe,' he reminded her again, wagging his finger back and forth.

'Yes … sorry. Thing is though, I've already made the commitment. You wouldn't want me to go back on my word and let another employer down, would you?'

He gave a wry smile. 'You're one in a million, Gema. It's very rare for temps to show that kinda commitment.'

'Well, I just like to do the right thing.'

He nodded, casting a licentious glance at her breasts. 'Well, how about meeting me for a drink after work one day next week?'

Oh, Christ – how do I get out of this one?

'I … I don't know what to say.'

'Just say "yes",' he laughed.

'I'm really flattered, Mr … I mean Joe, but the thing is my fiancé's rather a jealous type. I know that your intentions are completely honourable,' she said, knowing full well that the lecherous bastard's intentions were anything but, 'but I'm not sure Rick would quite see it like that. He's an ex-Marine you know.'

The colour drained from the man's face; for a second or two he seemed lost for words. He quickly regained his composure though.

'Well, as you know, I was only wanting to buy you a few drinks to say thank you for a job well done, but I certainly wouldn't want to create any waves, so I guess a plain "Thank you" right now will have to do.' He took a business card from his pocket and handed it to her. 'If you're looking for any temporary work in the future just give me a call.'

'Thank you, Mr Goldsmith' – he didn't bother to correct her this time – 'I will.'

'Now I must get on,' he muttered, '– lots of work to do.'

He shook her hand, rather formally, and headed back towards his desk.

Breathing a sigh of relief, she made her way back to the storage room and retrieved the box file she had left there. She tried to conceal it under her jacket, but it was too bulky. She stole a glance through the door back into the main office; everyone seemed to be busy with their own work, no-one looking in her direction. In the end, she just tucked the box file under her arm and walked as slowly and calmly as possible though the office and out into the corridor. No-one paid her any attention whatsoever; even Goldsmith didn't seem to notice her leave.

When Juanita stepped out into the cool evening air, her overriding emotion was not one of relief, but an intense feeling of exhilaration. The close brush with danger, combined with her eventual success, against the odds, had left her on a high that no drug could ever match. James would surely be proud of her.

***

'You did what?' exclaimed James.

'I just asked him for the password.'

'You just asked him?' repeated James. 'Are you completely crazy?'

'Crazy for you,' she said, laughing.

'No, seriously … if he had decided to start asking awkward questions …'

'Well, he didn't, did he? And now we've got all the information we wanted. Aren't you pleased with me?' she added, clapping her hands together.

He couldn't be angry with her. She had achieved everything he could possibly have asked and, as she stood in front of him, beaming with pride, his heart melted.

He stepped forward and encircled her in his arms. 'Of course I am,' he said, kissing her and brushing away a stray strand of hair from her cheek. 'You really are quite something, you know.'

'One in a million according to Mr Goldsmith,' she laughed.

'Was he coming on to you?' said James, relinquishing the hug and standing back a little, his hands on her shoulders.

'Well, he's not made of wood, is he? I can't help being irresistibly attractive to men.'

'You shameless flirt,' laughed James.

'Well it got the job done, didn't it?'

He had never seen her in quite this mood before: buzzing with excitement and seemingly oblivious to the danger she had placed herself in. 'Are you drunk?' he asked.

'Drunk on love,' she replied, pulling him to her and kissing him on the lips.

He savoured the kiss, but when their lips parted, he said, 'I think you need to come down to earth.'

'Don't you think I'd make a good spy … captivating men with my tempting charm and then snatching what I need from right under their noses?'

'OK enough,' he laughed. 'We need to start going through all this stuff. If we can figure out what this journalist was working on, then maybe we'll be able to find out what she might have uncovered.'

'And if something really evil is being planned, maybe we can stop it.'

'Not "we",' he admonished her. 'If we uncover something bad, we'll just give the police an anonymous tip off, pointing them towards whatever evidence we have found. *We* need to stay off the radar.'

'I guess,' she said, 'but you have to admit it's kind of—'

The sound of the doorbell cut her off, mid-sentence. The two of them locked eyes, exchanging the same unspoken question.

James raised a forefinger to his lips, stepping over to the closet and reaching into the safe inside, whose door was open while they were there in the room. He withdrew the Glock handgun inside, and screwed the silencer in place. Sliding the safety catch off, he moved silently over to stand alongside the hinged side of the door, motioning for Juanita to come over and open it. She put her eye to the security peephole, but evidently did not recognise whoever was there, for when she turned towards James she just shrugged. He nodded raising the gun by his shoulder, pointing it towards the ceiling, and flattening himself against the wall. Juanita opened the door, blocking his view.

A man's voice: 'Hello, Carla. It's been a long time.'

This could not be good: Carla was a name she had left behind in Miami, together with a life which could never be allowed to catch up with them again. James's finger tightened on the trigger.

Juanita's reply was hesitant. 'I … er … I'm afraid there must be some mistake.'

'Carla, it's me … Kyle.'

Chapter 22

It was Friday evening, and Mandy Jackson was enjoying a girls' night out with her besties, Mary-Jane Bailey and Dolores Faith. The venue was Pentangle – a rather upmarket bar in the heart of Manhattan. The ambience was well-judged: agreeable soft, blue lighting; smooth jazz background music, played at pleasantly low volume; and well-spaced groups of seats, which allowed enough privacy for a quiet conversation, while still affording a sense of inclusion in the rest of the bar. The drinks were pricey, but the place was so much classier than many of other joints in the area. As a special night out, once in a while, all three women considered it to be worth the cost.

The three of them had all attended high school together and, now in their early thirties, they had remained close friends ever since. They would get together like this at least once every couple of weeks, and *talk*: they could talk for hours on end without ever running short of things to say. The usual topic of conversation was men: all three were still single, and all three were still playing the field. They loved to hear about one another's latest exploits and, most especially, whether any of them had met someone just a bit special.

Sometimes a group of men would approach them when they were out together; after all they were – as Mary-Jane frequently asserted – three very attractive women. Occasionally, they would flirt with the guys for a while, maybe even give out a telephone number but, for the most part, they would politely give these guys the brush off: this was girls' time, not to be interrupted by the mating ritual.

Mandy was usually the most talkative: after a busy week in the hairdressing salon, talking mostly to complete strangers, she was always hungry for the opportunity to indulge in a more intimate chat with her two best friends. Tonight though, it was Mary-Jane who was doing most of the talking. Working in a pathology lab didn't afford many opportunities to meet eligible men in a work setting, but this time she'd met someone who'd clearly made quite an impression.

'So,' she said, 'this cop came into the lab the other day. My god he was *so* cute. Honest, he had real movie-star looks; blue eyes you could lose yourself in; and this real deep, smooth voice. And you know what? He *definitely* had the hots for me.'

'Oh yeah?' piped up Dolores, giggling. 'And how exactly do you know that?'

Mary-Jane tossed her head, flicking luxuriant tresses of wavy, blonde hair away from her face. 'Oh, come on … I know when a guy wants to get into my panties: it's clear as day. Anyway, by the time he left, they were getting pretty wet, I can tell you.'

Dolores shrieked in delight, then quietened down when she saw several customers turn towards the unexpected noise. 'Oh, Mary-Jane, you're *such* a tart!'

'Nothing wrong with getting a bit turned on by a handsome guy,' she retorted.

The three of them descended into a fit of giggling. When it finally subsided, Dolores took a sip of her improbably blue cocktail before enquiring, 'So you gonna follow it up? I mean you got his number or anything?'

'I can contact him at the NYPD, but I don't want to seem too obvious. But *he's* got *my* number, and I'll bet you a dollar to a dime that he'll find an excuse to call me.'

'You wish,' concluded Dolores, draining her glass. 'You guys want another?'

'Is the pope a Catholic?' replied Mary-Jane.

More giggles as Dolores swivelled in her chair in a vain attempt to catch the eye of one of the servers.

While all this banter about the hunky cop and his alleged desire to bed Mary-Jane was going on, Mandy had a slightly different question in her mind. 'So, what exactly was a cop doing at the lab anyway?' she asked. 'I mean, he didn't just drop in hoping to find a devastatingly attractive woman on reception, did he?'

'No,' agreed Mary-Jane, 'that was just his good luck … and mine too, as it happens. Didn't I already explain about why he came?'

'No, you didn't … I think you must have had one too many of those hideous-looking blue concoctions.'

At just that moment, Dolores finally succeeded in summoning a server. 'Two more of these please,' she said, holding up her empty glass, 'and another glass of Chardonnay for my boring friend here.' She gestured towards Mandy, who shot back a sour look.

'So,' said Mandy, as the girl moved away from their table, 'what exactly was this sexy cop doing at the lab?'

'Well,' began Mary-Jane, 'it's kind of exciting: we had this real weird incident at the lab.'

'Ooh, do tell,' said Dolores, she and Mandy leaning forward in unison across the table.

'OK … well, it started when we had a new stiff wheeled in recently. This one was a murder victim: half her head blown off when the perp stuck a gun in her ear before pulling the trigger.'

'Oh, yuk!' squealed Dolores, shuddering in disgust.

Mandy pulled her head back sharply, making a *moue*.

'Yeah, pretty gross, I agree. Anyway, a few days later this woman turns up at the lab, claiming to be the dead girl's long-lost sister.'

'You said *claiming*,' interjected Mandy. 'Why do you—?'

She was interrupted as the server returned with their drinks. She set them down on the table, gesturing towards the vividly coloured cocktails. 'Those're real good – my favourite, actually. Unfortunately, they won't let me drink while I'm working, but I always have one when I finish my shift, before I go home. Kind of a perk of the job like.'

'Yeah, well thanks,' said Mandy, a little irritated that the cloak-and-dagger tale, about to unfold, had been interrupted. 'I'll let you know if we need anything else.'

The look she shot the girl clearly had the desired effect. 'Sure,' she said, setting the revised check down on the table and beating a hasty retreat.

'So,' continued Mandy, 'why didn't you believe this woman who turned up?'

'Well, she had what looked like genuine I.D. and she had the right look: Latina, just like the victim. What's more, she knew all about the dead girl and her folks but, somehow, it just didn't feel right. And there was nothing in the notes about any sister.'

'So what did she want?' asked Dolores.

'She wanted me to give her a copy of the autopsy report. Now, the dead girl's mother and father had already had a copy, so it all seemed a bit suspicious that a supposed sister would turn up out of the blue asking for another copy. Anyway, I took her passport and went to see Rich – he's my boss. I wasn't about to give out confidential info like that without his say-so.'

'But you still haven't said why the cops were interested,' pressed Mandy.

'I'm getting to that,' said Mary-Jane leaning in a little closer to the other two, apparently enjoying spinning out this story as long as possible. 'Rich said he wanted to talk to this woman himself, but just as we went back to reception to see her, we saw her running out the door holding some papers.'

'Papers?' enquired Dolores.

'Yeah … turns out that while I was away for a few minutes she'd managed to get into the filing room – which is *strictly* out-of-bounds to visitors – and find the autopsy report she wanted. It was there, open on the photocopier, so I guess she had copied some or all of it.'

'Wow!' gasped Dolores, 'what on earth do you think she was up to?'

Mary-Jane spread her hands. 'Beats me. Anyway, she left without getting her passport back. Obviously, we reported the whole thing to the cops; turns out the passport was a fake. They seemed real interested in what this woman was up to: they came to see me twice. The first guy was old, fat, and certainly no looker, but the second guy – Mark – he was a real hunk.'

'Oh, so you're on first name terms with Mr. Hunky, huh?'

'Told you, he really fell for me the moment he saw me … I could tell.'

'Yeah, yeah,' said Dolores, rolling her eyes. 'So what you gonna do about it?'

Mandy's attention had drifted away from Mary-Jane's supposed fledgling romance with the hot cop. The first tendrils of suspicion began to snake through her mind. Before her friend could respond to Dolores's question, Mandy posed another. 'What did this girl look like?'

'Well, like I said, she was a Latina, probably mid-thirties … kind of pretty … well not "pretty pretty", exactly … but really quite striking looks. Why d'you ask?'

Mandy didn't answer the question, responding instead with another of her own. 'You still got her passport?'

'No … the cops have taken it away, but why—?'

'What was her hair like?'

'Long, black, glossy; she had real nice hair. What's with the questions?'

Mandy took a sip of her wine. 'Hmm … it's probably nothing, but I had a woman who fits that description come into the salon the other day. She had beautiful long, black hair, but wanted it cut short and coloured differently. I mean she still looked good with her new cut – after all, doesn't anyone after one of my cuts?' she added, modestly. The other two rolled their eyes in unison. 'But why would she mess with such lovely hair? It seemed to me like she wanted to completely change her appearance.'

Dolores gasped. 'You don't think it was the same woman do you?'

'Well,' replied Mandy, 'if I had committed some sort of crime and I knew the cops were after me, and that they had my passport, complete with a photo, I'd want to change my appearance as much as possible.'

'Ooh,' whispered Mary-Jane, 'you could be right – maybe it was her.'

'Thing is,' continued Mandy, 'this woman seemed kind of nervy. I just had the feeling she was scared or something. And she was carrying a *big* pile of cash in her purse.'

The three women looked at each other in silence for several seconds. It seemed they were all thinking the same thing.

'Do you think I should report it to the cops?' asked Mandy, eventually.

Dolores turned to Mary-Jane. 'You said the police have got this mystery woman's photo, right?'

'Uh, huh.'

She swivelled around to face Mandy. 'Would you recognise her from the photo … I mean if it's the same woman?'

'I … I'm not sure … I think so.'

'That's settled then,' declared Mary-Jane. 'We can see Mark – the hot cop – together. He'll have been trying to find an excuse to call me … but now he won't have to. It's perfect.'

'Gonna dress to kill, then?' enquired Dolores.

'Best push-up bra, low cut dress,' replied Mary-Jane, smiling conspiratorially, 'he could barely keep his eyes off my tits, even when I was in my work clothes.'

'Shall I call the police then?' said Mandy, still sounding a little doubtful.'

'I'll do it,' insisted Mary-Jane. 'I've got Mark's direct number, and now I've got the perfect excuse to call him.'

'Oh, you shameless floozy,' laughed Dolores.

'Shall we have another drink to celebrate then?' said Mary-Jane.

'Just the one then,' said Dolores, laughing as she drained her glass, her words slightly slurred.

Chapter 23

James tensed, ready for action, as Juanita opened the door to the unexpected visitor. Her voice sounded incredulous as she addressed the man standing in the doorway. 'Kyle ... is that really you? You look so ...' Her voice petered out.

The man gave a soft chuckle. 'I guess the beard makes me look a bit different from when you last saw me ... and, after all, it *was* quite a while ago. And I see that *you've* got a new look too ... the hair I mean.'

There were a few moments' silence, before Juanita spoke again, during which, James was uncertain what to do; he opted to stay put, waiting to see what happened.

'Oh my god ... it really is you, isn't it?' said Juanita. 'I hardly recognised you. Anyway, I guess you'd better come in.' She stepped aside, allowing him to enter the room. As he did so, James emerged from behind the door, still holding the gun at the ready as he tried to process what was happening.

'Whoa ... what's with the gun?' said the man, holding his hands up and backing away. He was tall; slim; muscular build; mid-thirties; short, dark hair; neatly trimmed beard.

Juanita placed a gentle, restraining hand on James's gun arm. 'It's OK, James ... it's Kyle ... Sylvia's boyfriend.'

He lowered the gun.

'Come in ... sit down,' she said.

The man came into the room and sat on the edge of the bed glancing nervously from one to the other. 'I ... er ... I guess you're a little bit surprised to see me, Carla.'

'First off, I'm not Carla anymore ... my name is Juanita now. But yes ... more than a *little bit* surprised.'

'Oh, OK ... Juanita then. But why the name change?'

'It's …complicated.'

'O … K …' he said, drawing out the letters as though treading very carefully, 'but you were Sylvia's best friend … why did you leave so suddenly?'

'Never mind about that,' interjected James, 'how did you find us?'

'Can you just put that gun away? It's making me kind of nervous.'

'Not until you—'

'It's OK,' said Juanita, 'he's a friend.'

James laid the gun down on the desk, still within easy reach should he need it. He was more than a little uncomfortable about the arrival of this stranger, despite Juanita's assurances. 'You still haven't answered my question.'

'What question?' said the man, his haunted eyes darting back and forth between Juanita and James.

'How did you find us?' repeated James.

'I, er … well, I'm a telecoms engineer by trade so—'

'Is that true?' asked James, turning to Juanita.

'I think so … yes, I remember that Sylvia mentioned that.'

'So, what if you are?' persisted James.

'I managed to hack the phone of Carla's friend at the diner where she worked.'

James was suspicious: if the two of them had managed to evade the police for over a year, then how come this guy had managed to track them down with such apparent ease? But then he remembered the strange text messages purporting to come from María. A surge of anger rose within him.

'What the hell gives you the right to deceive Juanita's friend, illegally hack her phone, and then come after us?' he demanded, rising from his chair and stepping forward to tower over the other man, still seated on the bed.

Kyle raised both hands, palms-outward in a defensive gesture, 'OK, I know … I'm sorry … but I was desperate to get in contact with Carla and—'

'Juanita,' James reminded him.

'Yes … OK … Juanita. Sorry, it's kind of hard to get used to the new name. Like I said, I was desperate to get in touch, and the girl in the diner—'

'María,' interrupted Juanita.

'Yeah ... M-María,' he stammered. 'She claimed she didn't know how to contact you, but it was obvious she was hiding something, so that was why I decided to hack into her phone. I know it wasn't right but ... well, like I said, I was desperate.'

'OK, so now you've tracked us down' said James. 'Why ... what do you want?'

'Sorry,' said the stranger, now looking a little more emboldened as he turned to Juanita, 'but just who is this guy giving me the third degree?'

Juanita seemed somewhat nonplussed by the whole situation: she took a moment or two to reply. 'This is James: he's my ... partner. I'd trust him with my life ... in fact, I already have, several times, as it happens. Why are you here, Kyle?'

He seemed to relax a little. 'I want to know why Sylvia died. I think you know who did it, and why.'

'Juanita, no ... no way,' interjected James. 'We can't get into this all over again.'

The look in her eyes, when she turned to look at him, was one of sorrow and regret. She took a few moments before replying. 'Sorry, James, but I think he has a right to know. The poor guy's been torturing himself for over a year now; I think he deserves some answers.'

Kyle gave a weak smile.

'In any case,' she continued, 'he's found us now; he knows our new identities. What is there to lose by telling him how and why Sylvia died?'

James really didn't have an answer; he spread his hands, helplessly, emitting a deep sigh.

In spite of all James's misgivings, Juanita began relating the incredible series of events which had taken place in Miami, more than a year earlier. To his intense discomfort she left almost nothing out. No matter how good a friend Sylvia had been to Juanita – or Carla as she was then – Juanita knew very little about her boyfriend, other than what she had told her. Could this guy be trusted to keep their secret?

***

It was more than an hour later by the time Juanita had finally finished relating the whole story. Kyle had barely interrupted her at all; he just listened, open-mouthed, as the details emerged, one by one. James said nothing during her account, still very unhappy at revealing all this information to this man who, to him at least, was a complete stranger.

Finally, Kyle broke the awkward silence which had settled in the room. 'So she really was an innocent victim, caught up in something she had nothing to do with at all?'

Juanita nodded, 'That's about the size of it, I'm afraid.' She sat down alongside him on the bed, placing a comforting arm around his broad shoulders. 'I feel so guilty, Kyle. The only reason she died was because she offered to let the two of us stay at her place when we were in trouble. Those two thugs were after James and me; Sylvia just happened to be coming down the stairs when they arrived.'

'So they shot her just because she was inconveniently in their way?' he said, an anguished expression on his face.

'I'm afraid so. Oh Kyle, we should never have asked to stay at her place.'

He looked away, silent for some seconds, evidently trying to keep his emotions in check. When he finally turned back and made eye contact with Juanita, his eyes were moist. 'From what you have told me, I don't think you had much choice. But regardless of that, I believe it's what she would have wanted; I know you two were very close, and it's typical of her generosity to want to help a friend in need.'

A tear welled up in the corner of Juanita's eye and, a moment later, the dam broke: she began sobbing, her shoulders heaving with each tortured gasp.

Kyle encircled her slim frame in a hug. 'Shhh ... don't ... it wasn't your fault.'

As James witnessed this outpouring of emotion and Kyle's sensitive reaction, his coldness towards the man began to melt. It looked like the poor guy really had been torturing himself all this time and, having finally learned the truth, it seemed he bore no ill will towards Juanita.

After a few seconds, Kyle eased himself away from Juanita, perhaps conscious of James's looming presence.

Juanita was still sobbing softly; James grabbed a handful of tissues from a box on the table and handed them to her. She wiped her face and took a deep breath, trying to compose herself before speaking.

She turned to Kyle. 'So now you know everything.'

Kyle nodded, slowly. 'It all seems so … oh, I don't know … senseless. I mean, she died for no other reason than that she was just in the wrong place at the wrong time.'

'I'm afraid so,' said James.

Kyle hung his head for a few seconds; when he looked up, his expression had changed completely: he seethed with barely suppressed anger.

'And what's even worse is that the bastards who murdered her are still out there somewhere.'

James shook his head. 'One of them is probably dead. As Juanita's told you, the car in which he was chasing us was involved in a really bad crash; I don't think there's much chance he'd have gotten out alive.'

'But you don't know that for sure.'

'No,' admitted James, 'but—'

'What about the other one?'

James spread his hands. 'I don't know. The police never found him and I have no idea where he might be now.'

'But he works for this shady network of professional hit-men you told me about, right?' Kyle's eyes had narrowed, and his jaw had taken on a determined set.

Suddenly, James realised where Kyle's mind was going. 'Don't even think about it. These people are vicious killers; you really don't want to tangle with them under any circumstances. And I couldn't help you find him even if I wanted to; I don't even know the guy's name.'

'But you'd recognise him, right?'

'Forget it,' insisted James. 'You'll never find him and, even if you did, he'd kill you in a heartbeat.'

Kyle hung his head once more, exhaling noisily. Suddenly, he looked up, as though another thought had just occurred to him. 'So, you and Carla—'

'Juanita.'

'Yes, sorry … so, you and Juanita have now made a new life in Canada, right?'

'Uh, huh.'

'So, what brings you to New York City?'

'That's another story entirely, and one you don't need to know about.'

'Oh, James,' interjected Juanita, 'We've told him so much, he might as well know the rest. Who knows? With his technical knowledge he might even be able to help us untangle what's on that computer.'

'What computer?' said Kyle, his interest clearly piqued.

'No ... absolutely not,' insisted James. 'Kyle, I'm really sorry for your loss, but you've got what you came for. Now you need to go home.'

Chapter 24

Mark Bowman was frustrated as hell at his lack of progress in trying to track down his suspect. He had her photograph, he knew she probably had an accomplice and that one or both of them drove a silver Toyota Camry, but that was it; now he seemed to have hit a dead end. Without the licence number it was virtually impossible to trace the car, and scouring more CCTV footage of New York's busy streets, without any clue as to where or when to look, was like searching for a needle in a haystack. If he was able to bring the full weight of the NYPD's resources to bear, he might stand more of a chance but, as he had been forbidden to involve himself in the Julia Turner investigation, this just wasn't possible. Furthermore, O'Reilly was constantly hassling him about the damned Patterson case; there was a limit to how long he could fob the sergeant off with excuses. It could surely not be long before it became obvious, even to a slow-witted dullard like O'Reilly, that he was spending his time on something else. Once that happened, he'd be severely disciplined at best, or worse still, fired. Then there'd be no hope of finding Julia's killer.

He considered his options. He could hang back for a while, let Don Lister, who had been assigned to Julia's case, do his work. Meanwhile he could put in a bit of effort on the Patterson case; if he made some progress there, then maybe he could get O'Reilly off his back for a while. But he had little confidence that Don would get far with his assignment; whatever spark of enthusiasm he may once have had for his job had long since died out, and now all he wanted was his service pension and a quiet life.

But maybe, if Mark *could* make some headway on the Patterson case, he might get O'Reilly to leave him be long enough to get back onto Julia's case without constant interference. Given his current complete lack of live leads on Julia's killer, it seemed his best option, even though it went against all his instincts. Reluctantly, he reached for the Patterson file, which had lain untouched on his desk for some time, and opened it. He emitted a deep sigh: *OK, where the hell do I start?*

As he pondered this question, the phone on his desk rang; since he had no enthusiasm for the task in hand, he was glad of the distraction.

'Detective Bowman,' he answered.

A woman's voice replied. 'Er, Mark, is that you?'

He didn't recognise the voice, so he was a little surprised that the caller knew his first name.

'Yes ... this is Mark Bowman. Who's calling?'

'It's Mary-Jane.'

The name meant nothing to him. 'Mary-Jane?'

The woman's voice was hesitant. 'Mary-Jane Bailey ... from the path lab. You came to see me the other day.'

The lightbulb went on. 'Oh yes, of course ... what can I do for you, Miss Bailey?'

'Oh, please ... call me Mary-Jane.'

'Sure ... I'll do that,' he replied. 'How can I help you?'

'Well, Mark' – her voice sounded more confident now – 'I'm hoping *I* may be able to help *you*.'

He waited for her to elaborate, but no further explanation was immediately forthcoming.

'How's that then?' he said, doing his best not to let his voice betray his slight irritation with her oblique reply.

'It's about the woman who came to the lab pretending to be the sister of the murdered journalist.'

Now she had his full attention. 'Go on,' he urged.

'Well, my friend, Mandy, is a hairdresser. She thinks a woman whose hair she cut recently may be the same person.'

'Interesting,' mused Mark, 'but why does she think that?'

'Well, she fitted the description perfectly, and Mandy said she seemed to want to change her appearance completely. Said she seemed kind of nervous ... edgy. Oh ... and she was carrying a hell of a lot of cash in her purse. Didn't seem to want to use a credit card.'

It was hardly conclusive, but it *was* interesting, and he didn't have any other leads. *Maybe ... just maybe.* 'That's very interesting,

Mary-Jane. If this woman *was* the same one who tried to copy the autopsy report, do you think your friend would recognise her from her passport photo?'

'Oh yes. Mandy says she remembers her very clearly.'

This was, indeed, an interesting development; Mark was keen to follow it up. 'OK, then perhaps the two of you could come down to the station to ...' He checked himself: if O'Reilly saw him interviewing these two women, he'd be bound to want to know what it was all about. 'Oh, wait a minute, all our interview rooms are busy right now. I don't want to waste any time following up this important lead, so could I see your friend at home, or somewhere else that's convenient for her?'

'Well, as it happens,' cooed Mary-Jane, 'Mandy's here with me right now ... at my place.'

'OK - what's your address?'

He scribbled it on his notepad. 'I'll be right over – see you in about half an hour.'

***

'See?' preened Mary-Jane. 'He's been just itching to find an excuse to come over and see me. All that stuff about interview rooms being full is a crock of shit: he wanted to get my address and to see me at home.'

'Actually,' Mandy reminded her, 'I believe it was *me* he wanted to see.'

Mary-Jane waved her hand, dismissively. 'Well, yes ... to I.D. the photo and ask you a few questions, but it's me he wants to get into bed—'

'You wish,' laughed Mandy.

'There's no doubt about it ... it was clear as day from the first moment he saw me at work.'

Mandy rolled her eyes. 'If you say so. Anyway, you've built this guy up so much, I'm kind of nervous about meeting him. What if it turns out that the woman whose hair I cut is not the one he's looking for?'

'Well, if she's not, she's not. You'll have done your public duty, and I'll have properly broken the ice with Mark. Next time, I can invite him over for a meal: nice candlelit dinner, a few drinks, and then maybe dessert in the bedroom.'

Mandy rolled her eyes, laughing. 'Oh, Mary-Jane ... you really are *such* a brazen flirt. Anyway,' she added, eyeing her friend's outfit up and down 'don't you think you're overdoing it a bit ... just to "break the ice"?'

'Overdoing it?' said Mary-Jane, rising to her feet and standing in front of the mirror. She smoothed down her short, figure-hugging, turquoise dress and adjusted the deep plunge neckline, checking that the sparkling, fake-diamond pendant nestled in just the right place to draw his eye to her generous cleavage, 'when it comes to men, there's no such thing as "overdoing it". Now, just time for a touch more perfume before he arrives. Watch and learn.'

Mandy shook her head in disbelief.

Chapter 25

It didn't take Mark long to find the apartment block, which was in one of Manhattan's less salubrious areas. Since he had taken a marked squad car, he didn't bother to waste time trying to find a parking lot; he just stopped on a yellow line right outside the block. It was an old, tenement-style, redbrick building, taller than New York City's zoning code would allow today. A zig-zag column of fire escapes clung to the façade, paint peeling from the rusty metal. It was clear that there hadn't been too much money expended on maintenance recently.

He grabbed his laptop bag and stepped out of the car, locking it with a press of the button on his key: you couldn't be too careful in an area like this, even with a marked squad car. He approached the front door, alongside which was an intercom panel. Checking his notepad, he located the button for Mary-Jane Bailey's apartment and buzzed her.

'Hello?' came the almost instant reply.

'Miss Bailey? This is Detective Mark Bowman.'

A whirring noise and click signalled that the door had been unlocked. 'Come right on up ... I'm on the third floor.'

In contrast to the general condition of the building, the dark green paint on the front door of the apartment gleamed as though only just applied. He rang the bell and, almost immediately, it opened. He barely recognised the woman who opened it: her hair tumbled over her shoulders in long, flowing waves; her makeup was heavy enough for her to be on a stage show; her short, stretchy dress clung to her body so closely that her generous breasts threatened to break free from the perilously low-cut neckline. In spite of himself, Mark couldn't help an involuntary scan up and down her body before regaining eye contact.

'Er … Miss Bailey?'

'Mary-Jane,' she reminded him, stepping aside to usher him inside. As he stepped past her, he was enveloped in a cloud of over-strong perfume, which eventually gave way to the aroma of freshly brewed coffee.

The apartment was immaculate: warm, welcoming colours; simple, minimalist furniture; a pleasing lack of clutter, yet nice feminine touches, such as velvet drapes, floral print artwork, and a vase of freshly cut flowers on a low table in the corner of the room. An attractive, dark-haired woman rose from one of the two couches which faced each other across the coffee table. She was plainly dressed in skinny denim jeans and a simple, white, polo neck sweater. Her hair was pulled back in a ponytail, and her makeup was minimal. Clearly, she was not headed for the same party as her friend apparently was.

'This is Mandy,' said Mary-Jane, closing the door behind her and gesturing towards the woman.

'Pleased to meet you, ma'am.' Mark stepped forward and extended his hand. Her smile, as she shook his hand, was beautiful, in spite of her lack of makeup.

'Likewise,' she replied.

'Please, do sit down,' said Mary-Jane, indicating the couch opposite the one where her friend resumed her seat. 'Would you like a coffee? I've just made some.'

Mark was anxious to get on with interviewing her friend, but he didn't want to seem ungrateful or offhand.

'Thanks,' he said, smiling, 'black, no sugar.'

Mary-Jane headed towards the kitchen while Mark set down his bag and sat opposite her friend. 'I understand that you think the woman who tried to steal documents from the pathology lab may have also visited your hair salon.'

Her reply was hesitant. 'W-ell … I can't say for sure that it was the same woman, but Mary-Jane thought I should talk to you. I do hope I'm not wasting your time.'

'Not at all,' said Mark. 'I appreciate your help. Now let me just … ah.'

They were interrupted by the return of Mary-Jane, carrying a tray, which she set down on the table. 'There, that one's yours, Mark,' she said – somewhat superfluously, as the other two were both white.

She sat down beside him, her dress riding way up her shapely thighs. Mark refused to be distracted; he directed his gaze towards the other woman.

'So Miss ...' he couldn't remember her surname.

'Jackson,' she said, smiling. 'Mandy Jackson.'

'Yes of course. You were saying ...?'

'Oh yes ... well I can't be sure about whether it was the same woman, but she did seem to fit the description Mary-Jane gave me.'

Mark delved into his bag and withdrew a blown-up print of the photo in the fake passport. 'Is this her?' he said.

She took the picture and studied it for a few seconds, before looking up. 'Yes ... I think it is.'

Mark's heart jumped. 'How sure are you?' he urged. 'Take a good look at the picture.'

She studied it for several more seconds; Mark waited, anxiously. 'Yes ... it's her,' said Mandy. 'I'm 100% certain.'

'That's fantastic, Miss Jackson. Now I need to get the details of what her new hairstyle looks like.'

'Well,' she began, 'it's much shorter, and kind of—'

Mark held up his hand. 'We can do better than just a description,' he said, leaning down and withdrawing his laptop from its bag. He moved across to sit alongside Mandy and placed the laptop in front of them. While it was starting up, he explained, 'I have some software on here which will enable us to play about with the photo, changing the colour and style of the hair until you are happy it's just right.'

'Ooh, can I see, as well?' said Mary Jane, standing up and moving across to plant herself on the couch alongside Mark.

The couch was barely big enough for three people, and Mark now found himself hemmed in from both sides by two very attractive women, his nostrils filled with the powerful scent which one of them was wearing. He was, however, determined to concentrate on the job in hand.

'OK,' he began, 'let's start with the length ...'

***

Twenty minutes later, the job was done. Mandy was happy with the hairstyle and colour, right down to the darker lowlights punctuating the medium-blonde main colour. The woman staring back at him from the screen now looked radically different from the one in the original photo.

'So, do you think that will help you?' said Mandy, sounding a little uncertain.

'It's incredibly helpful,' replied Mark. If we catch an image of her on CCTV, for example, it would be easy to miss it if we were looking for someone with long, dark hair. Now we stand a much better chance of spotting her.'

'I'm so glad to have been of help,' she said, smiling.

'Do you think I could have your contact details?' he said, 'just in case I need to talk to you again.'

She rummaged in her purse and pulled out a business card, handing it to him. It only gave her name and the details of the hair salon.

'Could you write your home address and phone number on the back as well?'

'Oh, sure.' She scribbled the details down and handed the card back to him.

'I'll give you my contact details too,' said Mark, fishing out a card from his wallet, 'in case you remember anything else. That's my direct line at the station, and my cell phone number's there, as well.'

'And you know how to get in touch with me, too,' interjected Mary-Jane, placing her hand on his arm. 'I'd be happy to help in any way I can.'

***

On his way back to the station, Mark's mood had lifted considerably; this latest discovery might just allow him to break through the impasse which his investigation had reached. Not only did he now know about the woman's completely different new look, but he could place her leaving the hair salon at a precise time: the hairdresser had been very sure about the time. This gave him a very good chance of picking her up on CCTV and getting on her trail.

There remained, of course, the tricky problem of keeping O'Reilly at bay; he'd have to make some headway on the Patterson case soon if he was to avoid the sergeant's wrath. Furthermore, he was increasingly sure that he'd be fired if O'Reilly discovered that he was putting all his efforts into investigating Julia's murder after having been expressly forbidden to do so. In spite of all this, he was buoyed by the prospect of perhaps finally making a breakthrough in the hunt for Julia's killer.

This was not the only thing which had lifted his mood: the hairdresser, Mandy, had made quite an impression on him. Despite the still-raw grief at losing his beloved Julia, he could not exclude from his mind the image of Mandy's delightful smile. For all her friend's sexy outfit and over-the-top makeup, it was Mandy, with her simple clothing, minimal makeup, and unassuming manner who had captured his attention.

Suddenly he felt a surge of guilt: it seemed disrespectful to his would-be fiancée's memory to even think about any other woman in this way. He banished the thought, hit the siren and stepped on the gas; weaving his way through the heavy traffic. Now he just wanted to get back to the station and see what he could do with this new-found information. He doubted very much that Don Lister, the detective assigned to investigate Julia's murder, would be making much headway, but even if he was, Mark was determined to track down her killer first.

This was personal.

Chapter 26

Against his better judgement, James had allowed himself to be persuaded by Juanita to let Kyle help them in their quest to discover what Julia had been working on before she was murdered. The three of them had now spent the entire weekend ploughing through the computer files which Juanita had copied. James had to admit that Kyle, whose flying fingers on the keyboard seemed far more practiced than either his own or Juanita's, had proven to be an invaluable ally in navigating the files.

There was a massive volume of material which seemed to be of no relevance, but it seemed that the girl, Emily, at the New York Times office had been right about Julia doing some sort of investigation into the employment of illegal immigrants. She had clearly been looking into the employment practices of several companies but seemed to have homed in on the one which Juanita had already seen a reference to: Johnson Brothers.

A brief trawl of the internet revealed that this was a small building company, based in New York City, which worked mostly on private projects such as individual homes and small apartment complexes. They didn't appear to do much work on Government projects, and there was little to indicate why the journalist would have chosen such an apparently insignificant company on which to focus her attention. Surely a bigger company whose main customer was the Government would have lent a political element and yielded a better story?

Try as they might, none of them could turn up anything which would shed any light on why Johnson Brothers was of such interest. It was time to take stock.

James had made three cups of coffee; he set them down on the low table together with an unopened pack of cookies.

'OK,' he said, 'so far, all we know is that she seemed to be interested in this Johnson Brothers outfit, but it just doesn't seem possible that anything she found out about them could be big enough to have warranted her murder.'

'I agree,' said Kyle. 'I think Johnson Brothers is a red herring … she must have had some other investigation – something more important – going on in parallel.'

Perhaps, suggested Juanita, the answer might lie in some of the many papers she had left behind in the New York Times office rather than in the computer files which they had spent the weekend scouring. 'I could always go back and see what else I can find,' she said. 'Goldsmith sort of left an open invitation if I wanted another posting.'

'Absolutely not,' insisted James. 'You've already taken far too many risks. In any case, the police will have taken all those papers by now.'

'But maybe if I was to talk to the girl, Emily, again? She seemed—'

'No – it's far too risky.'

Juanita could almost always talk James around when she was set on doing something, but this time there was no way he was going to fold.

'We'll press on with ploughing through the information we've got here,' he continued. 'Maybe we've missed something.'

'But—'

'No.'

Juanita emitted a deep sigh. James could tell from the expression on her face that, this time, she had accepted she could not change his mind.

'Look,' said Kyle, 'I know we've been through a lot of material, and it's damned frustrating that we've turned up nothing that looks promising, but maybe we *did* miss something. All I can suggest is that we start again, from the beginning … go through everything again with a fine-tooth comb.'

A gloomy silence descended. It was a very unwelcome conclusion, but James knew he was right.

Evidently Juanita knew it, too. 'OK, let's get back to it,' she said, exhaling wearily.

***

Back at the station, Mark was studying CCTV footage. Mandy had been spot-on about the time the woman had left the salon. There she was, right in front of him, pausing for a moment, looking left and right before hurrying off down the street.

He ran the footage in slow motion, studying every frame from the moment she stepped out of the salon to the point where she exited the field of view of the camera. At one point she seemed to look directly into the camera ... straight into Mark's eyes. A cold shiver ran down his spine as he locked eyes with the woman who was almost certainly Julia's murderer. He shook himself to dispel the eerie feeling.

Mandy's rendition of the woman's new hairstyle had been uncannily accurate: a short, choppy cut: medium-blonde main colour; contrasting darker streaks. She looked very different from the woman whose photo appeared in the fake passport, but virtually identical to the photo-fit picture Mandy had helped him create.

Once again, an image of Mandy's captivating smile infiltrated his thoughts; he quickly brushed it aside.

He noted the time stamp at the point where his quarry disappeared from view and brought up the record from the next camera. There she was, hurrying along determinedly, heading in the same direction – more or less northeast – as she had been when viewed from the previous camera. Where was she heading? Impossible to say.

He noted carefully the clothes she was wearing: skinny blue denim jeans over tan, high-heeled shoes; camel-coloured, close fitting sweater; and a thin – possibly silk – pale yellow scarf. If he lost her in a crowd somewhere, her clothing – especially the distinctive scarf – might just help him pick her out.

As she disappeared from view, once again he transferred his attention to the next camera. There she was again, still walking in the same direction. Apart from that brief moment outside the hairdressing salon, she showed no signs of being conscious of the cameras, and she didn't appear to be taking any steps to vary her route. *No*, Mark thought, *you have no idea I'm watching you. Maybe you'll lead me straight to wherever you're headed.*

But then she stopped, quite abruptly. *Why?*

She opened her purse and pulled something out of it. Mark zoomed in for a better view of what she was doing. She seemed to be holding a small, folding mirror and applying some lipstick.

Now why on earth would you just stop in the middle of the street to freshen up your makeup?

Next, she seemed to be checking on her new hairdo, tilting her head from side to side as though trying to get a view from more than one angle. Moments later she returned everything to her purse, closing it and slinging it over her shoulder before turning towards the nearest building and walking straight through the front door, and out of sight.

Zooming back out, Mark viewed the building which she had entered. It took him but a moment to identify it as the office of the New York Times: his dead girlfriend's former place of work. His heart leapt; this could surely not be mere coincidence. His brain began to race as he shuffled the various possibilities.

Could this woman also be an employee of the New York Times? Could Julia have been murdered by one of her co-workers? Or, maybe, she was someone with a grudge against the newspaper? Then again, she might have nothing whatsoever to do with the newspaper; she could be trying to retrieve some vital piece of evidence which could link her to the murder. Whatever the explanation, he felt in his bones that this was going to lead to the breakthrough he was looking for.

Now, if I can just—

The lumbering figure of Sergeant O'Reilly appeared in his peripheral vision. His heart jumped as he scrambled to kill the image on his screen before he O'Reilly arrived at his desk. He managed it with barely a second to spare.

'What the fuck's happening with the Patterson case?' he demanded. 'You've been on this for days now and you ain't come up with diddly squat.'

'Sorry Sarge, all the leads seem to have come to nothing so far.'

O'Reilly's jowly cheeks flushed red. 'Look, the chief's all over this one. If I can't get a result real quick, I'll probably be busted down to Detective rank.' He stabbed the air with a stubby finger, pointed directly at Mark's face. 'And I'm telling you … if I go down you sure as hell go down too. Got it?'

'Got it,' confirmed Mark. 'I'll find the perps … I'm on it.'

'You'd damn well better be,' growled the Sergeant, turning on his heel and stomping off.

Fuck the Patterson case, thought Mark, *I'm not stopping now.* He picked up the phone and dialled the number of the New York Times.

Chapter 27

Back at the hotel, James and Kyle continued to plough through the copied computer files, fuelled by frequent cups of coffee. Meanwhile, Juanita busied herself checking out the various papers she had copied. Although the material she'd copied represented but a tiny fraction of that which had been in the filing cabinets, it still took several hours to go through it all.

'Any luck?' enquired an exhausted-looking James.

She shook her head. 'Afraid not.'

James expelled an exasperated sigh. 'None here either.' He slammed the palm of his hand against the wall in frustration. After a few moments he seemed to have regained his composure. He turned back towards Juanita. 'Want another coffee?'

'Any more coffee and I'll start peeing the damned stuff.' She gave a weak smile. 'Oh, to hell with the coffee ... what's in the minibar?'

James stepped over to the miniature fridge and found her a small bottle of Chardonnay. He also grabbed two cans of beer, handing one to Kyle, who popped the ring-pull and downed about a third of the can in one. James did likewise, stretching his back and stepping over to the window, gazing out at the busy street below. 'Think I'll take a ten-minute break.'

'Me too,' added Juanita, collapsing onto the bed.

Kyle said nothing during this exchange; he set down his beer and resumed his work, gazing intently at the laptop screen as he tapped and clicked away. A few minutes passed before he broke the silence.

'I think I've changed my mind,' he said. 'It *has* to be something to do with this Johnson Brothers outfit,' he asserted. 'Practically everything on her computer which was saved within the last few weeks relates to that company.'

'Yes,' agreed James, 'but what could be so important about a tinpot little building company employing a few illegals?'

'Dunno,' admitted Kyle. 'Hey, Carla—'

'Juanita,' she reminded him.

'Yeah ... sorry. Anyway, didn't you say some of the hard copy stuff you've got is also related to this company?'

'Only one document as far as I can see,' she replied, levering herself wearily from the bed and heading for the pile of papers on the chair where she had been sitting. After shuffling the papers for a couple of minutes, she fished out what she was looking for: a slim document consisting of no more than about ten pages, printed double-sided and stapled together in the corner. 'It's headed "Employment of Illegals by Johnson Brothers".' She handed it to Kyle, who scanned the first sheet of paper.

'Yeah,' he sighed, 'I've got the original file right here on the screen.' He paused for a few moments, staring at the screen. 'Definitely the same document ... but it really doesn't tell us anything.' He handed it back to her.

She tossed it back onto the pile of papers on the chair.

And then she spotted it. The document had landed upside down, with the blank second side of the final sheet facing upwards. Except it wasn't blank: it contained a handwritten note.

Her heart jumped as she scanned the note. 'Guys ... guys ... I think I've got something here.'

Chapter 28

Mark Bowman sat opposite Cynthia Newman in the New York Times office. She slid the photo he had handed her back across the desk.

'Yes, she worked here as a temp …. just for a week. Nice girl, very efficient.'

Nice girl, he thought. *If only you knew.*

'What name was she using?'

'Using? What … you think it might not have been her real name?'

Mark metaphorically kicked himself for his poor choice of words.

'I'm afraid I can't discuss that with you, Mrs Newman. Now, if you could give me her name …'

'Sure. Gema … Gema López.'

The same name she used when visiting the hair salon; maybe she's starting to get a little careless.

'What kind of work did she do here?'

'Well … just general admin really. My secretary quit recently, and I needed some temporary cover to fill the gap before her permanent replacement starts.'

General admin? There had to be more to it than that. There's no way that she just happened to come and take a routine temping post `in the very organisation where her victim had previously worked.

'Can you be a little more specific? It could be important to our investigation.'

Cynthia raised her eyebrows and spread her hands. 'Usual stuff: filing, typing, answering the phone … that sort of thing. Mind you she was a very bright girl; I can't understand really why she wasn't looking for something much more demanding.'

Because she was looking for something right here, he thought, but didn't say.

'Anyway,' continued Cynthia, 'you said you were investigating Julia Turner's murder. What on earth could the work my temp was doing have to do with that?'

'Sorry, Mrs Newman ... like I said, I'm afraid I can't discuss the details of the case.'

She shrugged. 'Well, not sure there's much I can do to help you, then.'

'Are you quite sure there's nothing else she was working on while she was here?'

'Well, she did spend half a day working for Joe Goldsmith' – she tilted her head and rolled her eyes skyward – 'next floor up.'

'Doing what?'

'Oh, I think she was gathering together all of Julia's stuff for you guys to take away and examine.'

What? Mark was well aware that Don Lister had collected a bunch of papers and files to try to ascertain what Julia had been working on, but what the fuck was he doing allowing anyone to, potentially, tamper with evidence before seizing it? No wonder he'd never made it beyond Detective rank.

'Can I talk to this Goldsmith guy?'

'If you like ... no-one else wants to, if they can help it,' she added, acerbically.

Mark really wasn't interested in the office dynamics and who liked who ... or didn't. 'Can you call him then?'

'Sure,' she replied, reaching for the phone, 'I'll just—'

Before you do that, can you get me copies of everything you have on this Gema López: address, previous jobs ... everything you have.'

'OK, I'll have someone get her personnel file ... not that there'll be much on it; she was only here for a week.'

'You already said,' muttered Mark, starting to get a little irritated by this woman's rather offhand manner.

'So what do you want first ... the file, or to talk to Goldsmith?'

The intonation on the last word of her sentence, and the fact that she could only bring herself to refer to him by his surname, spoke volumes: Mark could almost taste the animosity which obviously existed between the two of them.

'Well,' replied Mark, 'perhaps if Mr Goldsmith is available now, I could talk to him while you get the personnel file sent up to me?'

'I guess,' she said, reaching for the phone once more.

While she was talking on the phone, Mark was trying to make sense of what he had learned so far. Assuming this woman – *'nice girl'* – was Julia's killer, why did she need a copy of the autopsy report? The only thing he had been able to surmise was that there was something in the report which might incriminate her. Other than the card with the scorpion logo – which had obviously been left deliberately – what could it be? He had scoured the report from cover to cover and had come up with precisely nothing.

And now she had contrived to get herself into the New York Times office, presumably with the express purpose of gaining access to documents and files which would reveal what story Julia had been working on. But why? If it was a random killing then, surely, what Julia had been investigating was totally irrelevant. Conversely, if she had been killed *because* of what she had been working on, then her killer would know what that was – unless, of course, it was a contract killing. If so, the killer hired to murder her might well ask no questions, as long as the fee was right. But then why would she – he was increasingly convinced that it wasn't a 'he' – want to dig through the autopsy report and, even more puzzlingly, Julia's files and papers?

None of it made any sense.

***

Juanita read out loud the handwritten note on the back of the final page of the document which had landed upside down. 'Mohammed and Ahmed Bashara – July 19/20'. She looked up and scanned the faces of Kyle and James, neither of which showed any sign of recognition or understanding.

'What does it mean?' James wondered aloud.

'I don't know,' said Juanita, 'but for her to pick out two specific individuals' names and highlight two particular dates must be significant.'

'Hmm ...' mused Kyle, 'the names sound Muslim. I'd have thought most of the illegals employed by this company – if indeed they are employing illegals – would be Hispanics … hardly likely to be Muslims.'

'Maybe,' suggested James, 'she picked these two guys out specifically *because* they didn't fit the usual mould.'

It wasn't enough, thought Juanita. She must have had a better reason than that. 'The girl at the New York Times said that Julia had previously been sharing what she was working on, but suddenly went all secretive. She thought Julia had stumbled across something much bigger than the employment of a few illegals. Maybe these two were up to something much more significant than working under the radar in the USA.'

'Or maybe …' suggested Kyle, 'they're not employees at all; they could be the owners of the company.'

James raise a sceptical eyebrow. 'Owners of a company with a name like Johnson Brothers?'

Kyle shrugged. 'Could be a cover?'

Juanita wasn't convinced, and judging by his expression, neither was James.

'What about the dates?' said Juanita. 'Mean anything to either of you?'

'Well, said James 'July 19th is Brian May's birthday.'

Juanita had no idea who Brian May was, and evidently neither did Kyle. 'Brian May?' he enquired.

'You know … Queen.'

'He's a queen?' said Juanita, completely perplexed as to where this was going.

James laughed. 'No … I mean the rock group Queen.'

She'd heard of them, but that was about it. Kyle looked totally blank.

'Oh, you philistines,' teased James. 'Brian May was their lead guitarist – one of the greatest rock guitarists of all time.'

Kyle shook his head in bewilderment. 'And how, exactly, is that relevant?'

James shrugged. 'She asked me if the dates meant anything to me. That's what July 19th means to me.'

Juanita let out a peal of laughter. 'How on earth do you even know that?

'It's kind of strange – although a lot of my memory is still hidden from me, I can remember quite a lot of my childhood and teenage years. As a kid, I was learning to play rock guitar—'

'I know … you told me,' she interjected.

'Well,' he continued, 'I was convinced I'd be the next Brian May. He sort of became my hero … I looked up everything about him. Did you know he's got a PhD in Astrophysics?'

Juanita began to laugh again, tears now streaming down her cheeks. 'No …' – she could hardly get the words out – 'I didn't know that.'

Kyle was watching this exchange with an expression of utter bewilderment.

'Anyway,' said James, 'as you know, I never did make it as a rock guitarist; instead I studied as a doctor, but then …'

His expression darkened as his words tailed off.

Juanita knew immediately what was going through his mind. She rushed over and hugged him. 'Shhh … it's all history now.'

It was completely bizarre: in the space of just a few minutes, the mood had gone from excitement, to intrigue, to manic hilarity, to sombre reflection. Juanita needed to break the spell; she unwrapped her arms from around James and stood up.

'So how are we going to find out what it means?' she said, her voice firm and determined.

James did not respond to her attempt to take charge and get the focus back onto the job in hand; he still seemed lost in his own thoughts.

But Kyle did. 'Seems to me we've got three possible strands to pursue.' He tapped the inside of the index finger of his left hand with the index finger of his right. 'First, we gotta figure out who these two guys are: employees, bosses, or nothing to do with the company at all.'

He tapped the inside of his left middle finger. 'Second, we gotta dig into their backgrounds … find out if there's anything to suggest they'd be up to no good.'

He tapped the third finger. 'And finally, we need to figure out what's significant about those dates … apart from the guitarist thing,' he added, making his own attempt to lighten the mood.

James finally emerged from whatever dark place he had fallen into. 'You're right,' he asserted. 'Let's divide our efforts: I'll go through the company data to figure out who these two guys are in the company; Kyle, maybe you can do an internet search to see if you can get any background on them; Juanita, you see if you can work out the significance of those dates. Come on, we've got a new lead here; let's not waste it.'

Juanita smiled. On the surface, at least, James was back to his old self: determined, driven, taking control.

Chapter 29

Mark was back at his desk following his visit to the New York Times office.

When Joe Goldsmith had been interviewed by Mark Bowman, he had concurred with Cynthia Newman's assessment that the Latina woman they had employed was 'a nice girl', although the licentious glint in his eye as he said it spoke of a different interpretation of the term from that which Cynthia had inferred.

Mark refrained from telling Goldsmith what a jerk he was to have allowed this woman – about whom they knew precisely nothing – to have access to all the evidence which had been requested by the police. In fairness, though, Goldsmith did not strike him as the sharpest tool in the box, and he was probably only trying to be helpful. The real fault lay with that no-hoper Don Lister, who should have just marched in there to quarantine the evidence while he got someone in to help gather it up. *Water under the bridge, I guess.*

He read through his copy of the woman's résumé and personnel record. Most was of little interest but, crucially, he had an address for her.

He pulled on his jacket and, taking care to avoid Sergeant O'Reilly, slipped away from his desk. He grabbed the keys to a marked squad car – once again, he had no intention of wasting time looking for a legitimate parking place when he found the address he was looking for.

Half an hour or so later, he pulled up outside the apartment block where his quarry lived: nice, upmarket area, devoid of the towering skyscrapers which dominated the older areas of New York City. He checked the copied document which lay on the front passenger seat of his car: she was on the 8th floor. He had no idea what to expect, but he wasn't taking any chances: he checked his weapon to make sure it was fully loaded and slipped off the safety catch.

He stepped out of the car – this time not bothering to lock it – and walked up to the main entrance. As he scanned the panel alongside the door, his heart sank. There were only 7 floors.

'Shit!' he muttered under his breath, before resetting the safety catch and holstering his weapon.

As he sank back into the driver's seat of the squad car, he slammed his hand against the steering wheel so hard that it hurt.

Another dead end.

***

Back at the hotel, James had drawn a complete blank. He had scoured the internet for all the information he could glean on Johnson Brothers. The owners were, unsurprisingly, two brothers named Johnson. Their photographs showed them to be White Caucasian; it seemed unlikely that they were the two individuals referred to in the handwritten note Juanita had discovered. As far as James could ascertain, there were no others who shared the ownership of the company.

The company was small: it employed eighteen permanent staff, plus a number of temporary workers which varied according to workload. It was likely that the illegal immigrants employed – if, indeed, there were any – would be found amongst this casual workforce. Frustratingly, James had been unable to unearth any details of the individuals employed – permanent or temporary – apart from the owners themselves. Probably something to do with data protection laws or some such.

Kyle's internet search had revealed that Mohammed Bashar and Ahmed Bashar were, in the Muslim world, names about as common as John or David Smith in the USA. He found dozens of references to individuals with these names, many of whom hailed from Iraq, Syria, or Afghanistan, and had made it onto the web by virtue of the fact that they were known, or suspected, terrorists. Equally, though, there were plenty of respected musicians, actors, politicians, and writers who shared one or other of these names. Regardless of who they were, there was no way he could establish a link between any of these individuals and a small building firm in New York City.

It was Juanita who had come up with the most interesting piece of information. Among a great many seemingly trivial and insignificant events associated with the dates she was investigating, there was one which was neither trivial nor insignificant: July 19th and 20th were the dates for the next G7 summit, due to be held at Camp David in Maryland. The leaders of the countries with the seven largest advanced economies in the world would all be together in one place for two days. Germany, France, Italy, Japan, Canada, the USA, and the UK would all be represented.

When Juanita revealed her findings to James and Kyle, she could tell by the stunned expressions on both their faces that they were thinking just the same as she was.

Could this be the target for the most significant terrorist attack since 9/11?

Chapter 30

Mark still couldn't figure it out. More than ever now, he was convinced that the woman he was tracking was responsible for Julia's death. Why else would the same woman have gone to such lengths to access both the autopsy report and Julia's files and papers at the New York Times office? And yet, try as he might, he could come up with no convincing explanation as to why she would put herself at such risk of discovery to do so. It still didn't make sense. But what was really eating him up was the fact that, once again, he had hit a brick wall. He was so tantalisingly close: he knew exactly what she looked like; he knew the make, model, and colour of her car; he had been able to track many of her movements; and yet still he was unable to—

The phone rang.

'Hello, is that Detective Bowman?' A woman's voice: one which he didn't immediately recognise.

'Uh, yes, it is. Who's calling?' he replied, somewhat disinterestedly.

'It's Mandy Jackson … the hairdresser … you spoke to me the other day.'

Now she had his full attention. 'Oh yes, of course, Miss Jackson. You were most helpful – I appreciate it. Now then, how can I help you?'

'Well, I've been thinking about this woman you're trying to locate … going over and over again in my mind everything she said to me while she was in the salon. I've remembered a few more details which might be of some help to you.'

'You have? That's great … uh, perhaps I could meet you again to go over everything you can remember.'

'Yes… of course.'

'Are you at home?'

'No, I'm at work right now, but I'll be on my lunch break in about forty minutes.'

'OK, where can I meet you?'

'There's a little diner right opposite the salon – it's called *Marco's*'

'OK … I'll see you there in about forty minutes then.' He hung up.

What could she have to say which might open up another lead? He supposed he could have just questioned her on the phone, but Mark always liked to interview witnesses face-to-face: sometimes the non-verbal communication spoke more loudly than the spoken words.

He tried to convince himself that this was the reason that he'd opted to interview her in person; it was, but truth be told, it wasn't the only reason.

***

Mark arrived at the diner before Mandy. It was nothing special: plain décor; laminate-topped tables; plastic-upholstered seats; and rather harsh fluorescent lighting. It did, however, look clean and tidy, and the only two staff he could see – a young girl working behind the counter and another, slightly older woman, clearing tables – were smartly turned out in their matching gingham uniform dresses and little white hats. There were only a handful of customers in the place.

The woman clearing tables looked up and smiled. She sported an abundant mass of blonde curls, somehow cajoled into a protesting pony tail behind the neat little hat she wore.

'Take a seat sir … I'll be right with you.'

He chose a seat by the window and waited for her to come and take his order. She was with him in less than a minute.

'Hi there - welcome to Marco's. I'm Tanya … I'll be your server today. What can I get you?'

'Just a black coffee for now,' he replied. 'I'm waiting to meet someone.'

'Sure,' she said. 'Let me know if you need something else when your friend arrives.' She flashed him a warm smile before disappearing.

While he waited for the server to bring his coffee, he looked across the street, where he could see right into the salon.

There were three girls working, two of them busy with customers, but the third – whom he instantly recognised as Mandy, in spite of the distance across the wide street – had evidently finished with her last customer before lunch. She slipped out of her overall and hung it on a coat stand, before pulling from her hair the band which secured her ponytail. She stood in front of the mirror and spent a minute or so brushing her hair before tilting her head from side to side, checking that she was satisfied with the result. She reached for her purse which was hanging on the coat stand and withdrew a small bottle of perfume, misting a short burst to either side of her neck. She replaced the perfume in her purse and slung it over her shoulder. Checking herself once more in the mirror, she seemed to say something to the other two girls working there before heading for the door.

'Here you go, sir … enjoy.'

He looked up as the server set down the steaming cup 'Thanks, Tanya.'

'You're welcome,' she cooed, smiling broadly, before turning away.

When he looked out of the window once more, he could see that Mandy was waiting at a crosswalk around thirty yards down the street from the salon. As the lights changed and she crossed the street, he watched her every step; her gait was elegant without being exaggerated. She wore a pale blue, knee-length dress, cut high at the neck: modest, but closely tailored so as to complement her slim, shapely figure.

Mark had not taken a single sip of his coffee by the time she stepped through the door of the diner.

He stood up and gave a little wave; her face registered recognition before breaking into a warm smile. She came over to his table, unslinging her purse from her shoulder and pushing it along the fixed bench seat opposite Mark, before slotting her slim frame effortlessly in after it.

'Thanks for agreeing to see me at such short notice,' said Mark, catching a faint waft of her perfume: much subtler than the overpowering scent which her friend, Mary-Jane, had worn the other day. She wore slightly more makeup than when he had first met her, but nothing over-the-top: just enough to enhance her natural beauty.

'Oh, it's nothing,' she replied, brushing away a stray tendril of hair from her face. 'I just want to help as much as possible. Like I said on the phone I—'

'Oh, hi Mandy.' The blonde server had arrived; she looked back and forth between the two of them. 'You never told me you were seeing a new guy.' She gave Mark an appraising look, up and down. He had seen this look many times, from many different women. She clearly approved.

'*Tanya* ... it's nothing like that at all,' protested Mandy. 'This is Detective Bowman of the NYPD. I'm just trying to help him with a case he's working on.'

The server looked at Mark. 'Wow! A real-life detective ... in my little diner. What's going on then?'

Mandy shot her a look which clearly spoke louder than words.

'OK,' said the woman, 'I guess this is top secret stuff or something.'

'Sorry ma'am,' said Mark, smiling, 'I'm afraid it *is* privileged information.'

'Sure ... I understand. I guess I'd better leave you two alone then, to talk your important talk. Want something to eat?'

'Just a coffee for now,' said Mandy, shooing Tanya away with a waft of her hand.

When they were alone once again, Mark smiled. 'I guess you're a regular here then.'

She laughed: a soft, gentle peal which, somehow, matched her lovely smile. 'Well it didn't really take a detective to work that out, did it?'

'I guess not,' he replied, also laughing now. 'So, you were saying ...?'

'Well ... as I mentioned on the phone, I've been going over everything I can remember and—'

The server turned up with Mandy's coffee, 'There you go, babe ... anything else I can get you?'

Mandy stared a volley of daggers at her; Tanya took the hint.

'Guess I'll leave you to it then. Just let me know if you need anything.' With that, she turned away.

'You guys friends then?' asked Mark.

'Sort of ... I come in here for lunch most days, so we've got to know each other pretty well. She's a nosey bitch, but I love her.' Once again, she gave that appealing laugh.

'So,' said Mark, finally taking a first sip of his coffee, which was now starting to cool, 'what was it that you wanted to tell me?'

'Well,' she began, 'you remember I said that this woman was carrying a lot of cash with her?'

'Uh huh.'

'Well, I remember her saying that she had left all her credit cards at her hotel.'

Mark's interest quickened; this could be a vital piece of information. He had already ascertained that the address she had given to the New York Times was false, but if she was, indeed, staying in a hotel it gave him two new leads: firstly, she was not a native New Yorker, but only staying temporarily; and secondly, he could start looking into New York hotels. There were, however, hundreds – maybe even thousands – of hotels in New York City. To check them all out could take a very long time.

'I don't suppose she mentioned *which* hotel?'

'No, but I do remember that when I offered to call her a cab, she said she didn't need one because she was going to walk, so I guess her hotel couldn't have been that far.'

His heart jumped; this was *really* useful. He could probably narrow the search to hotels within, say, a one-mile radius.

'That's incredibly helpful. It means that her hotel was probably quite close to the salon.'

'Pleased to help,' she said, smiling. 'Oh, and something else …'

'Uh huh?'

'She was having trouble with her feet.'

'Her feet?'

'Yeah, she was wearing pretty high heels, and her feet were sore. She kicked off her shoes while I was doing her hair and I remember that she kind of winced when she had to put them back on.'

Mark suddenly realised where she was going with this. 'And yet she didn't want to take a cab …'

'Right, so I'd say the hotel would have to be *very* close to the salon.'

Mark mentally narrowed the search radius to half a mile maximum. 'I can't tell you how useful your evidence has been, Miss Jackson.'

She smiled again. 'Can you just call me Mandy? Calling me "Miss Jackson" makes me feel kind of uncomfortable.'

'I will,' he said. 'Thank you ... Mandy.'

Mark suddenly realised he was very hungry; he had skipped breakfast that day to make an early start. 'Did you say you usually have lunch here?'

'Yes' – she checked her watch – 'I've still got time to grab a bite before I have to get back to work.'

'Well I haven't eaten either, so how about I join you for lunch?'

'Well yes ... if you have time, I'd like that.'

Chapter 31

James, Kyle, and Juanita were debating what to do with the potentially explosive information they had just unearthed.

'Maybe now's the time to give an anonymous tip-off to the police, and then get the hell out of New York City,' ventured James. 'Juanita's already put herself at considerable risk to get hold of this information … the police may be looking for her already.'

The three of them fell silent as this suggestion hung in the air.

After a few seconds, Kyle pursed his lips, giving a slight shake of his head. 'Do you really think the cops would take any notice of an anonymous call with no evidence to back it up? I mean even *we* don't know that there's actually some sort of attack planned. All we have are two names and two dates. We have no idea who these two guys are, and we can't even be sure that the dates refer to the G7 summit. Hell, they could be two innocent guys planning a barbeque for all we really know.'

Juanita didn't buy it. 'Come on Kyle … you don't really believe that, do you?'

'No,' he admitted, 'but I'm just trying to put myself in the cops' shoes.'

'OK, so why did Julia Turner think it was important enough to investigate? Why did her co-workers think she'd stumbled across something big? Why was she murdered, for Christ's sake?' Juanita let out a deep sigh of frustration.

Kyle raised both hands, palms-outwards, in a defensive gesture. 'Look, I'm with you on this; I'm just trying to think how the cops might view it. We can't say for sure what the journalist was investigating … beyond the possible employment of some illegals by this building company.'

Juanita jumped to her feet, spreading her hands wide. 'But there's no way that—'

James interrupted her; his voice holding an air of resignation. 'He's right Juanita.'

She looked at him in disbelief. 'But, a moment ago, you were all for contacting the police. Don't tell me that you've suddenly decided that we're not onto something sinister here.'

He shook his head. 'It's not that … I'd lay bets that there *is* something being planned, but Kyle's right about the likely police reaction. First off, we don't have any real evidence to back up our suspicions and—'

'Suspicions? You just admitted that all three of us are convinced.'

'But however much *we're* convinced – and I agree, we are – they are, if you look at it dispassionately, just suspicions.'

Juanita shook her head in frustration, blowing air through pursed lips. However much she loved James, he could be absolutely infuriating when he went all logical and objective on her like this. Every fibre in her body screamed that this was a time to go with her instincts. Before she could frame her reply, James had resumed his irritatingly logical analysis.

'Look at it from the cops' point of view: they get anonymous calls all the time, and they're always likely to be suspicious of anyone who won't come and talk to them openly. Their first instinct would most likely be to dismiss our approach as a crank call. Then, when we won't identify ourselves or offer any evidence to back up our suspicions, it'll only strengthen that view. Add to that the fact that Camp David is probably about the most secure venue that could possibly have been chosen for this summit, and I don't think they'd take us seriously.'

Juanita had lost the will to argue … and, annoyingly, she had to admit that he could be right. She looked up at him, enquiringly. 'So, what do we do then?'

He came over to her and placed his hands on her shoulders, looking directly into her eyes. The moment he did so, she could tell by the firm set of his jaw – an expression she knew so well – that he was hatching a plan.

'I'm not saying we give up: we've come way too far for that. But we have to find some more convincing evidence … something that the police will find hard to ignore.'

Kyle, who had remained silent during the rather fractious exchange between James and Juanita spoke up. 'I agree, but … well, what do you have in mind?'

'We need to get inside that building company: find out just who these two guys are. Then we stand a chance of finding out what the hell they are up to and getting hold of something that will convince the cops.'

Juanita's spirits immediately lifted. This was the James she loved: the determined, driven James. Her annoyance with the other James – the logical, analytical, clinical James – evaporated.

'Yes,' she breathed, 'let's do it.'

James gave a reassuring smile as he stepped away from her. 'We need to come up with a plan as to how we get in there.'

'And what we're looking for when we do get in there,' added Kyle.

'Well,' suggested James, 'a good start would be to find out whether these two guys work for the company, or if they're connected with it in some other way. Once we know who they are, we can try and figure out a way to find out what – if anything – they're planning.'

There it was again – 'if anything'; he just couldn't help himself; logical James had resurfaced for the moment. Juanita let it pass; at least, now, they were on the road to some sort of action plan.

'OK,' said Kyle, 'so let's get to it and try to figure out how we get in there.'

Juanita's mind immediately leapt back to the way she'd successfully inveigled her way into the New York Times office. 'Maybe,' she began, 'I could—'

James cut her off. 'Whoa! Stop right there. You've already done more than enough and taken way too many risks. Like I said, the cops may already be looking for you. This time it's down to me.'

'But this company's nothing to do with the pathology lab; even if they are looking for me, there's no reason on earth why they should be looking there.'

'It doesn't matter,' insisted James, 'it's still too risky.'

'But don't forget,' interjected Juanita, 'if they *are* looking for me, they'll be looking for someone with long, dark hair. You said yourself that the new hairdo has completely changed my appearance.'

His stern expression melted. 'Oh, Juanita, I know you just want to get to the bottom of this, and I love your commitment, but it's just too risky. The cops are not stupid; your change of hairstyle certainly helps, but they'll be well aware that you could have changed your appearance. You can't rely on just a change of hairstyle to keep you safe.'

She knew, deep down, that he was right. 'So, what then?'

He smiled. 'I have an idea ... but I'll need Kyle's help.'

Chapter 32

Mark sat at his desk, his head swirling with conflicting thoughts. He was energised by the new information that the hairdresser, Mandy, had provided, and he was now intent on narrowing down to the hotel at which his elusive quarry might be staying. Once again, the image of Mandy's engaging smile flashed through his mind, but he thrust it aside: the sense of guilt at even thinking about any woman other than Julia preyed on his mind, and in any case, he needed to stay focused.

But he had another concern: he was worried about the possibility of Don Lister getting to Julia's killer before he did. Don wasn't the sharpest of detectives, but he had the advantage of access to the full resources of the NYPD in relation to this case, while Mark had to work under the radar. He now knew that Don had seized all of Julia's papers and computer files from the New York Times office. Even though Don was too dim to have realised that her killer had been right under his nose, he now had access to information which might possibly explain *why* she had been murdered. That might just provide some clues about *who* had murdered her. Could that give him an edge in getting to the killer first?

Up until this point, Mark had always had an unshakeable belief in the rule of law, and the American justice system. Not this time though: he wanted to be the first to get to Julia's killer so that he could administer his own brand of justice. What that might mean for his job, his liberty, or his life, were considerations he just couldn't yet confront: he just wanted to make the murdering bitch pay for what she had done. His resolve was further strengthened when he put his hand in his pocket and fingered the small gift box containing the ring: the ring which he had never been able to offer to the love of his life, and which he now carried with him at all times.

He decided to wander over and have a word with Don Lister to try to find out how his investigation was going.

***

Some hours later that day, Mark and Don sat opposite one another in The Outpost, a middle-of-the road kind of bar, several blocks away from the vibrant hub of Times Square. The bar was crowded and dimly lit; the clientele were almost exclusively men, mostly in huddles of two or three, furtively discussing who knows what deeds and deals. Mark doubted that they realised two detectives were in their midst.

Mark and Don were not in the habit of socialising outside work, but when Mark had suggested they meet over a beer to discuss the case, Don seemed more than willing to do so. He had seemed genuinely moved by Mark's loss, and perhaps even appreciated the opportunity to share with him what progress – or otherwise – he had made.

'So, what's happening then, Don?' asked Mark, after taking a first sip of his beer.

Don's already-furrowed features creased up even further and his tired-looking, grey eyes drooped as he gave a slight shake of his head. 'It's a real puzzle, Mark,' he said running the fingers of his right hand back through his frizzy, grey hair and rubbing the nape of his neck.

As he didn't seem to be about to elaborate further, Mark prompted him. 'So, what do you know so far?'

The older man sighed. 'Well not much really. It doesn't look like a mugging or random killing: she had cash and credit cards in her purse, and some pretty expensive jewellery, but nothing appears to have been taken.'

Mark felt the bile rise in his throat as he recalled the horrific photograph in the autopsy report showing the diamond pendant which he had bought her for her twenty-fourth birthday, askew around her ruined, blood-soaked neck. He fought back the almost overwhelming urge to vomit.

'You OK, Mark? You look kinda pale,' said Don, a look of genuine concern across his face.

'Yeah, yeah … I'm OK. Go on.' Mark took a generous mouthful of his beer, swirling it around his mouth before allowing it to course down his throat, washing away the bitter taste lingering there, still threatening to erupt.

'You sure? I mean you don't look—'

'I said I'm OK,' shot back Mark, the words sounding much sharper than he had intended. 'Sorry, Don ... I didn't mean to snap at you at like that. It's just that I'm, well ... I guess the whole thing's still kind of ... raw.'

The older detective laid a comforting hand on Mark's wrist. 'Yeah ... I guess it must be. No offence taken.'

Mark gave a weak smile. 'Thanks ... anyway, you were saying?'

'Right, so it doesn't look to be a random mugging. Some of her co-workers at the New York Times seem to think that there's maybe someone out there who's got a grudge against the newspaper, but there's absolutely no evidence of that. And even if there was someone like that, why would he' – *or she*, thought Mark – 'just pick on a relatively junior journalist? It just doesn't make any kind of sense.'

'Sure doesn't,' agreed Mark shaking his head. 'So, what *have* you got?'

Don leaned forward, lowering his voice and glancing from side to side. 'To be honest, this has all the hallmarks of a professional hit.'

No shit, Sherlock, thought Mark. He did his best to hide his disdain at the other man's woefully inadequate detection skills. After all, he still needed to find out if Don had uncovered anything that might be useful to him.

'Why d'you say that, Don?'

'Look,' he replied, looking distinctly uncomfortable, 'I don't think I should be sharing all the details with you. O'Reilly would have my balls for breakfast if he knew I was even talking to you about this.'

It didn't matter. Don wouldn't have known that Mark had already seen the graphic details in the autopsy report, including the bizarre calling card.

He felt the bile rise in his throat once more. This time the urge to vomit was almost irresistible. 'I need to visit the men's room,' he blurted, rising to his feet and rushing away, barging past a couple of other customers in the process.

He didn't make it as far as a cubicle; he just barely avoided throwing up all over the floor by diving for the wash basin nearest to the door. Thankfully, there was no-one else in the room to witness the unedifying spectacle as his stomach erupted. Still gasping for breath, he turned on the faucet and flushed the stinking mess in the basin away, finally taking a few gulps of water, before wiping his face with a paper towel. He took a couple of minutes to compose himself before returning to the table.

'Christ, man … you look like shit,' declared Don, upon his return. 'You sure you don't want to leave this whole thing for a while?'

Mark gave a dismissive wave of his hand. 'I'm fine … let's carry on. Look, I know you're not supposed to share every detail of your investigation with me; I really appreciate you even meeting with me like this.'

Don acknowledged the comment with a nod.

'So,' continued Mark, 'if Julia really *was* the victim of a professional assassin, the question is "Why?", what had she possibly done to deserve such a fate?'

Don lowered his voice to a conspiratorial whisper. 'She was an investigative journalist, right?'

Mark nodded.

'So, my guess is that she was probably investigating something which someone, somewhere didn't want investigated. I reckon she was about to expose something important and she was killed to keep her quiet.'

So, Don wasn't quite as clueless as Mark had assumed. It was the only logical conclusion, and the one which Mark had also reached. The central question was *what* she had been investigating. She hadn't shared anything about it with Mark before her death.

The most obvious place to find an answer was among the files and papers which Don had seized from the New York Times office. Frustratingly, Mark had no access to these crucial documents, so how Don would respond to his next few questions was absolutely critical.

'I see where you're coming from, Don. I think you're probably onto something there.'

Don's tragic expression lightened a little, there was even a hint of a smile.

'So,' continued Mark, 'any clues as to what she might have been digging into?'

The smile – if it could be described as such – evaporated, and the gloomy visage returned. 'Well that's where the trail goes cold. We've collected all her files and papers from the New York Times office, and as far as I can see, the only thing she seemed to be working on just prior to her death was an investigation into employment of illegal immigrants in the building industry.'

Actually, Mark *had* been aware that Julia was working on this, but it was hardly something which was likely to provoke such dire retribution from someone intent on shutting her up. There had to be something more.

'That's it?' he said.

'Yeah I know,' replied Don, 'not exactly headline news that a lot of the workforce in the building industry is made up of illegals is it?'

Mark's heart sank as he sensed another dead-end looming. In desperation he asked, 'There must be something else … did you find anything specific which she might have been concentrating on?'

Don shrugged. 'Well she did seem to have been looking into one particular outfit over in the Bronx … Port Morris area.'

It was a straw that he readily clutched. 'Ah, so maybe there's something to be learned there. What's it called?'

'Johnson Brothers … but I'm afraid I've already been to see them. It's a rinky-dink little outfit owned by two brothers scratching a living out of small projects. I don't doubt that some of their workers are probably illegals, but I wasn't about to get distracted by pulling them up over that. There are plenty of much bigger companies out there doing exactly the same.'

Mark didn't buy it: if Julia had focused on this little company, she must have had a reason. Don must have missed something important.

'So, right now, you don't have any good leads?' said Mark.

Don's droopy face drooped even more. ''fraid not. I'm gonna go through all Julia's stuff again, in case we've missed something but, right now, I'm kinda stuck.'

Mark sensed that it was time to wrap things up. 'OK, well, I appreciate your bringing me up to speed, Don.'

'Sure thing.'

Mark didn't finish his beer: his stomach still felt too delicate, but as he shook hands with his colleague outside the bar, he felt re-energised. Now he had two, potentially-promising things to work on: investigating hotels close to the hairdressing salon and figuring out what secrets Johnson Brothers Builders might hold.

The net's closing, bitch.

Chapter 33

James and Kyle sat in the rented Toyota, surveying the dilapidated industrial unit just across the street. It had been easy to find the address of Johnson Brothers on the internet: they had a pretty slick-looking website, completely at odds with the ancient, down-at heel warehouse/office block that the two men were now looking at. The drab, grey paint on the block-built walls was peeling in many places and dirty everywhere. It was punctuated with numerous rust streaks crawling down the walls from the edge of the corrugated-iron roof. There were two large, slatted roller doors: one open, one closed. The closed one probably started life as blue in colour but was now a multi-coloured graffiti fresco; the dominant inscription read 'fuk the fuz'. The spelling left something to be desired, but the underlying sentiment was clear enough.

Their research had not managed to turn up any details of the internal layout of the building, so their plan would have to be flexible, according to what they found.

'Ready?' said James.

'Uh, huh ... let's do it.'

'OK then ... I'll give you about three minutes before I follow you in.'

The two men touched clenched fists before Kyle stepped out of the car and made his way across the street. There was no obvious sign of an office or personnel door, so he made for the large roller door at the front of the warehouse, which was open. He hesitated for a moment, but then stepped inside.

James was meant to wait for around three minutes, but when he checked his watch, time seemed to have slowed to a near-standstill as he watched the seconds tick by. One minute, one minute-thirty,

one-forty-five, two minutes … *Oh fuck it, I can't wait any longer –*
I'm going in.

He got out of the car and made his way towards the open roller
door, stepping through into a dimly lit space stacked with piles of
building materials: building blocks, sheets of corrugated metal,
plastic pipes, bags of cement, and more. As his eyes adjusted from
the bright sunshine outside to the gloomy interior of the building, he
could see a handful of guys at the far end of the room. Two of them
were deep in conversation over a sheet of paper which one of them
held; the rest seemed to be moving materials around. None of them
paid him any attention whatsoever. He could, however, hear faint
voices coming from his right. As he looked towards the source of the
sound, he saw an open door; above it was a faded sign reading
'Office'.

As he stepped through the door, he could see Kyle standing in
front of a desk. Behind it, sat a young woman, chewing boredly on
some gum. She wore exaggeratedly black eye makeup and bright red
lipstick. Her jet-black hair was piled up on top of her head in almost
a beehive style, highlighting the huge hoops which adorned her ears.
Her accent was pure Brooklyn.

'I told ya buddy … we ain't got no vacancies right now. Truth
is, we ain't got hardly any work for the people we already got. So it
don't matter how much experience you got … we just ain't hiring
right now.'

Suddenly she noticed James's presence. As she glanced up at
him, her expression changed: she stopped chewing and gave him an
inviting smile.

She turned back to Kyle. 'Look buddy, I got a customer waiting,
so why don't you just beat it? We ain't got no work for you, and
that's that.'

'OK, OK,' said Kyle, '… uh, can I just use your men's room
before I go?'

She laughed: a sound which could have shattered glass. 'Men's
room? You think we got separate Men's and Ladies' rooms here?
There ain't no "ladies" here, anyway, and I'm the only girl.' Her
strident laugh filled the air again. 'I just gotta make sure the door's
locked when I'm in there. Anyway, it's through there,' she said,
pointing, 'back into the warehouse and first on your right.'

'Thanks for your help,' said Kyle, his voice thick with sarcasm.
He disappeared back into the warehouse.

'Now sir, how can I help you?' said the woman, discreetly taking the gum from her mouth and disposing of it somewhere behind her desk. She smiled, batting her long, black, false eyelashes. 'My name's Jessica, by the way.'

'Well, Jessica,' said James, drawing out his words, 'I've just bought a plot of land over in Upper Montclair and I want to build a house there.'

The girl's eyes lit up. 'Well, you've certainly come to the right place. Why don't you take a seat, while we go through some details?'

'Thanks.' He pulled up the battered, metal-framed stacking chair and sat down.

Jessica grabbed a notepad and pen. 'Let's get your name and contact details first.'

'Wayne Robertson,' he said. 'Here's my card.' He handed her the false card he had printed back at the hotel.

'Say, Wayne ... I love your accent. You Australian by any chance?'

Why the fuck does nearly everyone I meet in the USA think I'm Australian? he thought.

'No,' he replied, smiling ... 'English.'

'English, huh? I'd love to visit England sometime. No chance on my salary though: it barely covers my food and rent. Nothing left over for fancy holidays. Guess I gotta wait for some rich guy to take a liking to me.'

'I'm sure you'll get a chance one day,' said James ... 'pretty girl like you ... I mean it surely won't be long.' He figured that a bit of flattery might help spin the conversation out long enough to avoid exposing the gaping holes in his story.

That piercing laugh rang out again. 'Well, ain't you the charmer then? So how come you want to build a house here in New York City?'

'Oh, I come here on business a lot ... I hate staying in hotels, and my rented apartment – that's the one on my card – just isn't right for me, long term. So ... I figured I'd build a house in a nice New York suburb.'

He could almost see her mentally assessing what level of wealth this English stranger might have.

'What sort of house you got in mind?' she said.

'Oh, my architect's already drawn up the plans: inside area six thousand square feet; five bedrooms, tennis court, games room, swimming pool, and a sauna.'

'Wow! That's quite a spread. You got a big family?' she said, obviously fishing.

'No, it's just me. I like a lot of space and I want to have plenty of spare bedrooms for visitors.'

Her eyes widened a little as she moistened her lips with her tongue. 'You know, I'd love to chat a bit more – you know, find out more about your business and so on. How about you invite me out for a drink sometime?'

Subtlety clearly wasn't Jessica's strong suit.

'Yes, I'd like that,' he said, judging that this was the best response to keep her onside.

She flashed him a broad smile. She actually *was* quite a pretty girl underneath all the paintwork and the downmarket hairdo.

'Here's my number,' she said, scribbling it in her notebook – the first thing she had written in it since he had arrived – and tearing off a page.

'Thanks, Jessica.'

'Oh, you can call me Jess … all my friends do,' she added.

She treated him to another broad smile – thankfully without the abrasive laugh this time. He was struck by what beautifully even teeth she had and their dazzlingly white tone. She might be on a pretty limited income, but he guessed she had spent a fair bit of it on dental work to achieve the perfect smile.

It's all about priorities, he mused: *dazzling smile or trip to England? Seems like she's relying on ensnaring a rich man to achieve the latter, but I guess the perfect smile is all part of the strategy to do so. Well, whatever, I wish her luck in finding Mr Right.*

'Anyway,' she continued, 'let's get a few more details down, and then I can make an appointment for you to see Mr Johnson. He's out on site just now, but I'm sure he'll be very interested in this project.'

James was fast running out of bullshit. *Come on Kyle – I'm out of time here.*

It was as though Kyle had somehow sensed his unspoken plea. A strident whooping sound split the air.

'Fuck it!' exclaimed Jessica, rather shattering her professional demeanour. 'Fire alarm. Right, we gotta get outta here right now. It's probably just some glitch with the system, but anyway we gotta get outside.'

***

The moment Kyle had stepped out into the warehouse he had started to look for a means of triggering the fire alarm, but he had drawn a blank. He couldn't see any smoke detectors, even though he was sure that there must be some, somewhere in the building. What about one of those 'break glass to activate' manual triggers? He couldn't see one of those either. In desperation he dived into the bathroom to which the receptionist had guided him and bolted the door behind him.

The room was filthy: greasy marks all over the greyish floor tiles; cracked white – well, once white – tiles on the walls; peeling, yellowing paint on the ceiling. When he looked into the toilet bowl itself, the tobacco-brown staining spoke of something which had not been cleaned in months – maybe years. There was no sign of any smoke detector.

He slammed down the lid of the toilet and sat down to consider his next move. On the back of the door, facing him, was a calendar; the tall, leggy model depicted wore only a tiny thong and white stilettos. She stood, legs apart, hand on hip, and enormous breasts thrust forward. Her left forefinger pulled provocatively at her lower lip as she locked her gaze onto the camera. How on earth did that girl on reception tolerate having to share these facilities with her male co-workers? Hardly relevant to the task in hand but... He banished the thought from his mind.

What to do next? To make any further progress, he'd have to venture further into the warehouse, at risk of being challenged by one of the workers there. Still, there was nothing else for it, so he unbolted the door and stepped outside.

He didn't have to go far: as soon as he tentatively exited the bathroom and turned to his right, almost the first thing he saw was a red, glass-fronted box attached to the wall, with a small, pointed hammer hanging on a chain alongside it. Taking a brief glance all around to ensure he wasn't being observed, he grasped the hammer and smashed the glass. Immediately, a piercing siren rent the air. He dived straight back into the bathroom to wait while everyone evacuated the building.

He gave it just two minutes before tentatively opening the door and looking around: there was no-one in sight; the deafening siren whooped unrelentingly on.

He rushed back into the office, now unoccupied. Where would he find what he was looking for? As far as he could ascertain, there was no other office area in the building, so it had to be here, somewhere. Behind the reception desk, were two grubby-looking, steel filing cabinets. He attacked the first, opening each drawer in turn and rapidly scanning the labels on the files. It all seemed to relate to various project details. Exasperated, he turned to the second.

The top drawer, according to the file labels, contained financial information: invoices, bank statements, debtors and creditors lists, and so on. He slammed it shut, without investigating further. The second drawer, however, contained what he was looking for: personnel files. There was a photocopier in the office, but he was nearly out of time; he decided to risk just taking what he needed. He grabbed the two or three files which looked promising and slammed the drawer shut, before stuffing them inside his jacket and heading back out into the warehouse area.

He quickly made his way to the large roller door through which he had entered the building. As he stole a glance outside, he could see around a dozen people, all gathered in a huddle in the parking lot. None seemed to be looking his way. The Toyota had stopped around fifty yards up the road, a whisp of smoke from its exhaust signalling that James had managed to slip away and was now waiting with the engine running. With a last quick glance to left and right, he stepped outside and walked, as calmly as possible, towards the waiting car.

Just as he approached the car, he heard a two-tone siren and, seconds later, a fire truck swung around the corner, racing towards him. He waited while the truck sped by, before crossing the street and sliding into the passenger seat.

'Did you get anything useful?' enquired an anxious-sounding James.

'I think so,' he replied.

'Then let's split.'

As they pulled away from the curb, they saw a police squad car swing around the corner, coming towards them. Unlike the fire truck, this car was maintaining a modest pace.

If he's responding to the emergency signal, thought James, *why is he going so slowly?*

They drove away, leaving the chaotic scene behind them.

Chapter 34

The scene which greeted Mark as he approached the building was not what he had expected. A fire truck, with emergency lights still pulsing, filled most of the small parking lot, a group of around ten or twelve people, huddled together, looking curiously on as two firefighters rushed into the building.

With practically no free space in the parking lot, he pulled up in the street and stepped out of the car, making his way towards the group of people watching the scene unfold.

'What's going on?' he asked, flipping open his warrant card holder and showing his I.D.

A rather rotund guy in jeans, grubby white tee-shirt, and a New York Yankees baseball cap responded. 'Fire alarm's gone off,' he said, taking a last drag on the stub of his cigarette before dropping it on the ground and grinding it beneath his boot. 'Pretty sure there ain't no fire, really, but I guess the fire department gotta come, just in case. Anyway, it don't bother me … gives me a break from work and a chance to have a smoke. We ain't allowed to smoke inside the building you see.' He lit up another cigarette, inhaling deeply, holding the smoke for a few seconds before blowing it out in a long, steady stream.

'OK, thanks,' said Mark.

He strode towards the open roller door just in time to meet the two firefighters emerging from the building 'What's happening guys?' he asked, flashing his warrant card once again.

'False alarm,' replied one of men, 'like most of the calls we receive.'

'Any idea what caused it?'

'No mystery there … come and take a look.'

Mark followed the two of them into the building, blinking as his eyes adjusted to the transition from bright sunshine to relative gloom.

'There … see, someone's smashed the glass and set off the alarm.'

'Why the hell would they do that?'

The firefighter shrugged. 'Who knows? Maybe someone thought there really was a fire, or maybe it was a disgruntled employee who just wanted to make mischief.'

Or maybe they just wanted a break and a smoke, thought Mark reflecting on the discussion he'd just had. 'OK, I'll take it from here if you like. I'll talk to all the employees and try to find out who did it. You guys get back to the station, so you can be ready for any *real* fires called in.'

As he watched the fire truck manoeuvre laboriously back and forth until it could exit the parking lot, a creeping doubt began to snake through his mind. It *could* just be coincidence but, in his gut, he couldn't help suspecting that there was some link between Julia's investigation of this company, and the deliberate triggering of a false fire alarm.

As the fire truck finally set off up the road, he approached the group of workers, still standing around, chatting in the spring sunshine.

'OK,' he said raising his voice just sufficiently to quieten the buzz of conversation, 'can I have everyone's attention please?' A dozen curious faces turned towards him. 'As you'll probably have guessed already, it was a false alarm; there's no fire, but *someone* deliberately set off the alarm by smashing the glass in the alarm box. I intend to find out who it was.'

A subdued murmur of surprise and indignation arose from the group of workers.

'Now then, who's in charge here?' continued Mark, silencing the grumbling.

Everyone looked at everyone else blankly, until the only woman present stepped forward: heavily made-up and sporting an improbably tall hairdo. 'Mr Johnson's out on site right now, so there ain't no-one in charge really.'

'And you are, miss?'

'Jessica Bianchi … I'm Mr Johnson's personal assistant.' A small ripple of laughter from the rest of those present prompted her to whirl around. 'Alright you scumbags … I'm the receptionist too, but I *am* his personal assistant.'

Mark couldn't help but smile at the way her strident rebuke instantly silenced all of them. He guessed that for a sole female to hold her own in this male-dominated environment, she *had* to be pretty tough.

'OK, Miss Bianchi … thank you. Now I'm going to need everyone back inside and then I'll want to talk to each of you separately.'

They all exchanged puzzled glances, before shuffling back towards the building.

If it really was just coincidence that the incident had happened right here, at Johnson Brothers, then he would be wasting a great deal of precious time, but somehow, he just *knew* there had to be more to it than that.

***

It was almost two hours later that he finished talking to all the male employees. All of them had denied breaking the glass and setting off the alarm … which of course they would do, wouldn't they? But Mark reckoned he was pretty good at spotting when someone was lying, and he got no sense whatsoever that any of these guys were doing so. He let them all get back to work while he conducted his final interview with the girl, Jessica, in the office.

'So, Miss Bianchi, you were here, in this office when the alarm sounded?'

She leaned forward, placing both elbows on the desk. 'That's right. I was talking to a potential client about a building project.'

'So, you wouldn't have been able to see who set off the alarm in the warehouse, then?'

'No, but … look, Detective Bowman, some of them guys are a bit, well … rough and ready, but I don't believe any of them would have deliberately set off that alarm. They really ain't bad people you know. And what's more, if one of them *did* do it, and Mr Johnson found out, he'd fire them on the spot, and building jobs ain't exactly growing on trees around here.'

Mark nodded, 'So who else might have been in the building at the time?'

'Well, like I said, I was talking to a client – English guy as it happens – but he couldn't have done it; he was here in the office with me when the alarm went off.'

'Anyone else?'

'Well, there *was* another guy who'd been in just a few minutes earlier. He was looking for casual work, but I told him we didn't have no vacancies. He was kinda persistent, but this other guy was waiting to talk to me, so I shooed him away.'

'He went back through there?' said Mark, indicating the door to the warehouse.

'Sure ... it's the only way in and out apart from the fire escape doors.'

'Hmm, you say these two guys came in just a few minutes apart?'

'Yeah, that's right.'

'So was it a busy sort of morning ... lots of people coming and going?'

She laughed: a shrill, harsh sound which startled Mark. 'Hell no ... business is real slow right now. Those two guys were the only visitors we had all morning.'

Just two visitors all morning, and they just happen to turn up within a few minutes of each other? The suspicions which had beset Mark ever since he had arrived now morphed into near-certainty.

'Is there anything which looks out of the ordinary since the incident with the alarm?'

She drew her black-rimmed eyes together in a frown. 'How d'you mean – "out of the ordinary"?'

'Anything out of place, or missing?'

She glanced around the office, still looking puzzled. 'No ... I don't think so.'

'Papers, files?' he prompted.

'Well most of them are right here,' she said, standing up and turning to point to the two metal filing cabinets located right behind her desk.

'Can you check them for me please?'

'Sure.'

She spent several minutes going through the drawers of the first one before concluding, 'I think everything looks OK here, but why—'

'Please, Miss Bianchi ... can you check the other one.'

'OK … whatever you say,' she said, shrugging as she opened the top drawer.

Mark waited patiently, not wishing to hurry her unduly. She leafed through the files in silence, before closing the top drawer and turning her attention to the second. As soon as she opened it, she froze for a moment, before turning back to Mark. Her eyes were wide and her mouth open, her scarlet lips forming a perfect 'O' shape.

'What is it?' prompted Mark.

'All the personnel files are all missing.'

Now there could be no doubt whatsoever: these two guys had been working together to create a distraction and steal those files. But what was the link to the mystery woman he had been tracking? He thought back to the CCTV footage he had studied a few days ago, when she had been driven away from the pathology lab by an accomplice. Maybe there had been *two* accomplices in that car. Then it struck him: the car – a silver Camry. His mind flipped back to the moment when he had first driven up to Johnson Brothers that morning. The car which was just pulling away from the curb as he drove past … a silver Camry.

Shit! He had missed them by seconds. And he *still* didn't get the licence number. What's more, he knew that there were no CCTV or traffic cameras in or around this old industrial park, so there was no chance of picking it up that way.

'Dammit!' he hissed, slamming his hand down on the desk.

The girl visibly recoiled. 'I … I'm sorry … I didn't realise …'

Mark raised a conciliatory hand. 'It's OK … OK. It's not your fault.'

'It's no big deal,' she said, still looking unsettled, 'we've got it all on the computer, so I can easily print off new copies of everything.'

'OK, well that's good,' he said, making every effort to level his voice and calm the mood. 'Perhaps you can make copies for me as well.'

'Oh, sure,' she replied, now managing a smile. 'Always ready to help the NYPD.'

'One more thing … and this is important.' She gazed at him, wide-eyed. 'Do you have any contact details for either of these two guys?'

The business card James had left, still lay on the desk. 'Only for this one,' she said handing Mark the card. 'He's the one who's a potential client.'

As Mark went to take the card, she hung onto it, reluctant to release it. 'Can I take a copy first?'

'Sure, but please don't try to contact him until you hear from me that it's OK to do so.'

Her face fell, but she nodded her acquiescence.

Thirty minutes later, Mark was on his way. Once again, he had come almost within touching distance of unravelling this perplexing situation, but once again failed. Just what the hell *was* going on?

Chapter 35

James was poring over the documents which Kyle had managed to purloin. The other two listened intently as he read out various pieces of information.

Johnson Brothers had eighteen permanent employees and, currently, fifteen casual workers. It was immediately noticeable that almost every name in the latter group sounded Hispanic. Two, however, stood out from the rest: Mohammed and Ahmed Bashara – the same names that appeared in the cryptic, handwritten note on the back of the murdered journalist's document.

'So,' said James, 'now we're clear about the link between these two guys and this building company. But that, in itself, doesn't prove anything. We still don't have any evidence that they're planning anything bad.'

'What else do we know about them?' said Kyle.

'Well, according to these profiles, both are US citizens, and …' He paused as he turned the page.

'I wonder how thoroughly the company checked that out,' interrupted Kyle, his voice dripping with scepticism.

Juanita felt a twinge of anger at the way Kyle kept letting slip his disdain for 'illegals'. He knew full well that she, herself, was an 'illegal' in his terms. She guessed he'd never known what it was like to try to escape poverty, hardship, or conflict in one's country of birth. She decided to let it pass.

James continued, 'Looks like they were originally from Syria … we've got names for their parents: Joram and Amena … seems they still live there.'

'Anything about how long these guys have been in the USA and what they've been doing since they've been here?' said Juanita.

James shuffled through the papers he was holding. 'The files are pretty thin, but we do have résumés for them … of sorts. Mohammed has apparently lived here for three years and it looks like he's just done a whole series of casual labouring jobs during that time.'

'And the other guy?' asked Juanita.

James leafed through several pages, taking around twenty seconds seconds to skim read them, before replying. 'Ahmed … yes, looks pretty much the same.'

'Anything about how they supposedly achieved US citizenship?' said Juanita.

'No, I can't see anything.'

'If they're US citizens, I'm the fucking pope,' spat Kyle.

Juanita fought back the urge to remonstrate with him. They were, after all, on the same side here, whatever Kyle's prejudices. 'Have we got anything else?' she said.

James flipped through the pages for a few more seconds, before shaking his head, exhaling noisily. 'That's it I'm afraid.'

'Dammit,' muttered Kyle, 'after all that we don't have a thing to confirm or refute our suspicions.'

An idea occurred to Juanita. While the two men continued raking through the papers in the hope of extracting something useful, she flipped up the lid of her laptop and powered it up. It took her barely a minute or two to find what she was looking for: the FBI list of most-wanted terrorists. It was a very long shot; there were just fifty-one names on the list, representing only the most dangerous and hunted known terrorists in the world. What were the chances that their suspects would be on that list? What were the chances that they'd even be using their real names? Nevertheless, she scrolled through the list. There were just four individuals whose last names began with 'B': Abas Badour, Dabur Burki, Kabir Beydoun, and … Mohammed Bashara. She clicked on the name and brought up a photograph.

A cold shiver crawled down her spine as she gazed into those dark, deep-set eyes, which somehow seemed to radiate pure evil. The hooked nose and sunken cheeks gave way to thin lips set in a grim, straight line, framed by a moustache and a long, bushy, black beard. She sat mesmerised for several long seconds before shaking off the trance.

'Guys, guys … I've got something!'

They both looked up. 'What? What is it?' said James.

'Come and look,' she said, stepping aside to make room for them and swivelling the machine sideways a little.

The three of them huddled around the laptop. As the two men gazed at the screen, it was clear that they had been struck by the same spell as she had been, seconds earlier; they were rendered silent for some moments.

Kyle finally broke the silence. 'OK, maybe … *just maybe*, that's our man … or one of them anyway, but remember what we said earlier: it's a real common name in the Muslim world. And we can't even be sure that this guy working at Johnson Brothers is using his real name.'

'I know, but …' she hesitated, fearing that what she was about to say would be ridiculed, by Kyle at least.

James seemed to sense what she was thinking; he laid a gentle arm across her shoulders. 'What is it Juanita? Nothing's off limits here.'

She turned and looked him directly in the eyes. 'I just … *feel* it. Somehow I know it's him.'

Kyle cut in. 'You can't *know* it. It's a very long shot at best.'

Her eyes blazed as she shook free of James's arm. 'Call it women's intuition … call it what you like. I *know* it's him.'

'Oh, give me a break,' muttered Kyle.

James intervened. 'Hey, back off, will you? We're supposed to be working together here.'

'OK … OK, I'm sorry,' muttered Kyle, holding his hands up in supplication.

The tense atmosphere eased a little.

James's voice was soothing, calming, when he turned back to her. 'You could well be right, Juanita. I know you too well to disregard your instincts.'

She felt a surge of emotion and hugged him to her. 'You mean that?'

'I do … but we'll need something more for the police. If only there was a photograph in the personnel file.'

'But,' said Kyle, having evidently now regained control, 'there is an address; both of the brothers have given the same address. Whether or not it's genuine is another question, but we could check it out.'

'You're right,' said James, 'if it checks out OK, maybe we can catch sight of this guy and find out if it's really the same person … maybe even get a photograph.'

Finally, thought Juanita, *we're closing in.*

Chapter 36

The business card which the receptionist at Johnson Brothers had given Mark was bogus: the address didn't exist, and neither did Wayne Robertson, the high-flying English businessman who had visited Johnson Brothers, purporting to be building a house in Upper Montclair. Mark wasn't surprised, just frustrated to have missed this guy by seconds.

He was also very, very puzzled. There was no doubt in his mind that the two men who had visited the company, just before he arrived, were working together. Equally, he was quite sure that they must have some connection with the mystery woman who had so far eluded his every effort to track down. But he just couldn't piece it all together.

It was clear that Julia's murder was the work of a professional assassin; the only logical reason for someone to arrange a contract killing was to silence her over something she had uncovered during one of her investigations. But if Don's conclusions from examining Julia's papers and files were correct – *by no means guaranteed*, he reminded himself – all she had been investigating was the employment of a few illegal immigrants by a tinpot building company. Surely, no-one would kill for that.

Then there were the strange actions of her killer: copying the autopsy report and stealing details of Julia's work from the New York Times office. And, assuming the two men in the silver Toyota were working with this woman, their theft of personnel records from Johnson Brothers.

Try as he might, he could not make sense of it all. His best hope now was to trawl through all the hotels within, say, a half-mile radius of the hair salon in the hope of finding where this woman was staying – if indeed she really was staying in a hotel as she had told

Mandy. Fortunately, Sergeant O'Reilly was on leave, so Mark would be able to research which hotels qualified, without the meddling bastard looking over his shoulder. His friend and colleague, Alex, knew full well that he was still working on Julia's murder, and had repeatedly advised him to let it go, but he knew she'd never shop him to O'Reilly. He grabbed a coffee from the vending machine in the office and set about his task.

Half an hour later he had his list of hotels. *Christ there are a lot of hotels in New York City*, he thought as he scanned the list: within just that half-mile radius of the salon there were no fewer than seventeen. He knew there would be no point in phoning them: they were very unlikely to be willing to divulge details of their guests to someone on the phone claiming to be a cop without seeing some I.D. And even if they were, it was entirely possible that this woman was using a different name now. No, he'd have to do it the hard way: trawl round each hotel in person, give them at least the name he had for her and show both the passport photo and the photo-fit with the shorter hairstyle. It wasn't going to be quick.

***

Three hours later, Mark had visited fourteen hotels, and no-one in any of them had recognised the name or either of the photos. There were only three left before he'd have to widen the search area. As he approached the Art Deco style frontage of the fifteenth, he wasn't feeling optimistic.

Inside, it was obvious that this fairly old hotel had been extensively refurbished; the décor was clean and modern, in muted tones of grey and beige; the seating around the square pillars which flanked the lobby had obviously been re-upholstered recently. He walked up to reception and was immediately greeted with a dazzlingly white smile from the immaculately groomed woman behind the counter. Her dark hair was scraped back from her face and firmly pinned in place at the back, her makeup perfect in every detail.

'Welcome to the Manhattan, sir. I'm Kayleigh' – a somewhat superfluous introduction, as she wore a prominent name badge – 'how may I help you?'

Mark flipped open the holder containing his warrant card. 'Detective Mark Bowman – I need to know if a Gema López Arteaga is staying at the hotel.'

The girl's eyes widened – maybe she wasn't used to cops rocking up at reception without warning. 'I'll just check,' she said turning to her computer screen. After a minute or so's clicking and tapping she announced, 'I'm sorry, Detective, there's no-one of that name staying at the hotel.'

Mark was getting used to this response. Wearily, he withdrew the two photos from his pocket and laid them on the counter. 'Recognise either of these?'

She took but a second or two to study the images, before declaring, 'They're both the same woman ... just different hairstyles.'

Mark was a little surprised that she had picked that up so quickly; to his eyes, the hairstyle made such a difference to her appearance that it could easily have been two different women until you studied the images closely.

'But do you recognise her?'

'Oh, sure ... she's been staying here for a few days now.'

Mark's heart leapt. *At last.*

Kayleigh continued, 'When she first checked in, I noticed her lovely long, glossy, black hair. We're not allowed to wear ours down at work,' she said, touching a hand to the side of her head. 'She's pretty, don't you think?'

'I guess,' he replied, unable to think of Julia's murderer as "pretty".

'Anyway,' said the receptionist, 'the other day she went out looking like that' – she placed an elegantly manicured forefinger on the counter by the passport photo – 'and came back looking like that' – the pearly pink talon stopped by the photo-fit image. 'I couldn't see why she'd want to cut such lovely hair short. 'I mean she still looks good with the new hairstyle ... it's kind of edgy ... but—'

Mark wasn't in the mood for a detailed critique of his quarry's new hairstyle; he cut Kayleigh off in mid-flow. 'Is she still staying here?'

Kayleigh turned her attention back to the computer screen. After a few seconds she replied, 'Sure, she's booked in with a guy for a few more days yet.'

Mark could hardly contain himself; after days of fruitless searching he'd finally struck gold. 'What name's she using?'

She checked the screen. 'Juanita Sanchez Ruiz. Pretty name, huh?'

Mark didn't bother to respond to her last comment. 'And what about the guy with her?' he pressed. She checked the screen again. 'James Connolly ... big guy, quite good-looking actually. And that accent ...'

'What accent?'

'English ... I just love the Brits' accent, don't you? It sounds so ... sophisticated'

My God, this girl could talk for America. Mark did his best to conceal his impatience. 'What's their room number?'

'309 ... you want me to call them?' she said, reaching for the phone.

'No, don't do that. I'll just—' His cell phone rang. 'Just hold on while I take this.'

'Detective Bowman?'

'Yes ... who's this?'

'It's Mandy ... Mandy Jackson ... you know, the hairdresser. We met the other day.'

As if he wouldn't have remembered who she was. Any other time and he'd have enjoyed chatting to her, but now just wasn't the moment.

'Hi Mandy, I'm kind of tied up right now, can I call you back in a little while?'

'Oh sure ... it's just that I've remembered a couple more things that might help you find—' She stopped dead, mid-sentence.

'Mandy?' More silence. 'Mandy ... you still there?'

'I think there's someone trying to get in,' she whispered.

'Get in where? Where are you?'

'My apartment ... I'm ... oh no, I can hear them fiddling with the lock.' He could hear the rising panic in her voice.

Oh Christ! He was within touching distance of catching up with Julia's killer, but now this. What to do first?

The woman he was after, and her accomplice, were going to be in the hotel for a few more days, but Mandy, for whom he had developed something of an attachment was, potentially, in danger right now.

He made his decision.

'You got a security chain, bolts … anything like that?'

'Yes … both,' she replied, her voice tremulous.

'OK, fit the chain and shut the bolts. Then call 911. But I'm real close – I might be able to get there first. Do it … now!' He hung up without waiting for her reply.

'Everything OK?' enquired the receptionist.

Stupid question.

'I gotta go …right now. I'll be back soon. Listen, under no circumstances say anything to this woman or this man about me being here, looking for them. Got it?'

She nodded, her eyes wide and lips parted. He dashed off without uttering another word.

Bursting through the main entrance, he sprinted the hundred yards or so to where his car was parked. By the time he slid into the driver's seat his breath was coming in ragged gasps. *Why the fuck don't I keep myself in better shape*, he chided himself. He hit the siren and sped off, with a squeal of tortured rubber, spewing clouds of acrid tyre smoke.

He drove as though the devil was on his tail, running red lights and weaving recklessly through the dense traffic, frequently in the path of oncoming vehicles. Against the odds, he made it without incident.

As he approached the main entrance, he could see that the door was slightly ajar, the wooden frame splintered where the lock had obviously been forced. He drew his weapon, flipping off the safety catch and cautiously stepping inside. Mandy's apartment was on the second floor; he decided to take the stairs.

As he crept upwards, everything seemed normal: no sign of any intruder, no sound of any disturbance. When he approached her apartment, though, it was obvious that all was not well. Like the door at the main entrance, her door also hung open, the wooden frame split and the flimsy security chain broken, hanging uselessly from the splintered frame.

He edged forward, as silently as possible, holding his handgun in a two-handed grip, finger poised on the trigger. He carefully eased the door open with the muzzle of the gun, straining to hear any sound which might betray the presence of an intruder; there was none. As he stepped inside, he quickly scanned the room, panning his weapon this way and that, covering every corner. Everything looked normal.

Unwilling to announce his presence by calling out, he crept forward, towards an open door at the far side of the room. As he stepped cautiously through the door, he immediately recognised the familiar tang of gun-smoke in the air.

Full of trepidation, he stepped around the bed; the sight which met his eyes hit him like a physical blow to his chest. Mandy lay on her back, surrounded by a rapidly growing pool of blood, glistening darkly atop the woodblock flooring, then, as it reached the edge of the white, deep-pile rug, soaking in and spreading as though being absorbed by a giant sheet of blotting paper.

There was a bullet wound in her chest, but it was the other wound which sucked the breath from him and made him fall to his knees: she had been shot through the ear, the exit of the bullet on the other side of her head having removed a jagged piece of her skull. He could hardly draw his eyes away from the hideous wound, but when he finally did, he noticed that, on her stomach, lay a small piece of card. Mark shuffled forward on his knees to see what it was.

The card bore no words, just the image of a scorpion.

Chapter 37

James checked the address on the scrap of paper he had withdrawn from his pocket; this was the place.

The apartment block, just half a mile from Johnson Bothers, was a low-rise, redbrick building, nestling between several other identical blocks. It was in an appalling state of repair: the pointing in the brickwork was badly eroded and ugly streaks of rust stain emanated from every one of the metal window frames, fanning out as they made their bid for earth. He checked the address once more: this was, indeed, where the Bashara Brothers supposedly lived. Well, at least it wasn't a false address.

Although Kyle had offered to join him, he had elected to come on his own. Although he had no intention of seeking any kind of confrontation, it was just possible that he might be about to come face-to face with one – maybe even two – of the world's most-wanted terrorists. Kyle was a telecoms engineer; he had no experience of such situations and could prove more of a liability than an asset if things turned ugly. But there was also another, more important consideration: he didn't want Juanita left on her own. There was no rational reason to suppose that she was in any special danger, as long as she stayed in the hotel, but there was something in his gut which didn't feel right. He just felt more comfortable that she had someone with her.

He took the Glock from the glovebox of the car, tucking it into his waistband as he stepped out of the car. He didn't want any trouble, but if trouble came seeking him, he wanted to make sure he was ready.

The paint on the front door of the block was so badly peeling that it was almost impossible to determine the original colour – maybe some sort of shade of blue or grey, he surmised. What surprised him, though, was that there was no security whatsoever. The door did have a lock, but no-one had locked it; entering the building required nothing other than a twist of the badly rusted iron handle.

As he stepped inside the building, the sharp tang of urine assaulted his nostrils; whether feline, canine, or human, he couldn't tell. He withdrew the gun from his waistband and flipped off the safety catch, before creeping up the stairs to the first landing. Apartment 203 – the one he sought - was right in front of him at the top of the stairs. Compared to the crumbling surroundings, the door itself wasn't in bad shape; the dark brown paintwork was largely intact, apart from a few scuffs at the bottom and a worn patch by the lock.

James stepped tentatively forward and put his ear to the door, listening intently; after about thirty seconds of absolute silence, he concluded that there was probably no-one in residence. He decided to test his conclusion; ringing the doorbell, he swiftly retreated to a dark recess just off the edge of the landing and waited, his gun held in readiness should it be needed. Nothing happened. After waiting for about twenty seconds, he stepped out of the shadows and approached the door once again, taking a close look at the lock; it appeared to be an ancient, and very simple, two-lever sash lock. This should be easy.

He laid the gun on the floor and withdrew from his pocket the lock-picking set, which he had brought all the way from Canada – just in case. It took him only a few moments to defeat the primitive lock.

Slipping the tools back into his pocket, he bent down and picked up the gun. As quietly as possible, he nudged the door open and stepped inside. It was pretty dark and gloomy, but as far as he could tell, there was no sign of anyone else there. He reached for the light switch alongside the door; a single light bulb – no shade – hanging from a cable in the centre of the room flooded the room with a harsh, unforgiving light. It took several seconds for James's eyes to adjust. The room was decidedly down-at-heel: the floor covering consisted of a few mismatched, threadbare rugs; the once-cream paint on the walls was grubby, and peeling in places; the only window was masked by a ragged piece of tarpaulin hanging from a couple of hooks screwed into the wall.

As he surveyed his surroundings, he was struck by the paucity of furniture: a single, saggy, brown couch; a battered, plastic-laminate-topped table with two metal chairs; and an ancient TV perched upon an upturned wooden box. That was it.

Apart, that is, from some pieces of wood propped in the corner of the room. There were perhaps a couple of dozen wooden poles, about five or six feet in length; their purpose wasn't clear. Curious, James stepped forward to take a closer look. He had taken just two steps when he froze in his tracks; he could hear voices outside the apartment.

Chapter 38

James stood stock-still, straining to hear what was being said outside the door. The language was foreign to him, but the tone was casual, jovial. It sounded like two men, laughing and joking. The sound was becoming gradually louder. He held his breath, with a growing trepidation, hoping against hope that they would just pass by.

His worst fears were confirmed as the conversation was overlaid with the sound of a key being inserted into the lock. *Shit!* He looked around desperately for somewhere to hide. There were two doors leading off the room he was in; he dived for the nearest, stepping through into what turned out to be the kitchen. He closed the door just enough to leave a narrow gap through which he would be able to look back into the main living room. Stealing a quick glance all around the kitchen, he quickly realised there was no way out of this tiny room other than the way he had come in: he was, effectively, trapped.

As he heard the two men enter the room, he withdrew the Glock from his belt; if these two men were who he suspected they were, they could well be armed ... and very dangerous. But at least he would have the element of surprise. He took several long, deep breaths as he considered his options.

There was no point in waiting until one or both of these men came through into the kitchen; better to act now. As he peered through the gap between door and frame, he could just see two pairs of denim-clad legs stretched out; they were both seated on the ancient couch. This was the moment. He flung the door open and stepped through, holding the gun ahead of him in a double-handed grip.

The astonishment on the faces of the two men confirmed that he had caught them completely by surprise.

'What the fuck …?' exclaimed the man on the left, his gravelly voice heavily accented.

'Stay right there, hands where I can see them,' shouted James.

Both men raised their hands in the air, the surprise written across their faces now giving way to fear. 'What's this about … who are you?' said the same man.

'Shut up … I'll ask the questions. Which one of you is Mohammed Bashara?'

The other one replied, his voice tremulous. 'I am, but how do you know—'

James cut him off. 'Stand up … slowly … keep your hands where I can see them.'

He did so. He was a short man – perhaps five feet six inches – with a rounded face and a short, black beard.

'Keep still,' said James, transferring the gun to his right hand while retrieving the folded piece of paper from his pocket with his left. With some difficulty he managed to unfold the paper, single handed, and examine the image of Mohammed Bashara, most-wanted terrorist. The gaunt face stared back at him from the page; the close-set eyes, the hooked nose … none of these features bore any resemblance to those of the frightened-looking face of the man standing opposite. The clincher was in the notes alongside the photograph: height six feet three inches. This was not the man standing in front of him.

James turned his attention to the other man. 'You,' he said gesturing towards him with the muzzle of the gun, 'stand up as well … slowly.' The other man rose cautiously to his feet. He was hardly any taller than the first man, and also bore no resemblance to the image of the terrorist from the FBI list. 'What's your name?'

'I am his brother … Ahmed. But who are you … why are you here? What do you want? We don't have any money if that's what you—'

'Quiet!' snapped James. 'What's the significance of the dates July nineteenth and twentieth?'

The two of them glanced nervously at each other, apparently reluctant to reply.

'Well?' insisted James, panning the gun from one to the other in turn.

The one who had said he was Mohammed finally responded. 'It's the G7 summit at Camp David.'

So, even if he wasn't the wanted terrorist on the FBI list, he had more or less admitted that he and his brother *were* planning something at the summit.

'Why do you just happen to know that, huh? What are you planning?'

His brother, who seemed to be the more confident of the two, spoke again. 'We have a perfect right to demonstrate against capitalist greed and exploitation. Muslim brothers and sisters have been oppressed for far too long.'

'Demonstrate? What do you mean?'

'You must know – otherwise why did you ask us about the dates?'

'Well, why don't you tell me anyway?' growled James.

The man raised his eyebrows, shook his head slightly, and emitted an exasperated-sounding sigh. The bastard didn't show any signs of fear now, considering he was staring down the barrel of a gun. 'There are big demonstrations planned. Obviously, no-one will be able to get close to Camp David itself, but there'll be a big turnout in Thurmont. That's where we're going ... and quite a few of our Muslim brothers from here in New York are going to be there too.'

'You're planning to join a demonstration?'

'I just told you that. Are you not listening?'

My god, this guy's got some nerve, thought James. He jerked the gun more forcefully towards the man.

'You sure that's all it is ... a demonstration?'

'Look, let me show you,' he said, lowering his hands and pointing toward the pile of poles propped up in the corner.

'Slowly,' said James, lifting the gun a little for emphasis. He turned his attention to the other man. 'You go with him, I want to be able to see you both.'

The two of them moved slowly towards where the wooden poles were propped in the corner of the room. But they didn't actually touch the poles; instead, the one called Ahmed went to bend down alongside them; he would have been obscured from James's sight by the sofa.

'Wait,' said James, 'stand still ... keep your hands where I can see them.'

He moved around the sofa, so that he could keep the two of them properly in sight.

'OK?' said Ahmed, holding his hands forward in plain view.

'Go ahead.'

James hadn't previously seen the stack of hardboard sheets on the floor. Ahamed bent down, slowly, and picked up the one on top of the pile. He held it up for James to see. It was crudely painted with the words, 'Justice for Muslim Brothers.'

'OK?' he said, waiting for James to nod his affirmation.

He laid that sheet aside and picked up the next. It read, 'Destroy the Corrupt Capitalist System.'

'You see?' said Ahmed. 'They're placards ... we still have to fix them to the poles but they're easier to transport like this. We'll fix them to the poles when we get there.'

A dead weight descended in James's gut; had he really made a monumental mistake? Were these guys really just two angry men determined to exercise their democratic right to protest? He had fallen silent, and the other man had clearly picked up on the vibes, now growing even more in confidence.

'So, who the fuck are you anyway? I don't get the feeling you're a cop. What right have you got to break into our apartment and threaten us like this?' His flabby chin jutted forward defiantly as he spoke.

James could hardly believe how bold this guy was, considering he was confronted with a loaded gun, but his own resolve had, by now, evaporated. 'Look,' he said, 'I think there's been a bit of a misunderstanding here.'

'No shit,' said Ahmed.

Mohammed cowered in the corner, hands still in the air, his frightened eyes pleading with his brother not to goad this armed intruder any further. But James knew he had screwed up, and now it was time to back out.

'OK, I'm going now, but both of you need to stay put until I'm long gone. If either of you try to follow me, it will end very badly. Got it?'

Mohammed nodded, his eyes bulging with fear. Ahmed just stared back, his expression cold and stony. James backed away, all the time keeping his gun trained on the two of them. He reached behind him to release the door catch and stepped through, before turning and heading down the stairs as fast as his feet would carry him.

It wasn't until he was back in the car and speeding away that the tension began to dissipate; it was replaced by a feeling of intense frustration.

Fuck, fuck, fuck! Were they really back to square one now?

Chapter 39

James returned to the hotel feeling utterly deflated. He had been so sure they were on the brink of discovering why the young journalist had been murdered, helping to avert a potentially devastating terrorist attack on a gathering of the world's most influential leaders. Now, it seemed, the whole thing with the dates and the names they had found in Julia's notes was a massive red herring.

But *why* had she written down those names and dates? Maybe she had gone down exactly the same blind alley as he, Juanita, and Kyle had. Maybe there *was* nothing sinister about Johnson Brothers or its employees. Maybe she hadn't turned up anything big at all. But if so, why had one of the world's most highly paid assassins been hired to kill her? None of it made sense.

He held his key card up to the lock, which made a reassuring click as the red light turned to green.

'Guys,' he called out as he entered the room, 'it looks like we've made a massive ...'

His words tailed off as he realised there was no-one there. The TV was on, but no-one was watching it. Maybe Juanita was in the bathroom, but if so, where was Kyle? He'd explicitly asked Kyle to stay with her while he was away from the hotel. The bathroom door was open and there was no-one inside.

Maybe they had gone up to Kyle's room, on the floor above, for some reason. He stepped outside and went over to the elevators, which were almost directly opposite their room and pressed the call button. *Damn! Three bloody elevators and not one of them anywhere near my floor.* One of them appeared to be stuck on floor six, one was edging toward him just one floor at a time, and the last was moving away from him. Frustrated, he stabbed the button several more times, which made no difference whatsoever to the resolutely stationary first elevator or the painfully slothful progress of the second. He gave up and hurried towards the stairs, taking them two at a time.

He knocked on the door of Kyle's room. No response.

He called out both their names. No response.

He hammered on the door, calling out their names, louder this time. No response.

The icy fingers of apprehension began to crawl through his mind.

He made his way back to their own room. If they had gone out together for some reason, then surely, they would have left a note. He looked everywhere; there was no note.

Then he saw it: Juanita's purse lay on the floor alongside the bed, tipped on its side with many of the contents spilt onto the floor. She never went *anywhere* without her purse. The creeping doubt that something was wrong morphed into a smothering dread.

What should he do? As he contemplated this question, the sounds from the TV playing in the background formed a meaningless hum: a sort of white noise which served only to interfere with his thought processes. But then two words jumped out of the aural miasma and penetrated his consciousness: 'Kyle Richards'. He was immediately on the alert, but he had already missed much of the news report.

He grabbed the TV remote from where it lay on one of the bedside cabinets and, with trembling fingers, rewound the live news report.

'... and the Dow Jones continues to slide on the news that ...'
He had rewound too far.

Desperately trying to remain calm and gain control of his quivering fingers he edged forward until he reached the point he was looking for.

'Police have confirmed that the body found in a dumpster near to Times Square was the victim of a brutal murder. The victim had been shot several times in the chest and head. He has been identified from his personal effects as one Kyle Richards, a resident of Miami Beach. Police are urging anyone who knew Mr Richards, and can shed some light on why he was in New York City, to come forward as soon as possible ...'

Oh Christ, what about Juanita? The scattered contents of Juanita's purse suggested that she had been taken against her will –

maybe Kyle too. If someone had abducted the two of them … The strength drained from his entire body, and he sank to his knees in shock.

Chapter 40

James just couldn't accept that Juanita might have suffered the same fate as Kyle. His fevered mind began frantically searching for other possible outcomes.

Maybe Juanita had evaded capture and they – whoever 'they' were – had only succeeded in abducting Kyle.

Maybe the murdered man was not Kyle at all; after all, the report said that the body had been identified from 'personal effects'. Someone could have planted Kyle's things on the body of another victim, couldn't they? But, if so, why?

Maybe it was another person with the same name. Could there be *two* people named Kyle Richards, living in Miami Beach? Well, yes – he supposed that was quite possible, but if so, what were the chances that they would both be in New York City at the same time? Surely, very slim.

Deep down, he knew he was clutching at straws.

The strident chime of his cell phone pierced his brain; in a daze, he withdrew it from his pocket and looked at the caller I.D. It was a message from Juanita. *Thank God!*

When he clicked on the message, he could not, at first, take in what he was seeing. It was a video clip: Juanita sat facing him, a gag pulled tightly between her teeth. Her hair was dishevelled and her makeup smudged across her cheeks. Her hands appeared to be tied behind the back of the chair. James stared fixedly at the screen, mesmerised.

A man's voice broke the spell: English accent, unmistakeably London. The man was out of shot but the timbre was cold and menacing.

'Hello, James Connolly ... or perhaps I should call you Stephen Lewis?'

James's blood froze: Stephen Lewis was a name he thought he had left behind more than a year ago when he had fled the shocking events in Miami. The only people who would know of that name were his erstwhile enemies from that appalling episode. And now, it seemed, one of them held Juanita captive.

'I've been looking for you for a very long time,' continued that ominous voice, slow and deliberate. 'You're a difficult man to track down.'

James shook himself free of the trance which had gripped him. 'Who are you … what do you want? Why are you—?'

He realised he was trying to talk to a recording, as his question was cut short by the disembodied voice continuing its sinister monologue.

'I expect you're probably wondering who I am, huh? Well, you'll probably know me best by my calling card … I think you may have seen it recently.'

The chilling realisation hit him like an icy bolt. His heart skipped a beat, and the breath was literally sucked from his lungs. This was not just a bad guy; it was one of the world's most feared assassins: a vicious, sadistic psychopath.

'As you can see, I have your pretty girlfriend here …' His tone changed as he addressed her directly. 'Would you like to say something to your boyfriend, darlin'?'

Juanita strained to pull her head away as a man's hand appeared in shot, reaching behind her to release the gag. As she shook herself free of the filthy rag, she struggled, for a moment, to find her voice. When she did, it was nothing more than a strangled croak.

'Oh, I guess it was a bit tight, huh? Sorry 'bout that darlin'. Never mind, take your time … I'm sure lover boy will wait to hear what you've got to say.'

Juanita worked her jaw from side to side until she was finally able to find a tremulous voice.

'James … don't listen to him. Please … he's trying to—' Her pleas gave way, abruptly, to an anguished scream, which pierced James's heart as surely as any spear.

The lighted cigarette which had been touched against her upper arm was pulled away and held right in front of the camera. Juanita's scream had subsided to a series of ragged sobs, her shoulders heaving with each tormented breath.

The man's voice continued, calm and unhurried. 'Now, as you can see, with just this simple implement' – he twirled the lighted cigarette between his thumb and forefinger – 'it is possible to inflict considerable pain.'

'You bastard!' screamed James, to no effect, as he was talking to a recording.

'Now the way you can stop this,' said the man, his tone casual, 'is to come right over to the location which I'm about to text you. Now, if you should be foolish enough to call the police, or to come armed yourself – 'cos I know you're pretty handy with guns – I'll blow her pretty head off before you can get anywhere near her. Got it?'

The cigarette, which had almost gone out, was withdrawn from shot, only to reappear a few seconds later, now glowing brightly just a few inches from the side of Juanita's neck. Her eyes bulged in terror as she sought, in vain, to pull away. This time the glowing tip was not just touched against her; it was viciously ground into her skin, eliciting from her a bloodcurdling scream. James's buttocks clenched as he tensed to prevent the involuntary release of urine which threatened to burst forth.

'Oh dear,' said the invisible man, holding the now-extinguished stub in front of the camera, 'I do believe this one's finished. Never mind, I have two more packs of twenty ... so I'm not likely to run out anytime soon. See you soon, James Connolly ... don't take too long, or I might need to have a little more fun with your girlfriend here.' The screen went blank.

Chapter 41

The location to which James had been summoned was a derelict warehouse in Brooklyn's rundown waterfront area. Once a bustling centre of commerce, this area was now a decaying monument to a bygone era. While much of Brooklyn's waterfront had been earmarked for residential development, this particular stretch was still home to numerous dark, crumbling edifices from an industrial age.

He had parked some distance away, so as to avoid announcing his arrival. Now he crouched behind a pile of wooden pallets around a hundred yards from the building where Juanita was supposedly being held, peeping around the edge as he surveyed his target.

The warehouse was, like most of the others strung out along the waterfront, of redbrick construction. Although the bricks were badly blackened – probably from airborne pollution – the basic structure looked sound enough. The windows were a different matter though: just about every glass pane was shattered, and the metal frames badly rusted, with barely a vestige of the original, dark green paint still remaining. The large, metal goods door in the centre – invitingly part-open, James noticed – was in barely better condition.

He had considered ignoring The Scorpion's threats and calling the police, but they would not know just what sort of psychotic monster they were dealing with. He was in no doubt that this bastard would have no qualms about killing Juanita at the first signs of police intervention, and he was willing to bet that the assassin would have some pre-planned escape route in place. He'd managed to evade the authorities for many years, in spite of his brazen advertising of his exploits by means of his calling cards; James couldn't imagine that he didn't have his escape fully prepared in the event of the cops showing up.

And then there was the not-insignificant fact that he and Juanita were both wanted in connection with the killings a year ago in Miami. So, even if the police were to succeed in rescuing Juanita, there would be a lot of awkward questions to answer afterwards. The truth about the events in Miami was so incredible that he doubted the police would believe what had really happened. And if they should be charged with murder, it was unlikely that a jury would believe them either.

No, in these most desperate of circumstances, he judged that his own, well-honed combat skills – albeit skills which had not been used recently, and which he had hoped he'd never have cause to call upon again – would stand him in better stead than letting the police confront an adversary whom they would almost certainly have underestimated.

He checked, for the third time, that the Glock was fully loaded, before tucking it into his waistband, behind his back.

Instead of approaching the building head on, he made for the adjacent warehouse, pressing himself against the wall, waiting stock-still for some seconds, looking for any sign that he had been detected; there was none. He took several long, slow breaths as he tried to prepare himself for the action which was to follow. His racing heart began to settle, and a strange, familiar calm infused him. Now he was ready.

He edged along the frontage of the building, stopping again at the gap between it and the one in which Juanita was supposedly being held. There was still no sign that he had been detected. He ducked into the darkened alley between the two buildings, pausing for a few moments to let his eyes adjust to the gloom before making his way, cautiously, along the side of the building looking for any means of entry other than the large goods door on the front of the building – his enemy would surely be watching that entrance. He found nothing.

Working his way around the back of the building revealed a metal fire escape, which was so badly corroded that the section between ground level and the second floor had fallen away completely and lay in a crumbling heap of rusty, twisted metal on the ground. As he approached the ground floor fire exit, he was dismayed to find that the sturdy door had been secured with a heavy chain and padlock. *Fat lot of good that would be in the event of a fire*, he thought: an absurdly mundane observation considering the desperate situation he was facing.

With no means at his disposal of forcing the lock and chain, the only way he would be able to overcome it would be to shoot out the lock. He swiftly dismissed the idea; there was very little ambient noise in this deserted area and, even with the silencer fitted to the Glock, he was sure the sound of the shot, and the shattering metal, would be detected by anyone inside. He abandoned any thought of entering by this route.

He made his way around to the other side of the building, entering another darkened alley alongside the adjacent building. He worked his way along the alley, searching for any other possible means of entry; he found none. There was nothing else for it: he would just have to go in through the front door and try to work out some way to avoid detection.

As he emerged from the alley and surveyed, once again, the front of the building, he noticed something else: a goods hoist. A short, metal boom projected from the building, just above an opening at the second-floor level. It was connected, via a rusty chain, to a wooden pallet, which was resting on the ground. As he gazed up at the metal structure, he tried to assess just how structurally sound it might be. It was certainly very rusty, but as far as he could see, it looked solid enough. Could he perhaps scale the chain and enter on the second floor? He wasn't the best of climbers, and he had always had a fear of heights, but it was only a short distance – maybe twenty feet – and it would avoid the potentially suicidal act of entering through the main door.

He made his decision.

He crept over to the goods hoist, pausing to check, once again, that the Glock was firmly tucked into his waistband, before taking a firm grasp of the filthy chain. He was a big man – six feet three and two hundred and thirty pounds – but strong and muscular. He managed to haul himself up a foot or so, before wrapping his feet around the chain and clenching them together to take his weight. Pushing down with his leg muscles while pulling with his arms saw him advance another foot or so. He repeated the sequence several more times until he was about halfway up the chain. But now the lactic acid began to burn in the muscles in his arms. He hung there, resting as best he could until he felt he could continue.

After resting for around fifteen seconds, he continued his ascent, edging upwards in ever-smaller increments until the burn in his arms forced him to rest once again. He made the mistake of looking down; his head began to spin as what looked like about fifteen feet when viewed from the ground now looked at least three times that distance when looking downward. He tore his eyes away and clung desperately to the chain. After a few more moments, the burn began to subside a little. He glanced upwards; only another four or five feet. *I can do this,* he told himself.

Forcing himself onwards, he scaled the last few feet until he was level with the opening. But there was one more hurdle to overcome: the chain was set away from the sill of the opening by perhaps three or four feet. How could he bridge that gap? Any mistake would see him plunge to the ground; at best, injuring himself badly; at worst, killing himself. Even if he survived the fall, he would probably have alerted his adversary inside the building. There was only one possibility.

Gathering his last reserves of strength, he relinquished the grip of his ankles on the chain, taking his entire weight through his hands and arms. He began to swing back and forth like a human pendulum, increasing the amplitude with each superhuman thrust. The muscles in his arms screamed at him to stop, the burn now in danger of breaching his breaking point. The pain which racked his fingers as he desperately clung to the chain ramped up to a level which he could no longer tolerate; in spite of his iron determination to prevent it, the muscles in his hands relaxed a little. His hands slipped a few inches, the rough chain sawing viciously into his skin. The self-preservation instinct kicked in, and somehow, he managed to clench his fingers tight once more and arrest the slide. The pain was excruciating.

One more swing: not enough. Two more, and ... He let go, propelling himself forward until his feet made contact with the sill. For a heart-stopping moment, he teetered on the brink, his balance poised between tipping forward into the opening and toppling backward into space. He struggled desperately to get his weight forward and past the danger point.

It was barely a fraction of a second later, though, that he sensed it: he had lost the battle between willpower and gravity. He knew he had tipped back beyond the point of no return. In this moment, when he knew all was lost, time seemed to slow to a near-standstill. His thoughts, though, were not directed toward the imminent crushing impact with the concrete below, or what injuries he might sustain. No, all he could think about was how he had failed; he had let Juanita down. The Scorpion had won, and now they would both die.

Chapter 42

A strong hand clasped his, arresting his fall backwards. Instinctively, he grabbed his saviour's wrist with his other hand and clung on tight as he was hauled forward and upward until his centre of gravity was in front of the tipping point. He fell forward, sprawling on the filthy floor, gasping for breath. Several long seconds passed before his heaving chest had settled sufficiently for him to drag himself, painfully, to his knees.

He looked up to see who had saved him, but the light level was very low, and his eyes had not adjusted from the bright sunshine outside. When, finally, a face began to come into focus, he could not believe the evidence of his own eyes. His head swirled as he tried to process what he was seeing.

'Kyle … is that you? But how …? I mean you're supposed to be—'

'Dead? Ah well, there's quite a story there but, before we go into that, there's someone you should meet.'

'Juanita … is she OK?'

Kyle ignored the question. His expression broke into a slow smile, but it was a humourless, menacing smile, the like of which James had never seen on Kyle's face before. The next thing James knew, he was staring up at the muzzle of a gun.

'Get up,' he snarled. 'Keep your hands where I can see them.'

James struggled to his feet, spears of pain lancing through his ravaged hands as he pushed himself up from the rough, wooden floor. He was still utterly bemused as to what was going on here, but the more pressing matter was that he had to figure out what to do.

He still had his gun; he could feel its hard shape pressed against his back. Could he reach for it, bring it to bear, and snatch a shot before Kyle reacted? Unlikely. Would a lunge forward to grab his gun hand and force it aside succeed? Possibly, if he could create some momentary distraction. But what about Juanita? Where was she? Would any attempt to tackle Kyle put her in even greater danger? As his mind raced through the possibilities he decided to play for time.

'Why, Kyle? What's going on?'

'Shut up and turn around … hands in the air.'

Damn, maybe I should have made my play straightaway. It was too late now though.

He turned, slowly, until his back faced towards Kyle.

'Don't move,' came the voice from behind him. A moment later he felt the gun being roughly wrenched from his waistband.

'OK, now turn around and head towards those stairs.' As James turned around, Kyle indicated the staircase with a sideways jerk of his gun.

James moved slowly towards the stairs, all the time desperately trying to come up with some plan to turn the tables. Perhaps he could try to trip his captor as they made their way down the stairs; if he slammed himself backward into the other man's legs, maybe he could upend him and seize the advantage. But just how far behind was he? How could he judge just where to aim his lunge? As they started down the stairs, he tried to steal a glance over his shoulder.

'Eyes front!' snapped Kyle. James complied.

When they reached the bottom of the stairs, he saw Juanita. She sat in a chair at the far side of the warehouse, bound and gagged, a single spotlight illuminating her plight. As he moved forward, ever conscious of the gun behind him, she seemed not to be able to see him, perhaps because of the light in her eyes. It was not until he was perhaps just twenty feet away that her frightened eyes met his. She shook her head, violently.

'Well, hello James Connolly,' came a disembodied voice from somewhere behind her chair. James felt a cold icicle of fear pierce his body. It was the same voice, the same London accent as he had heard on the phone.

The owner of the voice stepped forward, out of the gloom and into the pool of light. He was a big man; about six feet four; muscular build; shaven head giving way to a thick, bull neck. So, this was what the infamous Scorpion looked like.

He was smoking a cigarette and holding a handgun. He bent forward and released the gag from Juanita's mouth. A trickle of blood came from the corner of her mouth as she found her voice.

'James … I … I'm sorry. I never realised that—'

The man tapped the silencer of his gun against the side of her head. 'Oh, do stop babblin', darlin'.'

'Leave her alone, you bastard,' hissed James.

'Ooh, a little touchy I see,' said the big man.

Kyle moved away from behind James, came around the side of him and a little in front, where he could now be clearly seen. He held up James's gun in his left hand, while keeping his own in his right, trained on James. 'Seems he didn't heed your warning to come unarmed,' he said, addressing himself to the other man.

The big man tutted. 'Well that was very foolish … disobeying my instructions has consequences.'

He took a deep draw on his cigarette, coaxing the tip to a bright glow, before pressing it against Juanita's already badly burned left arm. Her scream cut through James like a rapier. He lunged forward, only to be checked by Kyle, stepping in front of him and thrusting his gun forward. Juanita's scream subsided to a series of tortured, ragged sobs.

The Scorpion pulled from the shadows another chair and placed it alongside Juanita's. 'Come here and sit down,' he ordered.

Kyle reinforced the instruction by stepping up to James and jabbing him in the side of his ribcage with the silencer on his gun. Reluctantly, James did as he had been ordered. His hands, still burning with the pain from the slip on the chain, were roughly bundled together behind his back and secured with what felt like a plastic tie-wrap, which cut painfully into his wrists. With the two of them now trussed up helplessly, the big man known as The Scorpion moved around in front of them to face them directly while Kyle stayed alongside them.

'I expect you would like some answers, huh?' said the big man, his tone taunting, gloating.

James was still desperately trying to figure out some means of turning around their dire predicament but, so far, he had come up blank. The longer he could keep the arrogant bastard talking, the better, though.

'You going to give me some, then?' he said.

The big man laughed: a gruff, low-pitched, menacing sound. 'Ask away.'

'What was that young journalist investigating? What had she uncovered that was so important that she had to die? Who paid you to kill her?'

'Whoa there ...' – the big man made a sort of downward patting gesture with his free hand – 'that's three questions at once.' He stroked his chin in an exaggeratedly theatrical display of mock thoughtfulness. 'Let me see ... I'll take them in order. Now, what was the first one again?'

James wasn't going to let the bastard get under his skin; he needed to stay calm if he was to come up with any sort of plan – though the chances seemed close to zero. 'I think you heard me the first time,' he said, quietly.

'Ah yes ... you wanted to know what the girl was investigating. Well, in all honesty, it really isn't important.'

Of all the possible answers that he might have expected, this certainly wasn't one of them. 'But ... she must surely have uncovered something big. I know you only get hired for the most important hits.'

'Ah, I see my reputation has gone before me,' he said. 'Nice to know my expertise is appreciated by a fellow professional.'

This remark *did* rile him, in spite of his best efforts to remain calm and unruffled. 'That's not me anymore,' he hissed.

His response elicited a humourless smile from the big man. 'Oh, did I touch a raw nerve there?'

James did not respond, asking instead, 'Was she investigating a possible attack on the G7 summit? Were you being paid by some terrorist organisation?'

'Goodness ... what an imagination you have.'

By now James was utterly bemused; he had been so sure – they all had – that Julia must have been working on something to do with the G7. Was this bastard lying just to taunt him? 'So who was paying you then?'

'Oh, that would be the same people that you used to work for ... and I still do.'

'But who's their client?'

'There isn't one.'

His infuriatingly cryptic answers were irritating James to the point of almost outranking his concern for the desperate situation in which he and Juanita found themselves. 'But *someone* must have paid them.'

His tormenter took a last drag on his cigarette before dropping it on the floor and grinding it underfoot. 'The thing is, James Connolly – as you now call yourself – you caused my employers considerable trouble and expense with your foolish heroics back in Miami. You foiled a potentially very lucrative assassination plot, which had taken over a year to plan. What's more, your actions resulted in the deaths of several of their operatives: assassins who had taken considerable time and money to train. They were *very* upset with you. They have been trying for over a year now to track you down.'

James was not too surprised that he had been on their wanted list, but he still couldn't figure out how Julia Turner's murder was connected to all this. 'OK, so now you've found me … but what does all this have to do with the murder of the young journalist? Why was she so special?'

'Oh, she wasn't special at all … she was just bait.'

Chapter 43

'Bait?' repeated James, confused and disoriented.

'Yeah ... I just picked an investigative journalist at random. My employers figured that if they got me to eliminate the subject, and made it obvious who had done it, you might pick up the news. Then, knowing that I only do really important hits' – he bristled with his own arrogant self-importance – 'you might decide to try to find out what was behind the assassination.' He let out a raucous laugh, which echoed around the empty building. 'And it worked a treat didn't it? See how being such a goody-two-shoes and poking your nose into things that shouldn't concern you has become your downfall?'

At last, the penny dropped. 'You killed that young woman just to get to me?' he said, incredulous.

The big man held up a forefinger in the air and wagged it from side to side. 'Not *just* you ...' – he glanced at Juanita, who visibly tensed under his gaze – 'your pretty girlfriend here caused as much mayhem as you. They want you both,' he concluded, with a chilling finality.

James's head was reeling at the way this animal had casually extinguished a promising young life, just as a means to an end. But he still couldn't put all the pieces together.

He turned towards Kyle, who was still pointing a gun at him. 'And how does this bastard fit in?'

'Oh, careful with your language, James,' said Kyle, thrusting his gun more forcefully in James's direction, 'I have a rather itchy trigger finger.'

'Not yet,' snapped The Scorpion. 'You know our instructions are to make this slow and painful.'

Juanita emitted a subdued whimper; Kyle gave a subservient nod, lowering his gun.

With the moment of tension passed, The Scorpion continued, 'OK, why don't you explain to this poor, confused fool what your part in all this was?'

'I'll be glad to,' said Kyle, smiling. 'Well, the thing is, I am not Kyle Richards; Kyle Richards is dead.'

'Dead? So the news report was …'

'… true,' confirmed the man they knew as Kyle.

Juanita, who had said practically nothing during the whole exchange, blurted, 'I'm so sorry, James. I really thought it was him … I didn't—'

'Shut up, bitch,' commanded the imposter, his face twisted with an evil intent which James had never seen before. 'I'm about to explain to your boyfriend.'

She did so, stifling a sob.

'You see,' he continued, 'there was every chance that you might not see the news reports about the journalist's killing or that, even if you did, you might not take the bait, so we needed a backup plan.

'We knew that girl, Sylvia, who got in the way, back in Miami Beach, had a boyfriend – Kyle Richards – who seemed determined to track you two down, and we thought he might just have an angle which we – and the cops – had missed. I was picked, as the person in our network who most closely resembled him, physically, to monitor his movements, and be ready to impersonate him if the opportunity arose. Our research indicated that you, Juanita, had only met him once or twice and that your boyfriend had never met him at all. We figured that some minor plastic surgery and a beard should be enough to fool you, as long as I came along with full knowledge of the backstory. And … it worked. I've tracked his every movement for almost a whole year, and when he finally set off for New York City in a hurry, I figured he was on to something. I followed him up to the point where he led me to your hotel, and then I killed him. Maybe you didn't pick up the fact that he'd already been dead for five days when his body was discovered.'

This was too much for Juanita; she wrenched so hard against her restraints that her chair moved a full six inches or so across the floor. 'You murdering swine,' she shrieked. 'How could you do that to an innocent guy who was just trying to find out why his girlfriend had died?'

The man – whose real name had still not been revealed – shrugged. 'Just a means to an end … nothing personal.'

'Nothing personal?' she screamed. 'What could be more personal than murder?'

He inclined his head, touching a forefinger to his chin as though considering this argument. 'I will be very well paid,' he eventually offered, as justification for his actions.

She glared at him; in spite of her restraints, the fierceness in her eyes seemed momentarily to unsettle Kyle's imposter.

He quickly recovered his composure. 'So now it seems that both plan "A" and plan "B" have worked, and we finally have you both.' He glanced at The Scorpion, as though signalling that he'd finished recounting his part of the story.

'So now we come to the end game,' said the big man. He stepped past his two captives, moving into the gloom behind them, emerging a moment later holding a camcorder mounted on a tripod. He set it down facing the two of them, fussing with it until he was satisfied with the view. 'Now, I think you know where this is going,' he said. 'As I said, my employers would like some video evidence of the pain you will suffer before you both die.'

The fear, the whimpering, and sobbing which Juanita had previously exhibited had completely gone; she stared defiantly at the man who was about to torture and kill her. Even *his* smug, arrogant demeanour seemed to falter for a moment. The lapse didn't last long, though.

'I always make a point of never letting anyone who has seen my face when … well, when I'm acting in a professional capacity, so to speak, live to tell the tale, so rest assured your pain and suffering will eventually end.'

Suddenly, he whirled around, with a turn of speed improbable for such a big man, to face the man they knew as Kyle. The expression on the man's face changed, in a split second, as the realisation of what was happening hit home. But he was too slow. *Phut*; the impact of the bullet punched him backward, and his gun spun from his hand, making a loud clattering sound as it hit the floor. His hands flew to the wound in his chest as he staggered unsteadily backward, trying to maintain his footing. He stayed on his feet for several seconds, astonishment written all over his face, before his knees finally buckled and he slid to the ground, gasping for breath.

He tried to drag himself forward, his bloodied hand grasping for his weapon which lay on the floor just a few feet away, but The Scorpion walked calmly towards him and kicked the gun far out of his reach. The man rolled over onto his back, gasping for breath.

'Wh-why?' he croaked.

The Scorpion did not answer his question; instead he addressed himself to James and Juanita. 'Now, on this occasion, I don't want to advertise who did this, so I won't be using my trademark killing shot through the ear.'

The man let out a pitiful whimper as The Scorpion stood over him and took aim. *Phut*; a neat, round hole appeared in the centre of the man's forehead, blood spurting freely from the wound.

This shocking turn of events, played out in mere seconds, reduced both James and Juanita to stunned silence.

'Like I said,' continued The Scorpion, locking eyes with James, 'I never let any witnesses live to tell the tale … plus which, I can make this look as though *you* killed him before I overpowered you. Then I get to collect his fee as well as mine.' His smile was one of pure evil. 'And anyway, I never did like the jumped-up prick.'

Chapter 44

James knew now, if he didn't before, that he was dealing with a sadistic psychopath. There seemed no hope of escape, but still he clung to the hope that if he could keep this man talking, something – any slim chance – might present itself. Maybe appealing to his inflated ego might delay things a little longer.

'I can see why they chose you to bait the trap.'

'Uh, huh?' said the big man, pressing the 'record' button on the camera.

'They must have known I'd think a top assassin like you would only be hired for a *really* important job.'

'Oh, please … I'm not *a* top assassin, I'm *the* top assassin. Name me another – anywhere in the world – who can command higher fees.'

'I can't,' admitted James.

The Scorpion grunted his satisfaction at James's reply before taking from his pocket a dark blue balaclava and pulling it over his head. 'Like I said, I don't want my face to become known, so this is for the benefit of the camera.'

The conversational tone which this vicious killer adopted while casually explaining everything to them was completely incongruous, considering he was preparing to torture and kill them both in the minutes, or hours, to come.

The man moved over to stand alongside the two of them. He laid his gun on the floor in order to leave both hands free while he lit another cigarette. 'Now then,' he said coaxing the tip of the cigarette to a bright glow, 'who first? Eeny meeny miny moe … I think I'll start with you, James. I've already had some fun with your girlfriend.'

If James was going to make a move, he would have to act now; they were out of time. Although his hands were bound to the chair behind his back, his feet were just bound together and not to the chair. Could he perhaps spring to his feet and swing around to bring the chair crashing into his captor? Even if he could, though, unless he was lucky enough to render the man unconscious with that first blow, there would be nothing he could do to follow up the attack, firmly bound as he was. The chances of success were negligible, but with no other plan available, he tensed for action.

The man took another deep draw on the cigarette, restoring its tip to a bright glow before bringing it within an inch of James's lips. Now was the moment; with the gun out of the man's grasp, he would never have a better chance. He tensed his leg muscles, ready for the strike.

'Armed police!' came an urgent shout from somewhere in the shadows behind them.

The big man acted with astounding agility, diving for the floor and lunging for his gun. He wasn't fast enough, though. The vicious *phut* of a silenced gunshot sounded before he could grab his own weapon, and he slumped to the floor. He had been struck in the chest, but the wound wasn't fatal; he was still trying to drag himself towards his gun. Another man stepped out of the shadows: tall, slim but muscular, probably aged around thirty. He wasn't wearing a police uniform. He walked up to the stricken figure on the floor and trapped the man's wrist under his shoe. He bent down and picked up the gun.

'You guys alright?' he said, glancing for a moment towards James and Juanita.

'I am,' said James, 'but she needs medical attention; she's been badly burned.'

'OK, but I need to deal with this motherfucker first.'

The wounded man was trying to drag himself to his knees, but the effort was too much, he shot the newcomer a furious stare before collapsing to the floor, rolling over onto his back. 'Who the fuck are you? What are you doing here?'

'My name is Mark Bowman; I'm a detective with the NYPD.'

'How did you find me?' gasped the injured man.

The other man did not answer the question; instead he responded with one of his own. 'Remember Julia Turner?'

The Scorpion's took a couple of seconds before answering. 'Julia Turner ... you mean the journalist who ...?'

'Yeah ... the woman you murdered in Central Park.'

'What of her?' growled The Scorpion.

'I was going to propose to Julia Turner on the night you murdered her.'

For the first time, James thought he could detect a glint of fear in the wounded man's eyes. 'You mean she was ...?' His voice tailed off.

'Yeah, she was ... got the picture now?'

'How long have you been listening?' said the stricken man, all the bravado gone from his voice now.

'Long enough to know you treated the woman I loved like a dispensable piece of nothing. "Bait" was the term you used, wasn't it?'

The man held up his hand in a defensive gesture. 'Look, I didn't know that she was—'

He was cut off mid-sentence as Mark Bowman shot him in the left kneecap.

The man's scream was ear-splitting. 'Why the fuck did you do that?' he gasped, grasping his shattered knee with both hands. 'Just what kind of cop are you?'

'The kind who's lost the only woman he ever really loved; the kind who despises scum like you.'

'OK ... OK, I get it. But look, we can work something out here. I'm a very wealthy man; I could—'

Mark Bowman shot him in the other kneecap. Another piercing scream rang out.

The man was now reduced to a blubbering wreck. 'P-please,' he pleaded ... I'll do anything you ask.'

'Then tell me this: why did you kill Mandy Jackson?'

The man drew his eyebrows together in puzzlement. 'Mandy who?'

'The hairdresser.'

'Oh yeah ... well I found out she was helping the cops, and I well ...' His voice tailed off as he gasped for breath.

'Spit it out you bastard!' yelled Mark, placing his boot on one of the man's shattered knees and grinding it forcefully down.

The man screamed in agony. 'Nooo ... stop!'

The newcomer relinquished the pressure on the ruined knee. 'Gonna tell me then?'

'I ... I don't like people who help the cops,' gasped The Scorpion.

'You killed her for no other reason than she was helping the police?' said Mark, the incredulity clear in his voice.

'Well, she might have helped them get to these two before I did. I mean ...' His voice tailed off as he registered the stony expression on Mark's face.

'You killed the woman I loved, and another who I was becoming quite fond of, when neither of them had done anything whatsoever wrong.' He was silent for a second or two, his jaw tightly clenched as the blood rushed to his face, a vein in his temple visibly pulsing. 'You absolute fucking bastard,' he hissed.

The terror in the man's face, as Mark levelled his weapon once more, was palpable. 'No ... nooo ... you can't—'

Mark pumped five shots into the man's chest, still repeatedly pulling the trigger uselessly after the magazine was completely exhausted.

He stood there, motionless, for several seconds, his chest heaving, staring at the bloodied corpse on the floor. James and Juanita were also struck dumb in the eerie silence which followed the preceding scene of violence and fury.

Finally, this cop – if that's what he really was – seemed to compose himself. He remained silent, though, as he reloaded his weapon, set the safety catch and returned it to its shoulder holster. Once that was done, he took from his pocket a penknife and approached Juanita.

'Wh-what are you going to do,' she stammered.

'It's OK, ma'am, I'm just going to cut through your bonds.'

'Thank you,' she whispered.

It took just a few seconds to release her; she stood up, flexing her stiff leg muscles and rubbing her sore wrists 'If you hadn't turned up when you did, we'd both be ...' She stifled a sob.

'It's OK now,' he soothed.

He turned to James and cut through his bonds, too.

'You really are a cop then?' said James, trying to ignore the pain which had now reasserted itself in his badly skinned hands; in those critical moments when they were both facing death, he had not been conscious of the pain at all.

'Uh, huh.'

'How did you manage to track that bastard down?'

'I didn't ... *you* were the one who tracked him down.'

'But how did you know he'd be here?'

'I didn't,' he repeated. I just followed the lady.' He glanced at Juanita.

'I ... I don't understand, how—?'

Mark held up his hand. 'Let me explain ...'

Chapter 45

Mark recounted the whole story, leading up to the point where he finally tracked them to their hotel, but was interrupted by Mandy's desperate emergency call before he could try to apprehend them.

'I was too late to save her,' he said, 'so I headed right back to your hotel.' He turned towards Juanita. 'Just as I arrived, I saw you coming out of the main entrance with that guy' – he nodded towards "Kyle's" body – 'right behind you. I could see immediately that you were leaving with him under duress: the way he held his arm under his coat meant he surely had you at gunpoint. With no idea, now, what the hell was going on, I decided to follow you both ... and ended up here.'

'But all the time, you thought it was *me* who had killed Julia,' said Juanita, incredulous.

He nodded, 'From the moment you impersonated her non-existent sister to try to steal the autopsy report, that's what I suspected. And then when you changed your hairstyle to help avoid detection ... Finally, when you inveigled your way into the New York Times office to gain access to Julia's papers and files ... then I was sure, in my own mind.'

'Seems all three of us had completely misread the situation,' observed James. 'We all thought she had been killed because of something she was investigating, and we all got it completely wrong.'

'We sure did,' said Mark.

'I can't believe I let myself be fooled by that animal impersonating Kyle,' added Juanita, shaking her head.

'It's not your fault,' said James. 'You had only met Kyle once, well over a year ago, and I do remember you saying you hardly recognised this guy when he first showed up at the hotel. But he was bloody convincing, and he knew all about Sylvia's death in Miami. He'd have fooled anyone.'

'I suppose so,' she whispered. She frowned, as another thought struck her. 'But if he wanted to kill us both, why didn't he make his move earlier … why did he go through the whole pantomime of helping us with an investigation which he knew full well was going nowhere?'

James shrugged. 'You heard what that other bastard said: they weren't supposed to just kill us; they were instructed to make us suffer first … and even film it.'

Juanita visibly shuddered, the colour draining from her face.

James continued, 'He could hardly have done that in the hotel: too messy and too risky. He was probably biding his time, waiting for an opportunity to lure us both to a remote location like this. Think about it: when I went to check out the apartment of those two brothers who we suspected of being terrorists, it was probably the first time he was alone with you. He just seized the opportunity to force you to come here, and then his psychotic partner used you to lure me here.'

'I guess you're right,' murmured Juanita.

'Can't believe I fell for the trap they set,' muttered James, 'leaving that goods hoist down at ground level, just inviting me to climb up, while Kyle – or whatever his real name was – waited at the top for me.'

'I guess we all made mistakes,' she said, placing a reassuring hand on his arm.

James turned towards Mark. 'How did you manage to get in unobserved?'

'Once they had captured you, they weren't expecting anyone else to show up; I was able to slip in right through the main door and then melt into the shadows around the edge of the building.'

'So, you saw and heard more or less everything then.'

'Yeah, I think so.'

'So, you know why these two were after us, said James. 'What happens now?'

An awkward silence ensued, Juanita now fearing that although they had cheated death that day, they would now be facing the long-dreaded encounter with the authorities in Miami.

'Look,' said Mark, 'I don't know anything about this shit that went down in Miami, but any good cop would be duty bound to take you both in for questioning about it.'

'I guess,' said James, his tone despondent.

'But any good cop would also have tried to take that bastard alive.' He hung his head for a few moments. 'I'm not a good cop … not anymore. Ever since Julia was murdered, all I've been able to think about is avenging her death. I knew that if I managed to track down her murderer, there was no way I'd give him – or her – any chance of some smartass lawyer getting the case thrown out.'

'So you always intended to kill him if you found him?' breathed Juanita.

He didn't answer the question directly. 'I wasn't even supposed to be working on Julia's murder – "too emotionally involved", they said. Damn right I was,' he muttered. 'If they found out I'd disobeyed orders and followed up the case, and then killed the bastard without giving him the chance of a trial, I'd be the one facing a murder charge.'

Juanita could sense the raw emotion in his voice as he poured all this out. She put her arms around him and hugged him. At first, he gratefully accepted the comfort offered, but after some seconds he pulled away, his eyes glistening with barely suppressed tears.

'So, the way I see it is like this: you two may have done some bad things … I don't know, and I don't want to. But you seem to me like good people. And in any case, I can't be associated with what's happened here today, either.'

'So, what are you saying?' said Juanita.

'See this?' he said, withdrawing his silenced handgun and holding it up, causing Juanita to momentarily recoil, before realising that he had no hostile intent. 'It's not my service pistol; the slugs in that bastard's body can't be traced back to me.' He replaced the gun in its holster. 'So, what I'm suggesting is this: you two get the hell out of here … you, lady, get those burns attended to, and then both of you need to disappear. Get the hell out of New York City and find somewhere in the world where no-one can ever find you. From what I heard here today, I'd guess you'll have even more of a price on your heads now. These people you have tangled with don't sound like the kind who'll give up easily.'

'For my part, I'll rearrange the scene here to make it look like some sort of gangland shootout.' He panned his gaze back and forth between the two of them, his expression intense. 'I was never here, and neither were you two.'

'I … I don't know what to say,' stammered Juanita.

'Don't say anything; just get the hell out of here.'

***

They needed to get out of New York City fast. Returning to their apartment in Toronto was out of the question, now that their adversaries knew that was where they'd been living. They returned to their hotel just long enough for James to hurriedly pack their bags and check out, while Juanita waited in the car. Then they just drove, with no particular destination in mind. They headed upstate, stopping when they felt it was safe to do so, finding themselves in the town of Ridgefield.

'We need to get you to a doctor,' said James, 'and get those burns attended to.'

She shook her head, wincing as it caused the neck of her shirt to chafe against the burns. 'Too risky – it'll be obvious that the burns aren't the result of an accident, and any doctor is likely to report it to the cops.'

He hated to see her in such pain, but he knew she was right.

'Let's just find somewhere to lay low for a while,' she continued, 'and then maybe you can get some first aid supplies. I know you'll do a good job of patching me up.' She managed a weak smile.

He felt a surge of love and admiration for this woman who had endured so much yet still showed such iron will. He leant over and kissed her cheek, taking great care not to touch any of her burns. 'Come on then – let's find somewhere to stay, and then I'll go and get some things to treat those burns as best I can.'

***

Three hours later, they were ensconced in the Paradise Motel – a somewhat ironic name, given what they had just been through. Anyway, it was comfortable enough, and the receptionist didn't start asking questions about why Juanita was making ill-disguised efforts to hide her neck and arms.

James had applied a soothing cream to Juanita's burns and covered the worst of them with gauze dressings. Some strong painkillers and a large glass of bourbon – admittedly, not a recommended combination, had now made her reasonably comfortable.

'So, what now?' she asked, holding out her empty glass; James poured a rather smaller measure this time.

'Let's just stay here for a couple of days and let your burns heal a bit … no-one could possibly know where we are right now.'

'But then what?' she insisted.

'We still have quite a bit of cash left, and several more fake passports. We need to get out of the USA, change our identities again, and settle somewhere where those bastards can never find us.'

'But where?' she said.

That was, indeed, the question.

Epilogue

Fifteen months later

They decided to flee to England. The first thing they had to do was adopt new identities once again. James chose the name Jason Hardwick, while Juanita became Gabriela Suarez Rivera.

The journey, travelling on fake I.D.s, had been stressful, but had passed off without incident. They had initially stayed in London for a week or so, but that was just a temporary arrangement. After much discussion, they decided that they could perhaps disappear more completely if they settled in a smaller, less well-known town. Besides, property rental prices in London were exorbitant, and their cash reserves wouldn't last forever.

They chose the market town of Chichester in West Sussex. Technically, it was classed as a city, by virtue of its cathedral, but with a population of just 25,000, it was pretty small by city standards. They rented a small, two-bedroomed house in the popular Summersdale area of the city, and to begin with, kept a very low profile. Although there was absolutely no reason to suppose that their erstwhile enemies could discover their whereabouts, they were taking no chances. James – now Jason – installed security cameras at the front and back of the property, and sturdy deadlocks on the external doors.

Trying to get hold of a gun was far, far more difficult in England than it would have been in the USA. After failing miserably to source one locally, he eventually resorted to taking a trip back to London and finding one on the criminal black market: a SIG Sauer P220 10mm. Once he had obtained the pistol, he always slept with it loaded and ready in the drawer of his bedside cabinet.

He regularly checked New York City's main news channels for any sign of repercussions from the shocking events in that Brooklyn warehouse. The original incident had been reported as the result of some sort of gangland vendetta, just as the cop who had saved their lives said it would. There was nothing in the news in the weeks and months that followed to suggest any further fallout.

As the months rolled by, they finally started to relax. It seemed that they had finally escaped the violence and mayhem in which they had previously become entangled.

Chichester suited them well: it had a theatre, which Gabriela absolutely loved, and was close to the sea; they both enjoyed walks along the seafront in the nearby towns of East and West Wittering. There were also numerous remains of Roman occupation in years gone by. Gabriela had never seen relics of such ancient times since she had left Mexico and became fascinated by learning about the history of the Roman occupation of Britain.

Jason managed to land a job as manager of a nearby clay pigeon shooting range. He didn't particularly like being around guns once again, but he was well qualified for the job, and he enjoyed the social interaction with the diverse range of people who came to sample the sport.

Gabriela had begun painting once again; her main love had always been painting wildlife, but now she had also fallen in love with the striking landscapes of the South Downs and the varied seascapes along the coast – the charming Emsworth harbour being a particular favourite. She soon started capturing these scenes on canvas, too.

After a time, they became friendly with their neighbours: a likeable middle-aged couple on one side and a younger couple with a small child on the other. James couldn't help noticing the wistful smiles which Juanita – now Gabriela – gave every time she met little Chloe – just two years old. Was it time for the two of them to consider starting a family? Or was it too soon to be sure they were safe enough from further pursuit?

***

It was Sunday morning, 10.00 a.m.; they were still in bed, luxuriating in the afterglow of a slow, passionate bout of early-morning lovemaking.

Gabriela yawned and stretched, rolling over to kiss Jason's cheek. 'You want some coffee, lover-boy?'

He smiled, pulling her to him and kissing her full on the lips. 'You making then?'

'Sure … stay there, and I'll bring it up.'

As she stepped out of bed and moved towards the door, seemingly completely unselfconscious of her nakedness, he could not tear his eyes away from her slim, shapely body, her hips swaying sensuously as she walked. As she reached the door, she looked over her shoulder, an impish smile on her face; she knew *exactly* what effect she was having on him.

'You brazen temptress,' he admonished.

She gave a toss of her hair, which had now grown longer once again, laughing as she left the bedroom.

While she was gone, Jason decided to check NBC News on his phone; with so much time now having elapsed since they had fled New York he was almost completely sure they were safe now, but nevertheless, he still checked the news at least once every day. As he scrolled through the various headlines, there was nothing of particular interest to him until …

NYPD Detective Murdered in his own Home – Professional Assassination Suspected.

With a growing sense of trepidation. he opened the article and read on.

> Police have confirmed that the man found murdered in his Manhattan apartment yesterday was a serving NYPD detective. They have released his name as Detective Mark Bowman. The motive for the attack is not clear, and the police have released few details about the nature of the killing, but our sources suggest this was a professional assassination.

> It is well known that the NYPD take any killing of one of their own very personally but, if this was indeed a targeted assassination, you can bet they will leave no stone unturned in their efforts to bring the perpetrator or perpetrators to justice.

Jason was barely able to breathe, as the impact of what he was reading hit home. He felt a deep sense of anguish that this man, who had saved both their lives, had fallen victim to these relentlessly vicious people. But that was not all; he felt a hollow dread eviscerate him as the implications began to sink in. If they were determined enough to wreak revenge on a NYPD cop in his own back yard, more than a year after the event, then—

Gabriela appeared in the doorway, still naked, holding two cups. The moment their eyes met, her warm smile evaporated, to be replaced by a fearful frown. 'Jason, what is it?'

'Put the cups down, Gabby. I think we may have a problem …'

THE END

About the Author

Ray Green is married with two daughters and lives in West Sussex, England. He graduated from Southampton University with a BSc in Physics and then went on to a career spanning some 30 years in the electronics manufacturing industry. For much of that time he was operating at Director or Managing Director level in several different companies, so he is well qualified to give an insight into the world of business and corporate politics and intrigue.

His business career culminated in his participation in a management buyout of his last company. It was an incredibly tortuous process, and the experience that provided the inspiration for his first novel 'Buyout' in which the principal protagonist, Roy Groves, battles similar issues in a fictionalised management buyout. The sequel 'Payback' tells what happens when the human desire for revenge takes hold. Ray's third novel 'Chinese Whispers' explores the shocking consequences when legitimate business is infiltrated by organised crime. The fourth book, which completes the 'Roy Groves Thriller' series is a comedy-thriller charting Roy's fortunes after he decides to quit the corporate rat race and retire to an upmarket expat community on Spain's Costa del Sol.

'Lost Identity', the first book in the 'Identity Thrillers' series, is a tense psychological thriller set in the criminal world of drug trafficking and murder. And the second ... well, I guess you've just read it.

There will be more to come from Ray Green.

www.ingramcontent.com/pod-product-compliance
Lightning Source LLC
Chambersburg PA
CBHW020106180626
46812CB00006B/2491